this wild silence

this wild silence

a novel

LUCY JANE
BLEDSOE

alyson books
los angeles

© 2003 BY LUCY JANE BLEDSOE. ALL RIGHTS RESERVED.

MANUFACTURED IN THE UNITED STATES OF AMERICA.

THIS TRADE PAPERBACK ORIGINAL IS PUBLISHED BY ALYSON PUBLICATIONS,
P.O. BOX 4371, LOS ANGELES, CALIFORNIA 90078-4371.
DISTRIBUTION IN THE UNITED KINGDOM BY TURNAROUND PUBLISHER SERVICES LTD.,
UNIT 3, OLYMPIA TRADING ESTATE, COBURG ROAD, WOOD GREEN,
LONDON N22 6TZ ENGLAND.

FIRST EDITION: MAY 2003

03 04 05 06 07 **a** 10 9 8 7 6 5 4 3 2 1

ISBN 1-55583-773-5

LIBRARY OF CONGRESS CATALOGING-IN-PUBLICATION DATA
BLEDSOE, LUCY JANE.
    THIS WILD SILENCE : A NOVEL / LUCY JANE BLEDSOE.—1ST ED.
    ISBN 1-55583-773-5
        1. WILDERNESS SURVIVAL—FICTION. 2. BROTHERS—DEATH—FICTION.
3. SISTERS—FICTION. I. TITLE.
PS3552.L418T48 2003
813'.54—DC21   2003040447

CREDITS
COVER PHOTOGRAPHY BY STONE.
COVER DESIGN BY MATT SAMS.

FOR MARGARET AND LAURA

acknowledgments

A heartfelt thank you to the friends and colleagues who have read various drafts of the manuscript, including Patricia Mullan, Martha Garcia, Barbara Sjoholm, Darieck Scott, Gina Covina, Linnea Due, Jane Futcher, Laura Green, Robin Ellett, MD, Gayann Hall, MD, Teresa Murphy, MD, Anna Kaminsky, MD, and Laura Bledsoe, MD. Any errors of fact that have persisted in the face of their generous comments and suggestions are my own.

A California Arts Council Individual Artist Fellowship arrived at a critical time and is hugely appreciated, as is a grant from the Puffin Foundation. I am also grateful for having the opportunity to work at the Soapstone Writing Retreat for Women.

I wish to thank Angela Brown and all the hard-working people at Alyson Publications, for embracing my novel with enthusiasm. Their contributions have improved every aspect of the book.

one: *dawn ice*

Scanning the horizon for Timothy is almost an instinct with me. I do it every time I'm in wilderness. It has never felt absurd, the idea that a little boy—and I always picture him still five years old—might come loping over the horizon and back into our lives. Never mind that by now he would be thirty-five and not a little boy at all.

This morning's horizon is violent with the colors of dawn. Blood red. Fire orange. Bruise purple. Smeared like pain across the sky, over the mountains and frozen lake. It's a raw morning, new as an egg, and for a moment I feel afraid. I glance at my sister, Liz, who futzes with the others around the splayed open truck, and I know she has changed; something inside her has slipped, let go, and settled in a new but not necessarily happy way. I also know my sister can't change, not significantly, without changing me, and that is the basis of my fear.

My theory is that change happens when there is a convergence of seemingly unrelated events that, despite their chance encounter, form a critical mass that overcomes the angle of repose and propels a person forward into new territory. Even in this first moment of the trip, long before anything consequential has happened, I am briefly aware that Flo is one stream of the convergence, this sunrise another, and of course Liz is somehow, as always, the controlling current.

The game, however, these thirty years since losing Timothy, has been that I'm the truth-seeker, the one to creep toward the uncomfortable precipice of our family secrets, so as the sun approaches the horizon and sears the brilliance out of the dawn, I let go of my fear, slip into my role, and regain my foothold on this planet by mentioning Timothy to my sister.

"Thirty-five," I say, reminding her of our brother's age today.

"Yep," she says, kneeling in the snow to snap Lenny's gaiters on over his size fourteen boots. Lenny is telling a story about an avalanche he survived by making swimming motions. He windmills his arms in the dim, icy air, demonstrating while Liz concentrates on his feet. He says his life— all sixteen years of it—passed before his eyes. He says that afterward he lay on the snow, his legs buried, for twelve hours before a Saint Bernard found him. He says he was clinically dead.

"So what was it like on the other side?" Mark, my sister's husband, asks.

"The other side of what?"

"Were you sweating and holding a pitchfork or were you floating on a cloud and wearing a white gown?"

Lenny smiles a crooked smile. Mark is good at teasing without making you feel bad. He's the butter in our family, the one luxury that makes everything go down easy.

"I don't remember ever skiing with Timothy," I say to Liz. "Did we?"

"Nope."

"I guess he was too little."

Liz used to scowl or change the subject when I talked about Timothy, which would only egg me on. I didn't like her implying that my wanting to talk about him was as stupid as picking a scab. But lately she has taken a different tack, shining me on, which is more effective. In the city last week, after we had lunch together and I was walking her back to the train station, I saw a tall, pale man with raspberry lips. "Hey, Liz, see that guy? Don't you think that's what Timothy probably looks like?"

"Yep."

"Gray suit, though. Timothy would never be a suit. Do you think?"

"Nope."

Anyone could see that talking about Timothy does not help her, that she is perfectly content in her Timothy silence, but it helps me. I obsess on who he might be today. I keep a mental list of all the possibilities: a cowboy in Montana, dead of exposure in the woods, slave to a pedophile, dead from measles contracted in an orphanage, a banker in the Cayman Islands, beaten to death at age five, a victim of amnesia, killed in a car accident, adopted into a loving family, a suicide in some prison, a New Age guru-follower in an ashram, dead of AIDS, a street person in New York. Et cetera. I always make sure to list an equal number of dead and alive possibilities, although logic tells me dead is much more likely than alive. If he were alive, certainly he would have contacted us. We're not hard to find. But then, amnesia would prevent him from contacting us. In fact, several of the options would prevent him from doing that. After all, he was only five years old. He could have easily been adopted into another family and forgotten us.

Or, I think, looking out over the blue dusting of snow on the dawn-lit lake, he could be little remaining bits of organic matter locked into lake ice, frozen year after year, thawing out in the spring, becoming fish food, until the fishes died and became bottom-feeder food. Until they died and fed the plants. Little bits of organic matter that never disappeared, just changed form moment to moment, year after year.

I wonder now why I haven't told Flo about Timothy. As Liz likes to point out, I tell everyone who will listen. Flo would listen, but to tell her would be like touching an open wound with a hot poker.

Turning my back to the eastern sky, the icy lake, and the mountains, I face the parking lot, its dirty snow and big brown outhouse on the far end. The problem with extreme beauty is that it is excruciating. So is this cold. It's freezing out here at five in the morning. Even the air seems crystallized, hard to breathe. We are skiing in only a few miles, making the excessively early start unnecessary, but that's Liz for you. She isn't actually a morning person, and that galls her. She pretends to be one. It's part of her modus operandi. Part of the wilderness survival thing. She annoys everyone with her brisk dance, her silver thermos of too-strong coffee, her insistence on conversation at the crack. If she were a true morning person, she would know to keep quiet, to listen, to enjoy the only part of the day when time unfolds haphazardly. The light now is so fragile a sharp voice could break it.

What amazes me about sisters is that you can look through the same lens—if you can think of a family as a lens—and see entirely different worlds. Like me, Liz works in the city, but she wouldn't dream of living there. And she thinks I shouldn't live there either. She likes to confuse me with my patients, most of whom live in the Tenderloin, many of whom are homeless, a few of whom are crazy. In fact, she thinks of anything urban as a pathology. Many years ago, when land was still relatively cheap, she and Mark bought several acres of rolling hills and live oaks on the other side of the East Bay crest. They built their solar-heated house themselves, and also the barn where Mark runs his educational publishing firm. Even though they both work full-time, they keep what they call a garden but I would call a farm, growing all the vegetables they eat, plus much more, which they give to me for my patients. In the winter they have lettuce, broccoli, carrots, cabbages; in summer peppers, squashes, watermelons, beans, tomatoes, herbs, strawberries, everything. They keep a few goats to do their "mowing" and for milk for their morning coffee and whole grain cereal. They also have a small orchard that provides buckets of apricots, lemons, apples, plums, and avocados. They even tried to grow their own wheat for making bread, but that didn't pan out. I feel accomplished if I manage to pick up a loaf of bread that isn't Wonder.

I like to tell Liz that I'm her dark side, and I am, literally and figuratively. Her long hair, which used to be straw-blond but is now caramel, hangs in a braid the length of her spine. Her skin always looks freshly scrubbed, glowing with lovely pink health, and her eyes are a cool and practical gray. Next to my sister, I look chunky and big-breasted; my light auburn hair and brown eyes seem muddy, lacking in clarity. I have our mother's heavy eyebrows and Liz has our father's trim lips. Despite these differences, it's obvious we're sisters; she just looks lighter and thinner and fresher.

Besides tending plants, Liz and Mark take on human projects too, such as Lenny, who now stands like a child, all six feet of him, while Liz adjusts his pack, cinching a strap, loosening another. His oversize feet, hands, and nose give him a look of vulnerability, making the stories of juvenile delinquency I have heard about him seem ludicrous. He appears quite tame now, tamer certainly than Liz, who struggles to fiercely overcome the morning.

Liz opens her thermos and pours a cupful of black coffee. She holds the cup out to her husband. He shakes his head. Mark is barely five feet five inches tall but has a powerful build. In a life drawing class I once took, the teacher had us draw the human form using all ovals, but if I were to draw Mark, I would use all rectangles. He's a flame blond with a ruddy face that makes his hair look all the brighter. He could be a Southern California surfer if he didn't scorn everything about California. Until he was fourteen and moved to Portland he lived in rural Oregon, near the Rogue River, and prided himself on his survival skills, as he now prides himself on his and Liz's anti-urban lifestyle—even though they live less than an hour from several Bay Area cities, including San Francisco. Liz and Mark are more than a couple—having been together since they were fourteen years old, they are more like twins.

After downing the cupful of coffee, Liz reaches into the front seat of the truck and pulls out a sheet of paper. "Mark, stove?"

"Check."

"Lenny, two space blankets?"

"Aye, aye." He salutes her.

Giving up on silence, I fit earphones over my head and let Janis Joplin's rasp ease the tension my sister infuses in me. I slide my finger along the ridged volume dial and crank up Joplin telling me to get it while I can. I've often tried to imagine what it would have been like to be Joplin's lover. To have sat on the back of that motorcycle with her. To have leaned my face into her badly damaged hair. To have felt all the fury in that small, also badly damaged body of hers. It could have been good. It could have been as wrenching as her voice. But then maybe not.

I knock a cigarette out of a pack and grip it between cold lips. Liz, still going through her checklist, glances at me and I see an appeal in her gray eyes, which I mistake as concern for my health. I shrug apologetically and tear off a match. I can't hear the scratch of the match with Joplin in my ears, but I can smell the mini-explosion of sulfur and draw it into my lungs. Next the glorious nicotine. Joplin's voice and the cigarette almost warm me up.

I watch Liz for a moment and reconsider that look she gave me. An appeal. She's afraid I won't be a help on this trip, but a help with what? Without sound on my sister, irritation morphs into affection as I watch her command our little expedition. Liz can be annoying, but when I'm with her I can almost feel the loneliness hiss out of my body, like air from a tire, leaving me flat and malleable. Her authority is comforting.

We're nearly ready to go. Mark stows our wallets in the hidden compartment and locks the truck. Melody, who works for Mark, has been ready for twenty minutes, and she skis back and forth in the woods next to the parking lot, a look of concentration—which could be joy, could be anything—on her face. Liz told me that Melody is a Buddhist.

I walk a few steps away from everyone, facing the lake once again, and savor the end of my cigarette, enjoying the contrast of fresh air and tobacco smoke, and let Joplin tear out a piece of my heart. The sun crests the horizon at last, its light seeming to clean away the debris of nighttime, offering up a crazy burst of hope. I think of Flo's room, where I slept night before last, laden with burning candles, the flames like little bits of the sun. I imagine Flo's previous life resembled Joplin's, but Flo didn't self-destruct. She changed. I wonder what she would think of this alpine morning. I can't imagine her here.

I let out a little scream, which I can't hear myself, when two giant fingers snap in my face. Lenny. He wants a ciga-rette. I slide the earphones down to my neck and pull out my pack. Standing behind Lenny, Liz scowls. Contributing to the delinquency of a minor. Well, smoking isn't illegal. The only problem is, I've brought a rationed number of cigarettes, fig-uring that on a camping trip I should smoke less than usual. If I have to split them with Lenny, I'll have even fewer for me.

Since Lenny's hands are encased in Gore-Tex mittens that on him look like boxing gloves, I light a cigarette and reach up to place it between his lips. I would like this kid, just based on his looks, if I didn't know anything about him. He has straight jet-black hair and bovine eyes, the lower lids drooping down, and upper lashes so long the tips actually touch his eyebrows. His too-big adolescent nose, matching his huge feet and hands, looks so out of place on his face. Mark and Lenny were matched in the Big Brothers of America program two years ago. Since then, Lenny has landed in juvenile detention twice, once for setting fire to a garbage can at school and once for helping to rob a 7-Eleven, and he's recently gotten into some fresh trouble—"having something to do with a woman," was all Mark said. Lenny is the alleged reason for this weekend. Mark and Liz believe hard labor in the wilderness can cure any personality malfunction.

Which I suspect is why Liz wanted me to come along. Like Lenny, I am in need of rehabilitation, a weekend's exertion in the mountains. But in my case, it's for my inability to "settle down," in Liz's words. Specifically, for my colossal misstep in breaking up with Robin and thereby denying myself the possibility of finally having a home, a *real* home. All Liz's interpretation, of course, but Liz is never entirely wrong.

When I told her about the breakup four months ago, I knew she'd be upset. She and Robin got on like bandits. My sister had practically offered the woman a dowry. So I embedded the information in an enticement, like giving a dog a pill wrapped in meat.

We were on the phone when I asked, "Hey, do you and Mark want the Bonnie Raitt tickets I bought before Robin and I broke up?"

"You *what?*"

"Bought Bonnie Raitt tickets but can't use them."

"Tina!"

"Yeah, yeah, I know," I said, trying to forestall the lecture. "But it wasn't working."

"*It* doesn't just work on its own," Liz informed me. "*You* have to work it."

"I'm not in love with her."

"You didn't give yourself a chance."

"Look, Robin broke up with *me* so—"

"Did Robin know about Lucienne?"

"Of course she knew about Lucienne. I have a lot of faults, but I'm not a liar."

Oh, boy. I didn't mean to say that. I could almost hear Liz wince, as if I had called *her* a liar. I hadn't meant to. I don't think I had, anyway. But every conversation Liz and I ever have reverberates back to losing Timothy. Everything that happens between us is rich with the possibility of shedding light, which is what we never want to do, on that accident for which we share responsibility.

"What I *mean* is," I backpedaled, "that even if I wanted to give up Lucienne for Robin, and maybe I did, it wouldn't last. *I* wouldn't last. I can't stand the way Robin wants to live under my skin."

I heard Liz breathing on the other end of the phone, long huffs from her nose, almost as if she were trying not to cry. Then, "You're forty years old and you have no center to your life."

"Whoa, Liz." Advice I could handle, but she was going for the jugular. "Most people think being a doctor is highly respectable. And I've got a nice house."

More deep breathing. Finally, "I'm sorry. I didn't mean to say that. It's just that…oh…Robin is really great. And you deserve a wonderful partner. That's all I'm saying."

It wasn't all she was saying. She was saying I'm incapable of sustaining an intimate relationship. She was saying I'll spend my life alone.

As Lenny and I take final drags on our cigarettes, Liz reaches over, pulls the headphones off my head, tearing the jack from the tape player housed in the side pocket of my backpack, and heads for the truck with them.

"Give those back!"

Liz stops at the truck, turns around, and slowly says, "Christine."

I'd never admit it to her, but even now my older sister speaking my full name in that reproaching tone makes my bones twitch. I hold my ground though. "Only two tapes, and they're already packed. As is the Walkman." I reach around to pat the side pocket of my backpack, where my tape player is stowed.

"Unpack them. It's not safe. You need all your senses out here. We have to be able to communicate. Come on, Tina."

Lenny grins; I guess it's funny to see adult sisters bicker.

"One comfort," I argue. "This is your venue, Liz, but I get freaked by the sound winter makes in the mountains." I try for a bantering tone but can feel my throat constrict and hear my voice squeak.

"Come on, Tina," she says again, this time clearly annoyed. I reluctantly hand her the tape player, which Mark stashes in the truck.

"I'll sing for you," he says, and opens his mouth to begin a rendition of something, but Liz whaps him in the stomach, a little harder than what I would call playful.

I grimace at Mark and he shrugs. Liz is in a doozy of a mood.

I dab my cigarette out in the snow and walk the butt over to the outhouse. Then, after throwing it into the overflowing pit, I walk a few yards away until I can breathe deeply, free of the outhouse stench, and where I can think about Flo, free of my companions' voices. The dawn light on the frozen lake is thin and fierce, like my sister—so different from the buttery light of the hundred candles burning in Flo's room. The difference maybe between found light and created light. Whatever would Liz make of Flo?

two: flo's landscape

As a doctor in a Tenderloin medical clinic, I know a lot of people in the neighborhood. My patients include immigrants struggling for a foothold in this country that, even at the millennium, draws newcomers as persistently, and often as disastrously, as it did a hundred years ago. My patients are elderly folks, clinging to their apartments and sparse pensions and memories of a middle-class life that somewhere along the way abandoned them. I see eighty-year-old ex-strippers, ex-doctors who drank their way to the Tenderloin, and ex-wives of corporate executives who failed to get a piece of the pie in their divorces. I see a few of the priests and nuns from the church next door, men and women who believe in their community so wholly that they will not leave it for more upscale services. I see the babies and small children of my adult patients. The older kids in the neighborhood, runaways and others who are not welcome in—or cannot tolerate—the families into which they

were born, rarely come to the clinic on their own but sometimes stop me on the street to ask for, or even demand, pills.
Occasionally a blue-jean-wearing priest or nun from next door
will escort a youngster to the clinic, see to his or her appoint-
ment, then work with me to try to make the kid understand, or
care about, mortality.

A lot of artists live in the Tenderloin too, including Florence
Hughes. She teaches a women's writing workshop in the
church. Some of my patients attend and have told me about the
autobiographies they are writing under her tutelage.

I knew Flo by sight long before she introduced herself.
I'd see her out the window of my office in the clinic, striding down the street, her loose black curls bouncing, her
rounded muscles filling her T-shirt and jeans, her wide
mouth animated and open, even when she wasn't talking. I
imagined that she taught with her whole body, and could
see, just by looking at her, why her students loved her. But
she also scared me. Her skin is bronze translucent, like
stained glass, as if it is very sensitive. And occasionally a
fleeting scowl seizes her face, almost like a tick, instantly
transforming her vitality into something much less appeal-
ing. One time I saw her on the corner of Golden Gate and
Ellis telling off a man in a business suit. "No, *you* shut up,
you motherfucker," she shouted, the knuckle of her first finger punching just centimeters from his mouth. The guy was
trying to hold his ground, stomping his Italian loafers, opening and closing his mouth, but he didn't stand a chance.
Even if he was a good foot taller than Flo, she'd kill him if
he gave her a reason. It was as if that shadow of a scowl that
played between her eyes had occupied her entire body. And
then there was the dog, the little white poodle always at her
side, prancing six steps for each one of hers. When we'd
meet, Flo would say, "Susan B, say hello to the doctor," and
the dog would yip once quietly.

Susan B has curly hair like Flo, but white, and she is usually adorned with a pink, rhinestone-studded collar.
Sometimes her fur is shorn in a traditional poodle cut, other

times left long and shaggy, but it's always fluffy, clean and brushed. On the windy day in October when Flo first introduced herself, Susan B wore a Scottish plaid dog jacket with a matching bow on top of her head. I was passing the two of them on the street and couldn't stop myself from laughing out loud. Then, thinking of that scowl, I shut up fast, worrying Flo wouldn't take well to people laughing at her dog. But she smiled. "I know, I know. She looks ridiculous. How am I supposed to know how to dress her? She needs someone more feminine in her life. Someone who knows about accessorizing. She looks like a fucking terrier in this outfit."

"She needs bagpipes," I said, which tickled Flo. I found myself wanting to touch the skin on Flo's face, where the harsh wind had drawn the blood to the surface. Instead I bent down and petted Susan B.

"Top of the head, between the ears," Flo said. "Only place people she doesn't know can touch her."

When I stood up again, Flo said, "Say, Doc—" and she paused.

I nodded, bracing myself for the litany of ailments. People stopped me on the street daily, pulling off socks to reveal sores or hawking up phlegm for me to analyze.

"I'm Florence Hughes. We've never actually met."

I shook her hand.

"Your name?"

"Oh! Christine Thomas," I said, embarrassed by my lapse but pleased she wanted to know me.

"I like calling you Doc."

"That's fine."

"Well, I gotta run, but we never, you know, formally met."

I didn't mean for my eyes to leave her face as she backed up but they must have, because she looked down suddenly at her paint-splattered shirt and, as if I had requested an explanation, said, "Paint. I'm a poet slash house painter. Gotta support my lady here. Susan B!" She spoke sharply. "Say goodbye to the doctor."

Yip.

I was relieved at the relative simplicity of the exchange—no sores, no phlegm—and started down the street.

Flo called after me, "Hey, come catch my show some time."

"I'll do that," I said, and kept walking, wondering if she knew I had already seen one of her performances, or part of one anyway.

She'd had a big audience that Friday afternoon on Market Street, mostly tourists. I recognized her as the poet-in-residence from the church next door to my clinic, so I stopped for a moment in the back of the crowd. I knew she was working with the women in her workshop on some serious writing, so I was surprised that her act was stand-up comedy. She opened with some pretty ordinary jokes, nothing hilarious, but it soon became clear that she wasn't the real show; Susan B was. A lot of the jokes were about the plight of starving artists and she referred often to the brown derby on the pavement in front of her. Every time Flo said the word "hat," Susan B stood on her hind legs and howled. People laughed. A few reached into their pockets. Then the real show began. When someone dropped a bill into the hat, Susan B stood on her hind legs again and danced in a full circle, but when someone left change, the dog trailed the cheapskate for a few steps, her hung head shaking slowly back and forth. The audience loved it, and the laughter drew a larger crowd.

Then Flo launched the more serious part of her show, the poetry, but she didn't handle the transition gracefully. While that physical vibrancy of hers made the jokes funnier—made the jokes period—that same energy nearly bulldozed her poetry. People drifted away. Apparently, Flo had experienced people's waning interest at this juncture, because she leaned down and whispered something to her dog. Susan B tiptoed, the way poodles do, over to a woman who had opened her wallet and taken out a bill. Susan B stood on her hind legs. The confused woman was stunned for a moment, the dollar bill dangling in her fingers, until Susan B leapt up and snatched it. She trotted back and dropped the money into the brown derby. After that, tourist children begged their parents for dollar bills to dangle for Susan B.

Meanwhile, as the audience ogled and laughed at her poodle, and as her brown derby began to overflow with cash, Flo continued performing her poetry. But the dog tricks were like too much sugar on a bowl of cereal; no one tasted the poetry at all. I didn't hear any of her words, could only see Flo's effort, which looked like desperation overtaking her body as she tried to communicate to her audience. Her willingness to dance right to the very edge of that desperation broke my heart. I left before the crowd grew too thin to hide me.

Right before Thanksgiving, a few days after Robin and I broke up, I stood at my office window, three stories above the street. I had just seen my last patient, a young man with a rash I couldn't diagnose, and I felt depressed. I was supposed to see my friend Alice for dinner, but I didn't know if I could stand her cheerfulness. I wished the evening was with Lucienne, actually. Lucienne is so good at irony, at holding the muck of life in her hands and turning it into something nameable. As I stood and watched, dusk socked the city streets with its thick dinge. A young man stumbled into the picture framed by my window, then slumped into the darkness of an entryway across the street. The greenish light of a street lamp swarmed up his legs, but his torso and head were lost. He was probably getting high. From this window I'd seen just about every human act imaginable. A moment later I saw his two legs kick spasmodically, then still. His head and shoulders fell forward into the dim light.

There was a time, a few years ago when I first began working at this clinic, when I would have carried an army surplus blanket across the street and covered him for the night. It's not cynicism that stops me now. Something more like practicality. My budget allows for only so many blankets. I have to figure how much mileage I can get out of each one. Sometimes this job reminds me of a "game" my eighth grade teacher made us play. He divided us into groups and told us we had a certain amount of money. We had to come to an agreement on how to use it: build a library, save a child's life, or fund researchers working on a cure for cancer. The only true answer is that there is no answer. It's tempting, at first, to think in terms of who "deserves" our resources more, but the deeper you think yourself into that box, the more lost you get. So I think in terms of mileage. Someone who actually comes to the clinic, seeking medical help, might make better use of the blanket.

One of the things I admire about Liz is her ability to order human values, choose one over another. As executive director of an environmental nonprofit, she commits herself wholly to rescuing wilderness. How does she believe so fully in its inherent importance? The part of my work I like best is walking from one exam room to the next, following my nurse Lynne's orders, taking care of one patient at a time. I can only manage what is directly, physically, in front of me. Liz looks at the entire planet and makes decisions. She sees into the future and believes in the possibility of stemming the flow of poisons into our environment. It's as though she thinks she can work in partnership with God.

As I looked out the window, I saw a paper plate fly off the pavement and plaster itself against the slumped man's legs. Then a flurry of paper products, probably the remains of a homeless family's meal, fluttered by in the autumn wind. Flo came in their wake, walking briskly with Susan B off her leash. She stopped and squatted in front of the man in the entryway. Susan B looked longingly down the sidewalk as she waited, perhaps impatient for supper. Flo glanced around, said something to Susan B, then the two of them crossed over to my side of the street. I left the window.

After turning off the lights and locking up the clinic, I pulled on my wool overcoat and headed down the three flights of stairs, anxious for a cigarette. The elevator was broken again, which meant my patients in wheelchairs couldn't get to the clinic. Hopefully the repairman would come tomorrow. I found Flo bounding up the stairs two at a time with Susan B on her heels.

"I was coming to get you," she said. "There's a dead man across the street."

"He's just high. I saw him shoot up a few minutes ago."

"He's dead now."

I held onto the smooth worn wooden handrail. Why didn't she go next door and get the priest? Why would a dead man need a doctor? I'm not a coroner. My job is keeping people alive. I felt angry and exhausted. I missed Robin intensely, suddenly realizing she'd be the perfect company tonight. Calm, sane, stable Robin. Why the hell did I let her break up with me?

I sat on the stairs for a moment, as if every muscle cell in my body had collapsed. Flo stood in front of me, Susan B now gathered in her arms, and waited. "Okay," I said. "Okay." I got up, and together we walked to the bottom of the stairwell and into the cold November night. The stiff wind blew between the buildings as if the street were a canyon, piercing my overcoat and making it nearly impossible to light my cigarette.

I knelt in front of the man. His hands were crusted with filth and he reeked of urine. I placed two fingers on the artery alongside his neck. Nothing. I pulled my cell phone out of my coat pocket and called an ambulance. It would be forever, standing there in that cold wind, waiting for an ambulance to come to the Tenderloin. If one came at all.

Flo sat on the curb with me, the dead man to our backs. Susan B whined, and I felt an absurd tug of loneliness as Flo comforted her. I remembered my date with Alice and pulled out my phone again. "Hey, Al. An emergency has come up, and I can't make it tonight," I said to her voice-mail. "I hope you get this before you come over. I'm really sorry. I'll call you when I get in."

"You go on. I'll wait," Flo said.

"It's okay."

"It'll be here soon. You don't have to cancel your date."

I sighed deeply.

"Weight of the world, huh?" she said.

I looked away from her. I was used to being mocked—what did a doctor know about suffering, right?—but got sick of it anyway.

"Hey."

I ignored her.

"Hey," she said again.

"What?"

"Have you seen the comet yet?"

I shook my head.

"It's pretty spectacular. Do you have a car? We could go up to Twin Peaks after the ambulance comes and have a look."

"I'm tired."

"Yeah, me too. Besides, to really see it you pretty much have to get out of town. *Really* out of town."

I looked at Flo. Her wide mouth, punctuated with a dimple on each side, warmed me. At the same time, those eyes, with their hint of a scowl, gave me pause. I saw her notice that pause, and her whole face softened, as if she knew what I saw and wanted to say something but didn't know me well enough to say it.

"My sister wants me to go up to Tahoe with her in March," I said. "You think the comet will still be visible then?"

"Until just about then. Maybe into April. God, it'd be really awesome up there. Without the city lights and pollution, you'd see the tail. You should go."

I didn't want to go; I didn't want Flo's enthusiasm for the comet to lure me into Liz's snow-camping trip. "It's just a big snowball," I told her.

"A cold stone, plummeting."

"Orbiting."

"Huh?"

"A comet orbits, it doesn't plummet. And it's not a stone, it's gases and—"

"Technically, you're right. Poetically, it's a cold stone plummeting."

I couldn't argue with that.

"Don't you think the tail implies a plummet?"

"Yes," I conceded. I guess I had gotten out of the practice of thinking of the natural world as poetry. I remember as a biology major, and even later, in medical school, being occasionally stunned with delight while reading about nature's successes, like the way bears locate and use several different kinds of botanical medicines, or even just thinking deeply about something as basic but miraculous as photosynthesis. Where I worked now, the miracles weren't so apparent.

As Flo and I waited, I thought about Liz's invitation, which had come shortly after I'd told her about my breakup. She'd said nothing about Robin in that phone conversation, but I knew the breakup was why she was inviting me. She thought I needed the brisk mountain air, hard cold exertion, a weekend to ponder my homeless soul. I hadn't even let her finish her invitational sentence. I interrupted and told her I was busy.

"It's *November*, Tina. You already know you're busy in March? Doing what?"

She was right; I wasn't busy. So I took a different tack. "Why would I want to go snow-camping? You know I gave that up."

"We haven't done anything real together in a long time."

The plea in Liz's voice took me off guard. Normally I would have jumped on the word "real," challenged her to tell me exactly how sleeping in the snow, in the mountains, in the winter—she would have interjected "late spring"—was more real than, say, a nice dinner in a warm San Francisco restaurant. Instead I said, "I'll think about it."

That night, sitting on the curb with Flo, I did wonder what the comet would look like from the Sierras. I had seen a comet, years ago, through my father's high-powered telescope. He's retired now but taught physics at the community college, and his concentration—passion actually—was astrophysics. After losing Timothy, he rarely used the telescope, but when I was a child he often woke up Liz and me in the night, ignoring my mother's protests, and carried us outside in our pajamas to look at something spectacular in the night sky.

The ambulance eventually arrived. Flo squeezed my shoulder and said nothing before striding away with Susan B. I wished I had asked if she wanted to have dinner.

A month later I stepped out of one exam room, where I'd had to tell a woman she was HIV-positive, and, rather than stopping in my office for a breather, I followed Lynne's orders and stepped right into the next exam room. There was Flo, sitting on the end of the exam table.

I hadn't even looked at the name on the new chart Lynne had put in the bin outside the door. I looked now: Florence Hughes.

"I don't wear those white gowns," she said. She had on her paint-splattered jeans and an oversize button-down white shirt. Her curly black hair was just long enough to wear in a stubby ponytail.

"Fine," I said. "What's up?"

Her hands rested on her thighs, and she spread out her fingers the way my cat Martin does. I had a doomed feeling, the feeling I get at least once a day, when I know, just know, I am going to discuss someone's mortality with her, someone who isn't ready to discuss it. *Two in a row*, I thought. I didn't let myself think, *This is Flo*. At least I thought I didn't. But her smile made me think she read the dread on my face. My doctor armor vanished, leaving me bare as an animal.

She began unbuttoning her shirt, and I saw the raw skin across her belly and right breast. "Poison oak," she said. "And I'm going out of my mind. I mean I cannot, *cannot*, keep myself from scratching."

I laughed hard with relief. Here I thought she was going to show me a lump the size of a golf ball in her breast.

"It's all down my leg, in my crotch. I'm not going to have any skin left by the end of the week."

I asked her how she got it.

"Um, Golden Gate Park during a romantic interlude?" She paused. "That is to say, I think Susan B rolled in the stuff and then I hugged her."

I wrote her a prescription and told her to stay home from work for a few days. Paint fumes weren't going to help.

She jumped off the table. "Thanks, Doc."

"No problem."

"See you around?"

"Yes."

"Okay, baby." She spoke to the big purple bag on the floor under the table. Susan B leapt out from the open zipper. "Say hello to the doctor." *Yip.* Then to me, "I know, I know, dogs don't belong in clinics. But she hates for me to leave her. Hey, you really should catch my show some time. I'm usually down on Market near Powell. I don't perform here in the neighborhood because no one has any money, right? And it's not exactly like tourists come through the Tenderloin." She held an imaginary microphone to her mouth. " 'And here, ladies and gentlemen, is where the homeless and addicts live.' " Then she smiled at me, those two dimples caving in her cheeks, motioned Susan B back inside the purple bag, hefted it, and was gone.

I stayed alone for a few moments. When I emerged, my nurse looked at her watch and said, "Forty-five minutes."

Lynne, who makes Nurse Ratched seem like a slacker, was very good at keeping me informed about how behind I was. This place would have folded years ago if it weren't for her.

After that, I didn't see Flo on the street for several weeks, not until the middle of January. I was leaving the clinic late, well after dark, and she approached me from behind, startling me so much I gasped.

"Damn, Flo," I said when I realized it was her.

"Sorry! I didn't mean to scare you. I just wanted you to know that the poison oak is gone. Totally gone. What a relief. Susan B, say hello to the doctor."

Yip.

"Hey, I was just about to catch a bus up to Twin Peaks. It's such a clear night, I want to see the comet. Come with me." As she spoke, she picked up Susan B and hugged the dog to her, keeping it between us, making me feel as if she were ambivalent about asking me. Which made me feel safer accepting the invitation.

An hour later we sat on the stone ledge bordering the parking lot on Twin Peaks, swinging our legs to keep warm. The night was clear and cold, perfect for comet-watching, and there it was, a pale smudge in the sky.

On the bus ride we had talked about mutual acquaintances in the Tenderloin, but it was awkward and I felt as if she regretted asking me along. So now I chose a topic I felt certain would engage her. "How long have you had Susan B?"

"Seven years. I got her as a puppy as soon as I moved out here."

"From where?"

"Philly. Do you have any animals?"

"A cat. A big old Maine coon."

"Ooh, they're luscious," she said. "What color?"

"Brown tabby."

"Susan B loves cats. She really does."

"Martin has never met a dog. I keep him inside."

"What a shame. No creature should be kept inside."

"You're making me feel awful!"

She shrugged. "Listen. I pimp my dog. Who am I to talk?"

"Why did you name your poodle after Susan B. Anthony? She seemed so austere, and your dog is anything but."

"I know, I know. She *was* austere, but I love the way she had that single-purpose life. Day after day, week after week, year after year, knocking on doors, explaining about votes for women, collecting support person by person. She spoke in *hundreds* of lecture halls to *tiny* audiences. There she was in her mousy hairdo and plain face and clothes. But Doc, she won. Susan B. Anthony *won*. I love her for that."

The canine Susan B wore a purple sweater tonight, an improvement over the Scottish plaid, and lay with her chin on Flo's thigh. I stroked the fur between her ears. She didn't lift her head but swung her eyes around to peer at me suspiciously.

"It's okay, Susan B," Flo told her. "It's okay."

"I have some patients who are in your writing workshop. They're devoted to you."

Flo looked pleased. "Really?"

"Yeah, really."

Then we sat silently, staring at the barely visible comet, and as the minutes passed I began to feel a rare sense of being somewhere. As if the comet were a private hideaway, an intimate place that Flo shared with me. For a few moments, I felt still, located, not lost.

When the bus rumbled into the parking lot behind us, my usual disorientation returned and I said, "Should we catch that one?"

"Yeah." She told Susan B to hop in the purple bag and zipped it most of the way closed. Then she pushed down on the stone ledge with her hands and lifted her butt into the air, swung her legs around, and leapt to her feet. I scrambled down more clumsily, and we ran across the parking lot to meet the bus. The driver had already closed the door by the time we reached it, but he hadn't started rolling, so we knocked. The man looked at us, then wagged his finger and shook his head, as if we'd just vandalized the side of his bus. He pressed the accelerator and the bus began to pull out of the parking lot.

"What the fuck?" I said, bewildered.

"Idiot shitface!" Flo screamed. Her open-faced hand slammed the length of the bus as it eased past us. "Fucking bastard!"

Two teenage couples sat on the hood of a '57 Chevy, drinking from a bottle in a paper bag. They laughed at Flo and she turned slowly to face them, like a big old bear on its hind legs, containing a power she could unleash at any moment. The kids laughed harder, elbowing one another, but knowing to not make eye contact with her. I turned my back on Flo, not so much afraid of what she was going to do as unwilling to watch. I felt a little like that lumbering bus as it started down the hill, swinging wide to get around the summit of the peak. Dodging, giving a wide berth, leaving a gaping question mark in the middle. Like Liz said, a big life with no center. By the time I turned around, Flo was stalking back across the parking lot, carting her big purple bag with Susan B inside. I followed her, and we sat on the stone ledge, in the exact same spot as before.

"There'll be another bus in half an hour," she said quietly.

"That driver was a jerk."

"Yeah."

"But the world is full of jerks. If you gave each of them that much energy, you'd have none left."

She looked at me and almost smiled. "You should have seen me when I was drinking and using. What you just saw would have been my loving mood."

"When did you get sober?"

"Few years ago."

I touched one of her black curls, then pulled it gently so I could watch it spring. Susan B ran back and forth, sniffing in the grasses at our feet. Then she jumped up on the ledge, and the three of us waited silently for the next bus.

When it came I leapt up, ready to run, but Flo remained seated. "Coming?" I asked her.

"I think I'll walk home."

"Walk?"

"I prefer to walk."

It was hard turning my back and leaving her then. I felt dismissed, like the real event of the evening would be the walk home, which I knew better than to question. *Walk from Twin Peaks to the Tenderloin? Are you crazy?*

I hugged her shoulders from behind and said, "Good night. And good night to you too, Susan B."

Flo lifted her dog's bony little paw as if it were a fist and said in a high dog voice, "Votes for dogs! Votes for dogs!"

"You're nuts," I said, then ran for the bus.

"Hey!" she yelled after me. "You're gonna go on that trip with your sister, aren't you? The comet will be gorgeous out there."

I climbed onto the bus with relief. I like small landscapes, limited territory that I can know. In medical school a professor once told me that most of us have trace bits of iron in our noses that give us our sense of direction. Those without these bits are the ones who get lost—on city streets, on forest trails, everywhere. I've always suspected that I'm one of those missing the trace bits of iron, which makes me uncomfortable in expansive places where the possibility of getting lost is so much greater.

Flo, I bet, had plenty of iron in her nose. She seemed to have lots of geographical reference points—from street corners in the Tenderloin to the comet in space.

I stood and pressed the metal releases on the bus window, and the pane slammed down. The driver looked in his rearview and called back, "Keep the windows closed." Before shutting the window again, I searched the sky and took one last look at that ball of frozen gases and dust.

three: blind date

When I return to the truck after dumping my cigarette butt, Liz, Mark, and Lenny—and, of course, Melody—are waiting for me. I want to ask Liz how she knows the lake ice is frozen solid, that it won't crack as we ski across, but she shoves off and skis down the short embankment to the lake shore before I have time. Mark motions for Lenny, who is trying to look cocky, to go next. At six feet, Lenny has legs like saplings and shoulders like a cement mixer. The poor kid has never been on skis, but Mark tells him it's just like running hurdles only the movements are less exaggerated. Lenny pushes off and Mark shouts, "Bend your knees," which Lenny does, but he still lands on his face at the bottom of the hill, not too far from the trunk of a fir tree on the lake's shore. He laughs, but I can tell that he's angry. I don't blame him. I remember being on ski trips when I was his age, and the adults' expectation that they would build my character. Of course, the trips did build Liz's character, set her on her life path. My father and Liz relished learning wilderness skills as well as the names of trees, lichens, birds, wildflowers, even kinds of ice. For a while I tried to be just as avid. I felt the awe—oh, I felt it—but for me it was awful as well as awesome. All that space, those huge cold mountains, the lurking but unseen presence of wild creatures merely tapped the native terror already inside me. When Mark came into our lives, so eager, I relinquished my place to him. In retrospect, I know I was regretful, that I had experienced what my father and Liz felt but just couldn't embrace it as fully as they did. I hadn't meant to let it go entirely.

Now I'm completely out of practice being in such big, wild places. I need commotion, activity, and bodies. The denser the human population, the more comfortable I am. In pure places, like on this deserted mountain lake, pain is too easy to feel. In the city, where pain sweats out of the very concrete, something in the human spirit—in my human spirit anyway—surges forth to overcome. It's just easier.

Liz dusts the snow off Lenny, getting him to smile with whatever she is telling him. She and Mark are so dedicated. I bet Lenny will be in law school within ten years.

As Melody skis expertly down the slope to the shore, her hips swaying with grace, the sun rises over the mountains in the east, its light leaching the rest of the color out of the sky. I get into a waving dispute with Mark, he waving me on, me waving him on, both of us grinning, until he finally goes. Then I push off, surprised at my own grace after so many years of not skiing. I glide onto the lake ice like a pro, thrust out my poles, dig in, push off, and ski forward.

With the arrival of the sun, a haze of warmth, like desire, infuses the endless space over the lake. For a moment I think it might be possible that Liz is right: Maybe I need this. Maybe I too can learn to use all this space like medicine. But as I breathe in deeply, the cold air scours my lungs, and the snow smells like an ache, hard and sharp and metallic. My resolve of the moment before gives way, and I fantasize about Sunday afternoon, thirty-six hours from now, when we will return to the parking lot and drive to a truck stop restaurant. Liz promised. I'll have the salad bar, including the Jell-O jeweled with fruit cocktail and the fake crab salad, followed by a rare steak, and a baked potato piled with butter, sour cream, imitation bacon bits, and chives. Maybe even a gooey, overly spiced piece of apple pie with cardboard crust. I know I'll feel proud of myself then for having slept in the snow, but tomorrow evening seems far away.

We make our way across the mile-long lake in single file like a family of ducks, Liz in front. Mark skis directly behind her, which surprises me because I expect him, as one of the trip leaders, to take up the rear. Melody follows close in his tracks, and I wonder why she is along. She isn't unemployed or a Latin American refugee; she isn't one of Mark and Liz's projects. She hardly looks like anyone's project. Tall and strong, she has a cloudless face, clear to the bottom. She wears a red-and-white-striped stocking cap, the kind with a long tapering tail, over her short and ragged-cut light-brown hair. There is a lemony innocence about her, a freshness that almost stings. She strikes me as very young.

At lunch last week, when Liz told me that Mark's employee was coming along on the trip, she had raved about the woman.

"Wait until you meet her. She's beautiful and really smart."

I picked up a hidden agenda and wanted to ask "So?" but kept quiet.

"Mark hired her to be the receptionist and do some data entry, but he says she's brilliant. He'd hire her in a second as an editor, but he can't afford another editor."

"That's great," I said. "She's young, right? She has time to find a better job."

"As if Mark wants to let her go! He figures he *has* to promote her or she'll leave. Sooner or later."

Mark started his educational publishing firm fifteen years ago and still struggles to find a market for his environmentally conscious, multicultural science and history texts. He does find one, but it's small and cash-poor.

I changed the subject, asking how the new kids, as in goats, were doing.

"Fine," Liz said, then persisted with, "Melody has been with women."

So that was it.

"But she considers herself straight," Liz added.

"Is that right?" I pretended to suppress a yawn.

"So she says. But I think maybe she just needs the right woman. She's only thirty, after all. She probably hasn't had that much experience of any kind."

I thought this was an interesting remark for Liz, who had never been with anyone but Mark, but, distracted with the need to get back to the clinic, I said, "Well, if she says she's straight, I guess she's straight. It's her call, right?"

Liz gave me her exasperated look.

"Liz, I have a waiting room full of patients. I have to go."

Our lunch was supposed to have been a planning meeting for the snow-camping trip. Liz had presented me with a list of what to pack and what to rent. I didn't care who else was coming along, and I *really* didn't care about her sexual orientation.

I hugged Liz goodbye, made tracks to the nearest pay phone to call Alice, who I knew had the day off from work, and begged her to go over to my house to feed Martin. I had been at Lucienne's the night before and hadn't made it home in the morning. By the time I got back to the clinic, half an hour late, and endured a lecture from my nurse, I had forgotten about Melody.

Only now, out here on the lake ice where I have nothing but my own thoughts for entertainment, it becomes suddenly obvious. Melody was invited along for my benefit. This is a weekend-long blind date. I groan so loudly that Lenny, skiing in front of me, turns to look.

"Having a good time?" I ask.

"Fuck, yeah," Lenny says. "See that mountain over there?" He points with a ski pole, loses his balance, and almost goes over. "Fuck," he says.

"Yeah, I see it."

"I'm climbing it."

"By yourself?"

"Oh, yeah," he says. "Fuck, yeah."

Lenny is not my responsibility, I tell myself, but I guess I had better mention to Mark that Lenny thinks he's going mountain climbing this weekend.

"I want to climb Everest by the time I'm eighteen."

"It's good to have goals."

"You see that show on all those climbers who died trying to climb it?"

"I did, but I can't say it inspired me to put Everest on my to-do list."

"They were totally stupid. You gotta know what you're doing."

"Always a good idea."

"That part about the guy calling his wife from the summit, you know, while he was dying? That was fucking awesome."

"I doubt she thought it was fucking awesome."

"That's how I want to die."

"On the phone?"

"Hell, no. On the highest spot in the world. *Living.*"

How can you die living? Lenny's contradictions weary me. What I suddenly want to know is, if this trip is a blind date for me and Melody, why am I saddled with the kid, this talker with a healthy imagination? Shouldn't Mark be doing male-bonding with him while I get to know Melody? Yet he, my sister, and my blind date are skiing forward as if they've forgotten Lenny and me altogether.

"You like fish?" Lenny now asks, and I'm relieved he's finished with Everest. I don't want to hear any winter survival, or failure to survive, stories until we're in that truck stop, sitting on vinyl and eating something hot.

"If it's grilled and served with a good sauce," I say.

"I got mayonnaise."

"You have mayonnaise in your backpack?"

"Fuck, yeah. I figured I'd catch us some fish. I once fished through a hole in the ice in a lake like this and caught ten salmon."

"You mean trout."

"Hell, no. *Salmon.*" He stops skiing and holds his hands a good meter apart, the poles dangling from his wrists, to show me the size of his catch.

"Well," I tell him, "salmon would be a heck of a lot tastier than whatever slop Liz and Mark have planned. And I can eat salmon without sauce."

"It's good with mayonnaise."

"I could try that."

I glance ahead at the stalwart threesome, who are skiing forward in tight formation as if they are bound together.

Oh, hell, I think, let them go. I know Liz won't let me out of her sight entirely. At least this kid isn't a sulker—not yet, anyway.

"Want a cigarette?" I'm not above buying off people. I give candy to the children in my practice and placebos to the adults. People want medicine, and I usually don't have time to win trust the slow way. Besides, Lenny is a big strapping boy. Out here I want him as my ally. You never know.

"Yeah."

I look around, wondering if I really want to stand still right here in the middle of the lake. It is, after all, March. When do these alpine lakes start melting? My mind runs a quick-time movie, like the ones they show in national parks, of the ice melting around the edges, big blue puddles forming around our feet, long sharp cracks separating with a groan.

Now I *really* want a cigarette.

I manage to get the pack out of my pocket without taking off my backpack; I skin off my gloves and hold them between my knees while I knock out two cigarettes and light them both.

Lenny also has shed his mittens and holds his cigarette between his thumb and forefinger, like an old-time movie star, and smokes greedily.

"How come you didn't bring your own?" I ask.

He shrugs.

Actually I'm tempted to give him the whole pack. It's high time I quit again, but the thought of quitting makes me draw the smoke more deeply into my lungs.

"I can take all the salmon I want," he says. "I'm Indian. We have fishing rights."

"Is that right?"

"Fuck, yeah."

"Which tribe?"

"Apache." He spits on the ice and squints up at the mountains, exhaling a cloud of smoke. Mark never mentioned his being Indian. "If I win, I'll be the first American Indian Olympic gold medalist."

"You're going to the Olympics?"

"Fuck, yeah."

"In what?"

He taps some ash onto the snow, awkwardly, and suppresses a cough. He gives me a sidelong look, evaluating whether I believe him or not. I'm touched that he cares. Most tellers of tall tales—I'm not yet ready to call him a pathological liar; maybe he's just a kid with a little bit of difficulty in distinguishing between dreams and real life—don't seem to care if they are believed.

"Hundred-meter hurdles. I've been invited to training camp this summer."

I can't resist offering, "Most Olympic athletes don't smoke."

He comes right back at me. "Most doctors don't smoke."

"You're wrong there. A lot of doctors smoke and worse."

"I'll stop if you stop."

I'm surprised by this offer. He looks sincere, his bovine eyes on me, waiting for an answer. "We got a difficult weekend here," I tell him. "Maybe after."

He snorts as if I'm just another hypocritical adult.

Forget this kid, I think, annoyed. I'm getting worried about the sun, which is coming up with a vengeance. Maybe I detect softer-looking ice, possible melting. I'm also nervous about the retreating backs of Liz, Mark, and Melody, now the size of chipmunks.

I've always hated to lose sight of Liz, but standing on this lake makes me feel an even more acute need for her presence. On a gut level I don't approve of her spending so much time in wilderness, especially around lakes. Probably the same way she doesn't approve of how much I talk about Timothy. In the end we're doing the same thing, exploring the same terrain, only language is my geography.

"Has Mark or Liz ever told you we lost our little brother on a camping trip?" I ask Lenny. "On a lake like this one. But in Oregon."

He takes a hard drag on the last half-inch of his cigarette, squinting at the most distant mountain in what seems to be his imitation of a grown man, and shakes his head. I can't tell if I have his attention. So I wait, intending for my silence to ripen his interest. He gives me one of his askance looks. He's gorgeous in a big-nosed, all-eyelashes kind of way.

"I'm the only one who will tell you this story," I say, as if that makes it more valuable. "Liz doesn't like to talk about it."

He nods, manages another drag on the cigarette, which by now is all filter. I realize my talking to him about Timothy is pathetic. As if I'm trying to strike some sort of deal: I listen to your stories and you listen to mine.

I counsel myself to drop it but steam forward anyway. "I was only ten, so it's hard to remember everything. Liz was eleven."

Lenny drops his cigarette onto the lake ice. We both watch the orange butt fizzle out. He glances ahead at the distance growing between us and our partners.

"I'll tell you later," I say. "It's a long story."

I can't help feeling a little hurt that he hasn't lapped up the chance to hear my story, but I too am eager to catch up to Mark and Liz. I'm amazed they haven't stopped to wait for us. I'm not even sure any of them have turned around to see where we are. This is not like Liz. Nor like Mark.

I pick up Lenny's cigarette butt and shove it along with

mine in my pocket, and we set off again. Lenny's skiing makes mine look elegant. He's all muscle on his skis, working them like two shovels, as though if he skis *hard* he will ski better. And yet, despite Lenny's clumsiness, his strapping youth more than makes up for his inexperience. He's faster than me. With panic I realize that I'm the runt of this skiing pack.

Mark, Liz, and Melody are waiting for us, on the far side of the lake. It must be Mark who raises an arm and waves.

As Lenny and I approach the shore, I see that from there we have no choice but to ski uphill, into the mountains, and I miss the flat lake even before I've left it. As I shuffle into their rest spot, Mark is distributing dried pears, from their own tree and dehydrator, and homemade energy nuggets, both of which I eschew, knowing that all too soon I'll eat them ravenously. I'm determined to hold on to my culinary principles for as long as possible.

I shuck my backpack and see Melody noticing me, as if my noticing her for the first time as we crossed the lake drew her attention. She had slept yesterday evening during the long drive up to the mountains and was silent early this morning when we left our motel rooms and drove to the pass where we parked the truck. Now I hold her eyes for a moment and she smiles. It's a candid smile, as if she is a part of this unspoiled landscape. She has snatched off her stocking cap and her hair stands up in clumps all over her head. I feel my sister watching me and know she is willing me to find Melody attractive. I hate disappointing my sister. Melody *is* attractive, but I'm distrustful of her apparent purity—even her smooth, white-iris skin and five-foot-ten posture—though I've always wanted to kiss a woman who was tall enough to make me have to lean back my head.

I feel a kindling in my chest and avert my eyes, perhaps only a response to this wild landscape. I suddenly have the familiar urge to say Timothy's name, as if he's a foothold. I scan the horizon, which is sharpening up as the sun rises and the sky's color deepens. I wonder how far back into these mountains we will go. I calm a stab of fear by reminding myself that it is only for one night. I will be between my own flannel sheets, along with Martin's furry body, tomorrow night.

"I doubt Timothy would enjoy a trip like this," I say, unable to control my impulse. "He would whine."

"We wouldn't have taken him when he was little." Liz surprises me with an answer.

"No, but still. He hated the cold."

The reference to the cold is going too far. I've conjured the picture of him in his little red swimming trunks, his pale body covered with goose flesh, his eyelashes clumped with lake water.

"Everyone ready to go on?" Liz asks. "We'll follow the drainage until we get out of the forest. Then we can choose our route above tree line."

"Who's Timothy?" Melody asks.

"Tina's mascot," Mark tells her, stepping behind me to knead my shoulders. "How's the pack feel, kiddo?"

"Not as bad as I thought it would. I'm scared of those hills, though." I nod toward the drainage Liz said we'd go up but keep the rest of my body in place to receive Mark's hands. He gives the best shoulder rubs of anyone I know.

"Timothy," I tell Melody, "is our little brother. He disappeared on a camping trip thirty years ago."

"Disappeared?"

"Christine," Liz says.

"Come on, Tina," Mark backs her up as usual. "Later."

"Later," I tell Melody, winking, trying to communicate that it doesn't have to be as heavy as everyone makes it. "I'll tell you the whole story."

"She will too," Liz says. "As many times as you want to hear it."

"Be nice," I tell her.

She makes kissy lips at me and I laugh, saying, "Besides, I have to have a word with you."

"Me?" she says, all innocence.

"You."

"Later," she mimics me.

When I glance at Melody as I heft my backpack, I notice she's studying the exchange between me and Liz.

I smile at her. "Do you have a sister?"

She shakes her head.

"Lucky you."

"If it weren't for me, you wouldn't know how to get up in the morning," Liz says. "I've taught you everything you know."

"You don't know half of what I know."

"I don't want to either."

I throw a snowball at her legs and she laughs. Thank God. The weekend will be a lot more fun if she loosens up.

Lenny pantomimes smoking to me.

"No way," I say. "I thought you were quitting."

"Not if you're not."

"Since when is my life tied to yours?"

He looks away, embarrassed, and I feel bad. I hadn't meant to sound so harsh.

"Next stop," I tell him. "We got a minimum supply and an increasingly stressful weekend. Look at those mountains. We're on serious rationing."

He shrugs, and I resist the urge to pat his face. He has that adolescent boy combination of hulking animalism and tender confusion. I hope Liz and Mark succeed at straightening him out.

It's only a bit after seven as we start climbing into the hills above the lake. I want to ask how far we're going but don't want to appear whiny in front of Melody, who looks fresher than when we started. I wonder if her being a Buddhist affects her approach to skiing. Maybe it helps. I decide to try to stay in the moment myself. But as soon as I get there, in the moment, or as in it as I can get, I realize it's painful, the moment is painful. My legs hurt. My chest hurts. Almost immediately I give up the present moment and project myself into a possible future one. With Flo. If she is so keen on seeing the comet outside of the urban glow, maybe she'd agree to a trip to Portland, where we could look at it through my father's telescope. He would love that. Maybe it's my endorphins kicking in, but I get immersed in my fantasy, including the long drive up Interstate 5, the possibility of her and my father hitting it off, finding a good place out of town for viewing the comet, and then a long night, maybe in sleeping bags, as we talk about everything we haven't yet talked about and watch the comet travel across the sky. Who needs the present moment when possible future ones feel so good?

Mark is skiing out front now, and Liz takes up the rear. Melody, skiing beside me, asks if I've read any good books lately. I mention Alice Munro's newest collection, which pleases her, and for the next half-hour we talk about the authors we like, and not only do I forget the pain in my shoulders, I forget Flo.

"So what do you do?" Melody eventually asks.

"I'm a doctor."

Melody nods intently. Everything for her seems terribly, not serious exactly, but real, as if my words have a shape, color, and smell. She handles them, gives them what appears to be her full attention and yet feels more like a style than actual listening. She asks, "Do you have a private practice?"

I tell her about the clinic in the Tenderloin.

"What do you do with the rest of your time?"

"The rest of my time?" I ask, stymied.

"So," she says slowly, speaking as if she is placing a piece in a jigsaw puzzle, "you work all the time, like Mark."

"And Liz," I add automatically. Then, trying to think of a way to make myself sound more well-rounded, I say, "I also spend time with my sixteen-pound Maine coon cat, Martin."

"And read books."

"And read books." I decide not to mention that I read a lot more than literature, including tabloids. I have a feeling I would get a demerit. "And you? You work at Mark's firm."

She nods. "I've been there a year."

"That long?" I wonder why I didn't hear about her until just a few months ago. "Is publishing your chosen field?"

"I'm not sure."

Maybe it's the stuffy way I asked the question, but she suddenly seems uncomfortable, so I change the subject. "Do you ski a lot?"

"Whenever I can. I live to be out here."

"Ah." A definite fork in our interests.

We ski silently for a few minutes, and I realize that the other three have gone ahead. I like to think Melody is skiing with me because she enjoys my company, but it's probably just wilderness protocol. This is as fast as I can go, and you just don't leave someone behind.

Tree line approaches. I eye the harsh white mountains ahead with suspicion. There are only two colors above tree line, blue sky and white snow, and only two textures, whispers of air and crunchy spring corn beneath our feet. Melody and I push through the last straggly firs to the open slope, so brilliantly lit it looks hot. We're silent as we ski uphill into this open country, and that silence is too big. So I ask, "Would you like to hear what happened to Timothy?"

She says, "Okay," but I hear fear in her reply. She needn't worry. I'll only tell her the version I've been telling for years: short and matter-of-fact, the version Robin criticized as being "doctor-like." She was right, of course. Just as a doctor gets used to the details of disease—not hardened exactly, but accustomed—I've become used to my story of losing Timothy. Robin's prodding and inquiries served only to seal my official version. This landscape, though, as sharp as a scalpel, seems to lay the story open at my feet, revealing much more detail than I've seen in years.

four: losing timothy

It was Memorial Day weekend, too early for the mountains, particularly in the higher elevations where we liked to go, but an unseasonable heat wave had been forecast and my mother wanted to get away. "From the city," she said. "From everything. I'm so damn sick of it." On Friday evening we drove to a high-elevation campground that hugged the western shore of a large lake in the Cascade mountains of Oregon.

On Saturday, even at seven in the morning, the air was velvety with the promise of heat. Liz, Timothy, and I sat at a picnic table wolfing our cornflakes, already in our swimsuits, eager to be set loose in the mostly empty campground. My mother boiled coffee on the Coleman stove, joking about not having any eggshells to make it authentic. I noticed she had brought her brushes and watercolors and had already laid them on one end of the picnic table, and that made me relax. We all relaxed. Sometimes I blame that air, the heat, as if it lured us all into a kind of false comfort.

The early alpine light was wispy, like cobwebs, and if I had been older, more aware, that might have worried me, the absence of the usual clairvoyant blue. Then, I cared only about the lake. I don't remember its name, but I can picture it perfectly: big, oblong, brown around the perimeter and gray in the middle, lined sparsely with trees on the western shore, the side of the campground, and by boulders and smooth basalt cliffs on the eastern side. Undoubtedly carved by a glacier, the lake must have been unusually deep, deep and very cold.

From the vantage point of a little girl, it appeared to be a perfect swimming lake, and I anticipated being a fish all weekend. My mother finally let us loose, warning us to stay out of the water for a full hour and not to go in over our knees when she wasn't around. She settled into a camp chair with her novel, cup of coffee on the picnic table next to her, and put her feet up in another camp chair. I remember hesitating for a second, noticing her complete contentment, and per-haps that too was responsible for what happened, the way I trusted that her contentment meant something, that I could let go of the edge I had carried all the way up here in the car the night before, the tension from their fight.

"You gonna paint, Mom?" I asked.

"Mmm," she said, already smiling into her novel. Then she looked up. "Take your brother."

Liz and I waited in the road for Timothy to catch up. He grinned foolishly, happily expecting to take part in our adventure.

After walking the campground loop, we surveyed the lake shore, searching for an ideal swimming site, found it, and tested the water by wading in up to our shins. It was bitterly cold, so cold my legs ached to my crotch. After all, the lake had probably melted only recently. Even worse than the cold, though, was the lake bottom, ankle-deep silty mud full of scratchy little sticks, the possibility of fish hooks, and worst of all, an entire ecosystem of slimy mud dwellers. On a camp-ing trip the previous summer, I had waded out of a river to find nine leeches affixed to my legs. With that still fresh in my mind, and because we had to wait an hour before swimming anyway, Liz and I decided to build a pier on which we could walk out to a deeper part of the lake and avoid wading in the slime. We weren't yet ready to admit that the lake was far too cold for swimming, regardless of the composition of the lake bottom.

After that moment in which I realized my mother was, at least for the time, content, she dropped from my thoughts, and I indulged in the kind of freedom only a child truly knows, that freedom of complete immersion in a project. I'm sure Liz didn't think of our mother that morning either. I assume, though, that she remained happy, sitting in the warm morning shade, drinking coffee and reading her novel. She has always been an avid reader, perhaps an addictive one, but this was before she had moved from novels to self-help books. I know she didn't touch her paints that morning, because when we eventually returned to camp they were in the exact same position on one end of the picnic table, but I imagine she enjoyed the possibility of painting as she read, the choice. My mother worked most of her life as a medical illustrator, drawing pictures of intestines, tumors, muscles, and brains. Only on vacation did she draw or paint for fun, and less and less as her life wore on.

On Thursday night my mother and father had the last fight I remember them having, the last *actual* fight. After Timothy disappeared, it was war, cold war, but no more battles. At dinner my father had said, "The rings of Saturn should be phenomenal this weekend."

My mother's eyebrows did that little leap they do, while at the same time her lips compressed just as Liz's do. She knew exactly what he was saying, but gave him a chance by warning, "Visibility should be ideal in the mountains."

"Mmm," my father said, and remained quiet for a few beats. We all did. Then he said, "I really want to use my big telescope." Meaning, not the portable one. Meaning, he was canceling the family trip to the mountains.

"Damn it, Oscar."

"It's just that I have this pile of tests to grade—"

"The test you gave two weeks ago."

"That's right—"

My mother pushed back her chair and fled to the bedroom. We all knew she'd emerge again in just a few minutes, face scrubbed, and have a plan. That time, the plan was to go without my father. The way she announced this decision implied that it would be a grand adventure, that the four of us would have more fun without him, that we had just been dealt a stroke of luck. I knew my father would do the dishes and then try to rub her shoulders. She would refuse to acknowledge the fight, so she wouldn't exactly shrug him off but would find something to do in another part of the house. And he'd shuffle off to his telescope with relief.

My mother was in a bad mood all day Friday, but that warm air on Saturday morning must have melted away her fury. The warm air, coffee, and a good novel, the anticipation of a long weekend of pleasure.

As Liz, Timothy, and I built the pier, a bit of a haze drifted into the sky, but I can't remember from which direction. It seemed to thicken the growing heat, and drops of sweat formed on my upper lip.

In my memory of that day, the haze seals Liz, Timothy, and me into that spot by the lake, holds us eternally in the heat. I wish I knew from which direction the haze came: east or west? Liz could probably say, but we have never talked about the details of this day, even though our lives are an endless discussion of it.

Doesn't everyone hate their little brother at that age? We did. It wasn't real hatred, of course, just extreme annoyance. I was keenly aware of, and disappointed in, the fact that Timothy was a much less than ideal brother. The way this story goes, the way he becomes a tragic figure, you would expect him to have long black ringlets and ice-blue eyes. Or golden pale hair, like the tips of fire, and gossamer veins in his delicate skin. It wasn't like that. He was a regular boy with limp, mouse-brown hair, ears a bit too big, sticking out. His lips were overly red and always damp. And he smelled funny. I worried that he wasn't attractive enough for our family. I resented his needy wet lips, his slightly stinky scent, like milk about to turn bad. In real life, most of the time, I didn't like Timothy.

But I didn't dislike him any more than any girl of ten dislikes her five-year-old brother. I worshiped Liz, and Timothy was a constant obstacle to our exploits. We were expected to include him, particularly on vacations, and the truth was that we even loved him sometimes. He could be very funny. We read him stories and made up roles for him in our games— usually, as was the case that morning, roles that occupied him but kept him clear of us. I realize now that even before he disappeared, he threw Liz and me together. As different as she and I were, even as children, we were together against him. We became best friends because of him. It has never changed.

I was very excited about our pier. It was just the kind of project I loved. A long log, too thin and wobbly to walk on, stuck out into the lake. Our plan was to shore it up with rocks to make the pier. For a while we let Timothy help. We had found a good pile of stones in the woods and were carrying them, one at a time, to the lake shore. To do this we had to pass through an unoccupied campsite. In the course of the morning two or three cars pulled into the site, considering it, then moved on.

Timothy wasn't very good about carrying the stones, being so small, and he cried twice because of stepping barefoot on sharp objects. Liz thought up another job for him. We had found a small raft made of four boards nailed across two logs. We couldn't believe our good luck, and although there were no other children, no other swimmers at all, out this early, we wanted to make sure we had the raft for the day. Liz put Timothy in charge of guarding it.

I remember seeing him standing in the lake mud, the water midway up his shins, holding on to the raft. I also remember being a little afraid of the cruelty in giving him this job. Maybe the lake mud didn't terrify him like it did me, but he was covered with goose flesh and his quivering lips were magenta. I remember wishing he would grow up.

Then he started whining. We were taking too long with the pier, he said. So Liz waded out, enduring the ice-cold water and muck, and lifted him onto the raft. "There," she said, "float."

"I'll start placing the rocks," she announced to me. "You keep getting more."

"I want to build the pier too," I told her.

"You will," she said. "But we can't leave Timothy alone. You get rocks for a while and I'll build, then we'll trade."

"Okay." I glanced at Timothy, who now giggled on the floating raft. Liz waded out and put a hand on the raft and dragged it in closer to shore.

When I returned with another big rock and dumped it on our pile, Timothy was lying on his stomach, paddling his hands over the sides of the raft, making motor sounds with his lips. Liz was working arduously and didn't look up as she said, "More small rocks."

Back into the woods, I walked a little deeper to find a place out of sight so I could pee. I found a log covered with a carpet of bright-green mosses, a couple of lady ferns growing from them. I rested my thighs on the mossy log and hung my behind over the back and peed. The cool of the forest was pleasant, and I was tired of doing the rock labor, so I dallied for a while, kicking at the forest duff with my bare toe, examining the interior of the moss. I don't know how long I put off returning to my sister and brother. I carried an extra big armload of small rocks to make up for taking such a long time.

As I walked back down into the campground, I saw a yellow car pull out of the campsite by our pier. That car, I learned a moment later, carried away Timothy.

Of course I don't tell Melody all of this, only the usual story including the pier-building, the yellow car, the months-long search. I keep it short and undramatic, trying to convey with my voice that this was thirty years ago and that I have long since come to terms with the loss of my brother. Even so, we've stopped skiing and stand together on the slope, facing but looking beyond each other. She inhales a couple of deep breaths, I guess as a way of showing respect for my story, but she seems distracted, even a little annoyed, as if the story has something to do with her. Her mouth is slack with strong feeling. Fear? Sorrow? Dread? Sometimes people don't know what to do with the pain they assume other people carry.

"It was a long time ago," I tell her, trying to give her the distance I give myself.

"What about Liz?" she finally asks. "Has the loss been hard on her?"

"You'll have to ask her." I wonder why she would ask about Liz and know my sister would never answer her question.

Melody nods and I feel stupid, like I discussed something too intimate with someone I don't know. She seems unable to even look at me. How, I wonder, does a Buddhist experience this raw landscape? I take a deep breath and try to practice mindfulness. It is a bit too primitive out here. A haze suffuses the clarity of blue that led me forward moments before. Now it is white sky on white snow. Being mindful of the moment brings me to the sharp pain at the base of my neck. Of course there are dozens, maybe hundreds, of facets to any moment. Thirty years ago, and yet Timothy has been a part of every moment in my life since, including this one now. Another facet of this moment is Melody's clear-to-the-bottom face and that crazy hair, standing out raggedy all over her head. She wears fleece tights on her long legs and a Gore-Tex shell. I am very mindful in this moment that she is the only human being in close proximity, that besides her my moment contains snow and a sky filled with frozen ice crystals, a haze that could become snow later today.

I want to touch her, not from desire but because she is all that exists out here on this white canvas. And *seeing* her isn't quite enough. I'm afraid to blink; she might disappear. I'm also afraid of what I think is her desire for silence.

"Thanks for listening to my story," I say, controlling my urge to touch her, and begin skiing uphill toward Mark, Liz, and Lenny, who are tiny figures on the mountainside ahead of us. "What about you?" I call over my shoulder. I hear a sharp exhalation, a cross between a laugh and the sound you make when someone hits you on the back.

"I try to lead a simple life. No big stories."

The word "try" is a dead giveaway.

"Do you have a partner?"

To this she is silent, also an intriguing answer.

I let her be then, and we ski silently for the rest of the morning, never quite catching up with my sister and her crew. I see them stop occasionally, presumably to check on us. I have the feeling Melody feels burdened by me, that she wants to go on ahead but thinks, rightly, that she shouldn't desert me.

As we approach the summit, the distance to which seems to stretch continuously, I decide to propel myself the rest of the way by singing, silently, all the songs on my *Best of Janis Joplin* tape. But as soon as I start my off-key, imaginary Joplin concert, I get side-tracked thinking of Flo.

I like to assign musicians to the people in my life. Dylan is forever attached to Mark. Lucienne gets Aretha, in part because Aretha is the only nonclassical musician she'll listen to. Flo gets Joplin. The way Joplin threw a saddle on her pain and rode it hard. Except that Joplin's pain kicked back and killed her. But not Flo. She hung on.

Two days after the comet-watching night, I found Flo on Market and Powell, where the cable cars stop. Even in January there are some tourists in San Francisco, and they line up for the length of that entire block to ride the cable car up the hill. Flo and Susan B had a small crowd. She had just finished her jokes and the audience was dispersing. I hung back, trying to hide behind the easel of a man who was painting twenty-minute portraits, but she spotted me through the lace of people, just as she started the first poem.

I didn't like watching her perform her poetry, even if I

didn't listen to the words. The idea of standing on a street corner announcing your rawest truths to anyone who would listen appalled me. I wanted to drag her off the street, take her for a cup of coffee, a bowl of soup, a matinee, anything but watch her arms, legs, hands, curls, mouth on the street saying words that shouldn't be said, words that she pulled from...where? By the time she finished, I was one of only four spectators, not counting those who paused in passing. I moved from behind the easel and stood twenty feet away. Susan B stared at me the whole time, ready I suppose for me to put my hand in my pocket. I looked at Flo's feet, at her hands, only occasionally flicking my glance across her face. I was embarrassed by the size of her audience, but she continued, as if she had a pact with herself to finish, to always finish. No matter what. Susan B Anthony won because she never stopped, no matter how small her audiences.

Afterward, Flo thanked the other three, then grimaced at me and said, "Who let you out of the clinic?"

"Lunch. And I'm late."

"I'll walk you back."

The next time, two days later, I listened to the sounds of her poetry. Not the words, not that yet, but the notes and rhythm, as if her poetry was easy-listening music. I let it spill over me but made no commitment to the language. She had a crowd this time, but I felt as if I were her intended audience, as if reaching me was her goal. As if her poetry was a dialogue—only I wasn't allowed to speak. And yet, I left before she finished.

I was back within the week, and this time I listened to her words.

It wasn't that I was afraid of *what* she said. God knows I hear it all every single day in my practice, but I felt awed by the way she located, named, owned, and most of all, used her pain. Listening to her made me realize how losing Timothy sucked the center out of my life, created a permanent vortex into which anything was liable to fall. The loneliness I felt could not be handled because it was an absence, not a presence. I was jealous of the specificity of her pain, the way she connected the beating of her heart with the blows of her childhood, how they echo today as desire, even as joy, echo as primordial touch, the beginning of feeling. Those blows, she said, are the Adam and Eve of her sense database. Hearing her stand on the street and reel off words as wrenching as music made me feel as disoriented as this wild silence, this landscape of harsh air and mountains makes me feel now.

I stayed that time and asked her out for a bite to eat. We went into an old-fashioned diner on Market. I got coffee and she ordered a piece of cherry pie for Susan B and herbal tea for herself.

"I can handle the humiliation of being a circus act," she said, sneaking a bite of pie down to Susan B who was in the big purple bag at her feet, zipper open. "I hawk poetry. That's what I do. But I hate having to pimp my pup. Florence Hughes, performance poet and poodle pimp. At least my title has alliteration." She swallowed some tea, looked questioningly at me, but I hadn't any idea what she might be asking. I wanted to tell her I admired her, both her and her poetry. For having the guts to give it away. If I opened my mouth, though, I was afraid I'd tell her not that I admired her, but that I thought she was out of her mind, which was equally true.

"I've tried it without Susan B," she said. "I make maybe one fourth what I make with her. It pisses me off that people like dog tricks four times better than poetry. Still, if it keeps them standing there listening, I'll do it. Do you think I'm a shit for using my baby-dog that way?"

"No."

"Well. I'm glad you don't think so. I keep my house-painting business so I don't have to exploit her any more than I already do."

"Flo," I said. "Your poetry is…startling. It knocks me out. Do you write it down?"

"Of course I do, Doc. I'm highly educated. You don't have to worry about that."

"I'm not worried about that."

"I have a university degree and everything."

"Me too," I said, smiling and understanding her defensiveness. Because I work in the Tenderloin, full-time, not just a few hours of weekly charity work, some people assume I'm not a real doctor, and lots assume I'm not a good doctor.

She smiled back, getting it. "I've been published in a couple of dozen good journals. But I haven't been able to sell a volume of my poems."

"You will."

She looked into her mug of tea and scowled, then braced her elbows on the table and made two fists. I tried to imagine what it would be like to be tender with her, but I couldn't. It was as if she were more condensed than most people. Still, I longed to run two fingers along the length of her arm. That was when I decided that Flo gets Joplin.

As Melody and I ski switchbacks up the long side of the ridge, using the tracks already laid down by Liz, Mark, and Lenny, I swear I'll give the rest of my cigarettes to Lenny and quit today, this moment. Melody took the lead a while back, and I'm nearly hyperventilating as I try to keep up. Now and then she calls, "You okay?" and I answer, "Barely," but she doesn't slow down. She is obviously eager to rejoin the rest of the group. I add *join a gym* to my stop-smoking resolution.

As the top of the ridge is finally within actual reach, the white haze puckers and separates, forming into billowy clouds. With big parcels of blue, the sky looks much more friendly, and a private breeze blows through my chest. We crest the summit at last and look out over miles and miles of mountain peaks. In the distance a lake the size of a small sea lounges like royalty.

Melody doesn't even stop, hardly glances at the mountain range and Lake Tahoe. She skis over the top of our ridge and down the back side, toward the threesome below us, as if she just can't wait to get there. Very goal-oriented, I think, for a Buddhist. I stay for a moment, trying and failing to comprehend the 360-degree view. This vista is too deep and expansive to hold in my heart, but it flows in anyway, like some kind of fierce electric current. The horizon is the longest I've ever seen, a full circle, which makes it eternal. I turn my back, so that hopefully the others can't hear me, and shout, "Timothy!" I cup my hands around my mouth and call his name over and over again.

five: camp craft

I watch Melody ski down the slope, her hips gliding back
and forth as she makes turns in the crunchy snow. She
snowplows to a stop in front of Mark, Liz, and Lenny, where
they stand at tree line, waiting for me. I push off and tra-
verse down the slope, skiing nearly parallel to the ridge top
so that I lose only a few feet of elevation at every turn. When
I finally get there, Mark is passing out energy nuggets again,
and I eat three.

Liz announces, "About a half-mile through these trees
there's a really nice opening with a view. I'm thinking of
camping there. Everyone game?"

"Sounds perfect," Mark says. "Melody?"

"I like it."

"Tina and Lenny?"

"What do you think, Lenny?" I say. "Do we like it?"

"Fine with me."

"Do we get lunch then?" I want to know.

"Yep." Liz takes off.

I love the idea of being there already. It's not even noon. Do we get to set up the tents and take naps? What else would you do all afternoon in the snow? I'm sure Liz has plans, but skiing isn't a team sport; they don't need me.

Then I wonder who will be sleeping with whom. There are probably two tents. Of course Mark and Liz will sleep together. They wouldn't throw Lenny in with me and Melody, would they? Not if they want to set us up. Besides, they'd need to keep an eye on Lenny. So that's it: me and Melody in one tent, and the other three in the other tent.

I'm in a good mood at lunch. Our campsite is lovely, set in a few trees and looking across a long valley to more mountains. We're perched on the side of another ridge, not nearly as high or exposed as the one we just skied over. Mark scoops snow into a big tin pan and Liz fires up the stove.

"Portobello mushroom noodle soup," Liz says.

"Cheese sandwiches and raspberry newtons," Mark adds. They don't even have to talk about who does what. It's like a dance the way they make lunch.

Melody sits on her backpack, after placing her sleeping pad under it, so Lenny and I follow suit. Lunch is actually fun. We crack jokes and look at the view, which is manageable from this treed vantage point. Thinking the worst is over, I'm delighted with myself for skiing this distance with a pack and looking forward to lying in a warm down sleeping bag in a tent until tomorrow morning. I can handle this.

After lunch, Liz scrubs her soup mug with snow and says, "I'm going to look for a good cave site."

"Cave?"

"Snow cave."

"I'm sleeping in the tent, thanks."

"We don't have a tent," Liz says, as the sun slips behind a cloud.

"That's not funny."

"Winter camping isn't supposed to be funny. You have no

business being out here if you aren't willing to develop the skills you need to stay alive."

She at least has the decency to hold my glare, her basalt eyes the center of the gray, sunless world. "Liz!" I nearly shout.

She turns her back and trudges through the snow and into the trees, where she stops, puts her hands on her hips, and peruses the hillside.

"Liz!"

"We'll need two caves," she calls back to Mark, ignoring me. "One for Lenny, Melody, and Tina, and one for us."

"What?" My sister billed this weekend as a lark, a couple days of hardy, yes, but *fun* outdoor play. Some blind date.

"Don't you think we could all sleep in one cave?" Mark says, following his wife.

Liz stops and turns. "There are five of us."

"One big cave. All the warmer." Mark stands with his hands, gloveless, dangling at his sides. He looks oddly helpless.

I sputter expletives.

"I just figured the hillside wouldn't accommodate a cave that big," Liz says.

"Let's try," Mark insists.

"It's a lot of work if it fails."

"You know, Liz," I say, "this makes me really mad. You didn't tell me we'd be—"

"You'll love it," Mark cajoles. "Besides, it's a heck of a lot warmer than a tent."

"I can't believe you didn't bring a tent."

Liz has returned to her pack, and dug out her rubber-soled, felt-lined boots, and she pulls them on with as much authority as I would imagine her signing directives at work.

Mark gives me his sheepish look, as if to say we'll be better off if we indulge Liz. He too changes into his other boots and tromps off with Liz to look for a cave site.

All this time, Melody has been standing with her back to the rest of us, looking at the view. Do we irritate her with our bickering or is she contemplating meditating? I feel jealous of her…her what? Detachment? But a moment later, when Mark shouts for us to come look, she is the first to snap into her skis and dash off in the direction of his voice. I roll my eyes at Lenny and ask if he knew we would be sleeping on the snow.

"It's fine with me," he says. "I've been through a lot worse."

I pull out two cigarettes, light one and hand it to him.

He chuckles like an old man. "This is a hell of a different kind of journey than the Trail of Tears, though."

"Mm-hmm," I say, again wondering why I'm left with the kid.

"You know about the Trail of Tears?"

"Sure."

"I was there."

"Is that right?"

"You don't believe me?"

"Wasn't that in the middle of the last century? Like 150 years ago?"

"Between 1830 and 1842." At least the kid pays attention in history class.

"I remember every detail. My spirit inhabited my great grandmother's body."

I'm nervous about the next few hours and don't have the patience for Lenny's stories, so I'm quiet for a few beats, but then I realize silence might be worse. In a forced voice I say, "So, Lenny. Tell me what the Trail of Tears was like. From a firsthand perspective."

Two streams of smoke flow from his nose like a dragon. "Dusty. Real dusty."

"Yeah, Oklahoma's like that."

"We walked for ten days without a drop of water. My great grandmother's skin was like a hide. Her tongue was like a piece of wood."

"That's intense, Lenny."

"Fuck, yeah. It was intense, all right. If my spirit hadn't been in her body, she wouldn't have made it."

"Are you sure about that?"

"Am I sure? Look at me. I'm six feet tall. I'm strong as a fucking ox."

"Lenny," Mark says, returning from the trees, "watch your language."

"Your great grandmother might have been stronger than you think," I say.

"What I'm saying is that it's a fucking trip—"

"Lenny," Mark says. "I don't want to have to talk about this the whole weekend. Clean language, period. Got it?"

Something about me makes Lenny a little rebellious. The way Mark glances at me, I can tell he thinks so too. I raise my eyebrows and widen my eyes, defending my innocence.

Mark tries to give me a meaningful look, then says, "I want an answer in the affirmative, Leonard."

"Fine," he says, then continues to me, "—because if I hadn't been in my great grandmother's body, keeping her strong and alive, then I never would've been born. See what I'm saying?"

"I do."

"In essence, I brought myself into the world."

"That's heavy."

"Yeah, it is. I'm thinking of going on a vision quest. I might be able to communicate with her."

"When?"

"Today. Tomorrow maybe."

"We've talked about this," Mark says. "You're staying with the group the whole weekend. No exceptions."

"What about shitting?"

"Of course, buddy. No one's going to watch you do your private business. Now come on, both of you. I want to show you the cave site we found. Bring your shovels."

I glance at Lenny, who's looking at his feet, blinking hard. For a moment I think he might be fighting tears. But when he looks up and meets my eyes, I wink and he pulls the right corner of his mouth up. We change into our felt-lined boots and follow Mark. About fifty yards from our lunch site, Liz and Melody discuss a short but steep embankment they figure will be perfect for the snow cave. Liz is saying—it seems for about the tenth time—that the embankment is big enough for two caves.

Mark asks, with uncharacteristic annoyance, why she is she so dead set on two caves. One would be warmer and more fun.

"Fine," Liz hoists a shovel. She jams it into the snowbank, pulls out a load of snow, and throws it in the direction of Mark's feet.

Now I really am confused. What's she so mad about?

Mark explains the snow cave plan to me and Lenny. First we'll dig a three-foot-long tunnel, angled upward so that the warm air, which will eventually emanate from our bodies and gather in the cave, won't flow out. The hardest part will be when we start to dig the cave at the end of the tunnel where there's no room for wielding a shovel, but eventually we'll end up with a tunnel entrance that leads to a big, snowy, domed cave with a flat floor, supposedly big enough for five.

"Mark," I say, "you should have told me." It's hard to stay mad in the face of Liz's mysterious anger, but I've always trusted Mark to tell me the real deal and I feel betrayed.

"Grab a shovel and take a turn." He casts his eyes meaningfully toward Liz, who has already achieved a two-foot-long tunnel. *Don't aggravate her more* is the message, and I wonder, since when do we consider Liz a sensitive flower?

"Let me at it," Lenny says, relieving me, and Liz, of digging duties.

I stand off to the side and try to figure out what is going on. Liz has always been bossy, and it's not unusual for her to be somewhat blind to the desires of others if they're in opposition to her own, but I've always been her weakness, just as she's always been mine.

Now that I think about it, though, the last time we really had fun together was last spring, nearly a year ago, when we flew to Portland to visit our parents. We only had time to stay the weekend, so we took them out to a nice dinner on Saturday night. Liz isn't much better than they are at indulging herself, but something about their austere presence throws her into my camp, and we enjoyed ordering an expensive bottle of pinot noir, then another, and insisting on appetizers and desserts. Our father had on his khakis and safari vest and our mother wore her denim skirt, ever practical, as if always prepared for a natural disaster. Liz and I told them lots of stories, about the city and our friends, her land deals and my patients, and they shook their heads slowly as if we had put them on a merry-go-round and were spinning it as fast as we could. At the end of the meal, during coffee, my mother sat back and looked at Liz for a long time, then me. She had draped an arm across the back of my father's chair, and I noticed that her fingers rested on his shoulder. She looked old to me then, they both did. And while Liz leaned into a story, her face flushed with the wine and our not quite forced but somehow overly intentional laughter, a sheen of tears brightened our mother's eyes. It was Liz. Liz's effort. And I'm sure it was my effort too, the two of us a perennial team, perennially trying. My mother knew something we didn't, which of course is ironic because she hadn't been there, and we had. She and my father had found comfort with each other at last. But she knew Liz and I were still straining at the bit, and she was sorry for us.

At the time, I assumed Liz hadn't noticed anything different about our parents, but I never give her enough credit for her skills of observation, outside of scientific inquiry. It's just as likely that I had been the blind one, that the change in my parents had happened years before but I'd noticed it only then. If she had seen a change in them, she chose as I did to pretend she hadn't. Later that night, we lay in the twin beds of our childhood room, behaving like our childhood selves, telling stories and stuffing the pillows over our faces to muffle the laughter. I had just met Robin and was at the stage of wanting to describe every detail of her life and body, especially her body. Liz was high from having landed a huge deal for the agency, a deal that would save the lives of thousands of harbor seals, and her victory made her silly, allowed her to even make fun of the seals, not to mention the jowly attorney who headed up the opposition. That night we found everything hilarious.

Only now, standing next to my sister as Lenny assaults the snow with his shovel, do I remember my mother's comment as we headed up to bed that night. We stood at the foot of the stairs and she took each of our faces in her hands and kissed us good night. "I'm so proud of you girls," she said, "to think how many lives you've saved between the two of you."

I'm getting cold standing around waiting for a shoveling turn. Because the tunnel is so narrow, only one person at a time can work on the snow cave. Soon Lenny has completed the tunnel and he starts widening the end of it for the boudoir. To warm up, I shovel his debris away from the cave opening. After a while, Lenny emerges, wet and frustrated. It looks like painstaking work, laying in a snow tunnel on your back and scraping at the end of the hole. He brushes snow off his jacket and pants.

"Are we having a campfire tonight?" he asks.

"No," Liz says.

Lenny scowls.

"Why not?" I think of the warmth and color.

"You don't have campfires on snow-camping trips."

"Let's break a rule."

Liz, who hasn't let go of her shovel all through Lenny's digging turn, drops it now. She comes to my side and puts her head on my shoulder, and suddenly I realize I'm not what's bothering her this trip, that even my predictable needling reassures her somehow. She lifts her head and takes my face in her hands, just as my mother had that night. "We can break any rules you want. It's just that you can't build a fire on snow because it melts the snow and a fire won't burn in a puddle. Besides, there's nothing to burn. All the firewood is under the snow."

I smile at Mark, relieved that we're all falling back into our roles, and say, "She's got a couple of good points there."

She drapes an arm around my shoulder. "I'm not trying to ruin your fun."

Still, I persist. "How about that guy in Jack London's story? There was plenty of snow when he built his fire." I turn to Lenny. "This guy was lost in the winter wilderness. Nothing but snow, right? Him and his dogs. He tries to get a fire going and fails. In the end he has to cut open a dog and crawl inside to get warm. Inside the dog's opened body."

Lenny blinks, considering.

Mark grins.

Lenny says, "Who did that?"

"A guy in a story by Jack London."

"Let's build a fire," Lenny says. "If that guy could do it, we can."

"The point of that story," Liz says, "is that he *couldn't* build a fire."

"Look," Lenny raises his eyebrows and purses his lips. Screwed-up kids are often masterful negotiators. "Let's say something goes seriously wrong out here. Let's say a bear takes our packs and we have no food. Let's say the shovels break and we can't build the snow cave. We would *have* to build a fire or die, right?"

We all stare at him, adjusting to the improbability of his story.

He steps closer to Liz, towering over her, and quotes her verbatim. "You have no business being out here if you aren't willing to develop the skills you need to stay alive." He adds, "Building a fire in the wilderness is a skill everyone should have."

Liz looks at Mark and smiles.

"Touché," Mark says. "Okay, Shackleton. Go for it. Five people can't dig a snow cave anyway. You want to help him, Tina?"

"Who's Shackleton?" Lenny asks.

"A guy who explored Antarctica."

"Let's go," I tell Lenny. Having a project suits me, even if I'm yet again paired with Lenny. Let Mark handle Liz and her weird mood. And Melody is just too quiet for me. A voice is probably the warmest thing I'm going to get all weekend, so I'm sticking with the talker.

As we trudge back to the packs, in the area we have designated as the kitchen, I hear Mark say, "A fire could be fun."

"I think we need a strategy," I tell Lenny. "They don't think we're going succeed."

"Oh, we will."

"Right. But let's have a plan to make sure." I offer the idea of putting down a bed of green branches on which to build the fire. Lenny suggests digging a pit in the snow and then stomping on the floor of the pit until the snow is packed solid as ice, then laying the bed of greens on that. Hopefully the greens will keep the melted snow from dousing the fire, and the walls of the pit will protect the fire from wind.

"It's a plan."

We work together digging the four-foot-square pit, one foot deep. Through the sparse alpine trees I see the green, red, and blue parkas of the others. Long silences are broken occasionally by Mark's jokes and laughter.

"You find the green branches," Lenny instructs after we finish stomping the floor of the pit into as solid a base as we can. "I'm going to get benches."

"Benches?"

"To sit on."

I'm just along for the ride. No commentary. If Lenny wants benches, we'll have benches. I change back into my ski boots and skis, knowing I may have to go fairly far afield to find green branches. I'm tempted to break them off living trees but know Liz would be furious. As I ski downhill, deeper into the trees, I find some downed branches that must have broken and fallen in recent winter storms. I drag these back to camp and break them into pieces the length of our pit. An hour later, I've laid down a thick bed of branches, too green to burn, that will insulate the fire from the snow floor of the pit. I am struck by what a large project we've undertaken and also by how much I am enjoying myself. I've always loved construction, projects that have concrete results, measurable success factors.

I thought medicine would be like that. But on most days, with most patients, I'm mucking my way through thick gray areas. Where does mental illness stop and physical symptoms start? What is medication, that substance my patients want so desperately, and to whom should I give it? Reality hasn't stopped the fantasy, though. I long for that moment in a theater or on an airplane when someone suddenly shouts, "Is there a doctor present?" and I jump out of my seat and save a life. Without qualification. Of course there are moments of clear triumph. A kid *doesn't* bleed to death. A case of syphilis *is* caught before it's too late. But I spend most of my time begging women to insist that their partners use condoms or trying to convince mothers there's no cure for a cold. Most of the time I have to pretend that what I do is an absolute science, that I have definite answers, because people want that so badly. Then, alone with my doubts, I pray that my ministrations have some positive effects.

Liz's work yields far more tangible achievements than mine. She can tally up dollars raised, laws passed, and acres of wilderness saved. Her work strikes me as excessively tedious—the endless meetings, the writing of grant proposals, the baby-steps approach to getting something done. But in the end, on her global scale, she's likely to save many more lives than me.

Lenny spends the next couple of hours hunting down three logs, which he rolls, relishing his own brute strength, great distances to our campsite, where he arranges them around the pit. As he's doing that, I search for dry firewood. I finally find an entire dead tree lying across the snow in the forest. It's covered with dry branches that snap when I break them off the trunk. I ski back and forth with armloads of these, making a big pile behind one of Lenny's logs.

I'm surprised that neither Mark nor Liz come to check on us. I'm sure they can see us through the trees, as we can see them, and usually Mark is like a puppy in groups, running back and forth, eager to know what everyone is doing. I have been telling myself that Liz would never lose track of me out here, but my sense of security may be false. Perhaps it is the armloads of firewood I'm carrying, which remind me of the stones thirty years ago. Or perhaps it's noticing Liz's fierce concentration on her own construction task, which makes her oblivious to me and Lenny. Like before. Whatever the cause, I have this thought: Liz is not a safe person.

Just then Mark does come through the trees to check on us. Thank God for Mark, I tell myself for the millionth time, feeling a burst of affection for him.

"Whoa," he says when he sees the pit, green branches, log benches, and pile of firewood. "You two are the most serious campers ever."

Lenny grins. "Call me Shackleton."

"Yeah," Mark says. "Next year we're doing the South Pole. You game, Tina?"

"Sure. Oh, yeah, I'll be there." I plunk down on one of the logs. "Very comfortable," I tell Lenny.

"We're almost done with the cave. It's going to knock you out. You two okay for another few minutes?"

"We have some finishing touches to attend to," I tell him and he leaves.

Lenny and I pack the sides of the pit, divide the firewood pile into kindling, midsize pieces, and all-night logs. It's four o'clock by the time we finish, and shadows stretch across the blue, icy snow. Though the sun still hangs over the mountains to the west, it is a weak orange star, its long rays piercing the chilled air, more decorative than serviceable.

Lenny and I are inordinately proud of our preparations.

"Do you want to build the fire or should I?" he asks.

"I think you should. Do you know how?"

"Huh!" he scoffs. "That is something I definitely learned from my ancestors."

I think of the fire in the garbage can at school that landed him in juvenile detention. He probably thinks this is going to be as easy as tossing a match in a big metal can full of greasy french fry cartons.

In spite of his long body, Lenny squats delicately in the snow pit. He reaches behind him and breaks small twigs off the pile of dry branches. These he shapes into a tepee in the center of the bed of boughs. His huge hands are surprisingly graceful as he adds increasingly larger sticks to the tepee. He stands then and looks at the sky and mountains. "We'll wait for dark," he says, and gives me a full, beautiful smile.

"I wish I had a camera," I say. "This fire-to-be is f—, uh, gorgeous." For Mark's sake, I refrain from swearing.

"Yeah," Lenny says. "Fucking gorgeous."

It really is. I stare at the benches, pit, bed of boughs, and twig tepee like they are salvation. It will be dark in a couple of hours, and I can't bear the idea of spending the entire night in an ice vault. If I want, I can stay by the fire all night long.

Still restless, Lenny searches for more wood while I sit on one of the logs, exhausted, and wait for the others.

When Liz returns to the campsite, she looks as though we've slaughtered a grizzly bear and are cutting steaks off its rump.

"We didn't touch a single live tree," I defend myself before she can speak. "Everything we used was dead and down."

What we've done goes against every natural grain in Liz's body, but she refrains from saying anything. She even forces a smile and says, "It'll be fun." I get up and hug her, because I know she is being generous.

"I told you they weren't kidding," Mark says when he and Melody arrive a few moments later.

"I'm gonna ski back to the lake," Lenny says, "and get us some salmon to cook over the fire."

His delight is childlike, anything but delinquent, and I can see Mark mentally debating how to handle this. Of course Lenny can't ski over the ridge to the lake and back by dark. Of course he has nothing with which to cut a hole in the ice, nor a fishing pole. And of course there are no salmon in that lake.

"Aw right?" he asks, rubbing his hands on his thighs.

"Come have a look at our chalet," Mark says, trying to change the subject. "You have the space blankets in your pack. Why don't you grab them."

"Give me your sleeping bags," Liz orders the rest of us. "I'll lay them out in the cave."

"I'll do that," Mark says.

"It's okay," Liz insists.

I hand Liz my sleeping bag, but Mark intercepts it. He takes the space blankets from Lenny, gathers everyone else's bags, then heads to the snow cave alone, forgetting his invitation to Lenny, barely able to walk under his load. Melody busies herself with her pack, and Liz sits on the log with me. I feel bone-tired and lonely. I hate the tension between Mark and Liz.

"Well," Liz says when Mark returns, "what does everyone want to do? We've got a good hour before dark."

"Fish," Lenny says.

I say, "Hey, I want to ski to the other end of the ridge. Come with me, Melody? Lenny?" Maybe Mark and Liz need a little time alone. "Come on. A quick ski to the other end of the ridge. Just a few minutes."

But Liz chimes right in. "Hey, Lenny, we promised to teach you how to ski turns. Want to give that a shot for a few minutes? Then we'll light the fire and have dinner."

"You two go on," Mark says to me and Melody. A look of defeat slackens his face. "We promised Lenny we'd teach him how to ski turns."

"Lenny can come with us," I say. "We'll show him."

"What about fishing?" he says.

"Sorry, buddy. The lake is too far away and we don't have

the proper equipment. We'll go fishing this summer. What say we practice those turns?"

I give up trying to get Lenny to come along, figuring this is all part of Liz, and maybe Mark's, plan to set me up with Melody. Once Liz has a plan, it takes legislation to stop her from carrying it out.

Melody doesn't look enthusiastic. She glances at Mark. He smiles.

"Okay," she says with a shrug.

six: linguistics

As Melody and I ski away from camp, I don't even try for conversation. The late-afternoon light makes me pensive. The air feels substantive, yet clairvoyant, like an ether that can read a soul, that has zero tolerance for bullshit. It scares me in the same way Flo does, but unlike Flo, this air doesn't have a form I can embrace.

But then I can't embrace Flo either. When I tried to kiss her a week and a half ago, she told me she was celibate. If she'd left it at that, maybe I would have too, but when I stepped back she said, "Sometimes I can't see you in your eyes. It's like you disappear."

Because she touched the huge ache in me, and because I couldn't bear that, not even for a moment, I leaned in and tried to kiss her again.

"Hey, you have a girlfriend, don't you?" she asked, stepping back.

Not exactly. But if I were to explain to Flo that Lucienne

was a product of that vanishing point that is me, that shifting horizon, I would only prove her point. How could I tell her Lucienne helped to hold me up but was not central?

I met Lucienne in the summer before my second year of medical school, nearly ten years ago. I had been celibate since high school, a whole five years. Lucienne likes to say that we became lovers because I stalked her for so long she had to give in. If I'm present when she tells this story, I tell mine, which is that she placed an ad in the *Guardian* addressed specifically to me. She claims this is out and out false. Whether she wrote the ad or not, it—and not my stalking—is what brought us together.

The first time I saw Lucienne was at Café Flore on Market Street. She was smoking a Gitane cigarette, drinking an espresso, and speaking with a lusty French accent. She waved the cigarette in the air as she asserted her opinion to a mousy woman sitting across from her at a table on the patio. Lucienne, a solid 200 pounds on her five-foot-six frame, wore a tweed jacket with suede elbow patches, horn-rimmed glasses, and a white T-shirt. There, I thought, is every mother's worst fear. If Lucienne were a question on *Jeopardy!*, the answer would be, "What is butch?"

She was very compelling. Though all the details of Lucienne, from her short brown hair to her chubby hands, are as ordinary as dirt, the gestalt of the woman is mouth-watering. It isn't true that I returned to Café Flore every few days to see her; it was the only place that carried the kind of peppermint tea I like. I did notice that Lucienne was often at the café and that she looked at me frequently, almost the way people glance at mirrors as they talk. I had the sense that she thought I was watching her and liked seeing that in me. Lucienne has a healthy ego.

It never occurred to me to approach her. Then late one night while reading the *Guardian* on the couch in my studio apartment, after several months of this mutual reconnaissance, I found the following item in the personals:

> You have deep chestnut hair, not quite shoulder-length, with red highlights in the sun. Your dark eyebrows are full, nearly singular, and your lips

have the look of being gorged, dark and overripe.
Your eyes are brown but not chocolate-brown,
instead they are opaque and crisp, like autumn
leaves. You are gorgeous.

You drink peppermint tea at Café Flore. I dare
you to talk to me.

I sank back on my couch with a wistful lust. Oh, to have
someone write that for me. I mentally ran through all the
Café Flore regulars I could remember and tried to match the
description of this chestnut beauty. I thought of cutting out
the ad so that the next time I was at Café Flore, if I saw someone who matched the description, I could hand it to her. This
woman should not miss this opportunity. Things like this happen once in a lifetime.

It wasn't until about twelve hours later, while I was studying an immunology text, trying to get a jump-start on next
year's reading, that it smacked me in the forehead. *I* drink
peppermint tea! I had never in my life been called gorgeous,
but I do have dark chestnut hair and full, if not gorged, lips.

And of course it could only be the Frenchwoman who
smokes the Gitanes. Who else?

I couldn't go to Café Flore for a week. Every time I
approached, it was as if I glanced off some anti-gravitational
force when I got within sight of the place. By the time a week
had gone by, however, I felt ridiculous that I had even
believed it could be me. The place sold peppermint tea, right?
Clearly they wouldn't stock it if a lot of people didn't order it,
right? A lot of women have chestnut hair and full lips, right?

Convinced that the ad had nothing to do with me, and
tired of bad tea, I finally returned to Café Flore. I didn't see
her that time, nor the next time nor the time after. Then one
Friday evening when I couldn't have looked any less gorgeous,
there she was. My skin was yellow from lack of sleep, and the
half-moons under my eyes were small bluish pillows. I hadn't
washed my hair that day. I got my peppermint tea and took a
table on the patio with my back to her. This time she was

speaking in French to a man who spoke back fluently.

Rubbing my forehead, I thought of the "dark eyebrows, nearly singular" part. That, I had to admit, was not a common physical attribute. I turned slowly, feeling like I was in a novel—in fact, Lucienne always made me feel that way, as if the part of my life I shared with her was remote from my real life—and looked at her. She was listening to her coffee date, but that didn't stop her from looking back. Maybe it was the fatigue intoxicating me, but I didn't feel like wondering anymore. I pushed back my chair and walked over to her table. I held out my hand and said, "Hello. I'm Christine."

She hesitated for a moment, then dragged one of the metal chairs, creating a spine-tingling scrape, across the paved patio from the table adjacent to hers. "Have a seat," she said, and turned back to hear what her friend was saying.

But he pulled on his black leather jacket and said, in American English, "Actually, dear, I've got to run. We'll finish later." He stood, leaned across the table, and kissed her on the lips.

"Lucienne." She extended a hand, which I shook.

We talked the rest of the evening and made a date for the following day.

I didn't reference the ad, and neither did she, for several months. When I did mention it, I did so obliquely. "Do you meet all your lovers by leaving messages in newspapers?" I asked.

She inhaled on her Gitane, then stubbed it out in the tin ashtray. We were again at Café Flore. "What do you mean?"

"'I dare you to talk to me,'" I quoted.

She gave me a faint smile as she exhaled the smoke. "I'm not following you."

"Never mind." Embarrassment at believing I was that gorgeous someone stopped me from pursuing it. The idea of showing her the ad filled me with chagrin. What if it hadn't been her? What if it hadn't been written to me? It didn't really matter anymore anyway.

Later, much later, I asked her directly. I never showed her

the ad, claimed I had thrown it out, but I told her its contents, most of them. She laughed heartily but denied it. By then she had fully developed her stalking story, and the ad was my only defense. To this day, we both claim that the other first initiated contact.

Lucienne is my longest-term lover, though we rarely see each other as often as once a week. Most of the time I am Lucienne's only lover, but she's more comfortable when I have others. She likes lots of elbow room. When Robin decided to stop seeing me—mostly because of Lucienne—I knew Lucienne would love (a verb she has never attached to my name) me less with Robin gone.

Sometimes I think Lucienne and I could have, should have, fallen in love at the start. But we didn't. I was just trying to get through medical school, and anyway the mere thought of being in any kind of intimate relationship was a breakthrough. Big, solid Lucienne held me up. She was beginning work on her Ph.D. in linguistics, and that was passion enough for her.

I have, for years, blamed our loose arrangement on linguistics. Lucienne is obsessed with the intricacies of language, which makes it nearly impossible for her to make a commitment to specific words, or even to the things that words represent—but then Lucienne doesn't even believe there is a clear distinction between things and the words for them. I've told myself that Lucienne is too creative with language; that in her mouth, words and sentences are a medium that move as fluidly and brilliantly, and as fleetingly, as the aurora; that to pin her down verbally would be the same as physically restraining an extraordinary dancer.

I've had to use hyperbole to support my ongoing commitment to someone as elusive as Lucienne. But the truth is, if Lucienne liked me at a distance, that suited me too.

Robin, who of course hated her, said she was arrogant.

Flo would say she's just a bunch of talk.

seven: endless task

Melody and I ski past the occasional clusters of scrubby trees along the backbone of the ridge. Our two figures, scissored legs and swinging ski poles, cast long black shadows onto the snow. I watch the stretched exuberance of our likenesses as we ski; they make us look more athletic, more graceful, than we do in the flesh. Soon we glide to a stop on the nose of the ridge. Behind us is the much higher ridge, well above tree line, that we skied over this morning. To the east the mountains glow fire-red in the late sunlight.

We could turn around now, go back to camp, but I know that would disappoint Liz, our being gone alone together only fifteen or twenty minutes, so I say, "I have an idea. Let's ski down this slope, then around the front of the ridge, and come back up the other side."

You could mistake her face for placid, but it's not; it's composed, a composure she has worked for, a studied calm. I can't help wanting to know what she has had to hack through to get it. When my father, Liz, and I used to backpack, we'd bushwhack through tangled manzanita to reach pristine lonely lakes in basalt basins. What is Melody's manzanita? For that matter, what exactly is her pristine lake? Somehow I suspect it is not so pristine, but definitely lonely. Her reticence, her perfect skin, even the way she seems to approach her spiritual practice, strike me as parts of an oh-so-carefully-constructed solitary habitat. As much as I try to like her, I don't.

"Okay," she says to my proposition, and skis down the short slope.

At the bottom we look around, take bearings.

"What if there's a cliff or something on the other side?" she asks.

"It'll take us ten minutes to ski over there and find out. If it doesn't look like a straight shot back up to the top of the ridge, we'll come back and ski home the way we came."

"Okay."

I laugh. "Who would have thought I'd ever call an ice cave home?"

"For tonight it is."

Keeping above the big trees, we ski around the nose of the ridge. I venture, "I think Mark and Liz are trying to set us up."

She expels breath. "I don't think so."

"Oh, I know my sister."

She shakes her head. "Did you and Liz learn to ski together?"

"My father taught us."

We had always been car campers, but after Timothy disappeared my father became obsessed with skiing and hiking and river rafting and travel, anything adventuresome. He left us for weeks at a time to trek in the Himalayas or kayak in Alaska, while my mother's anger calcified at home. There were no fights after Timothy disappeared, the stakes were too high, but I know that each of my parents tried to strike a deal with the other and that neither recognized the other's terms. My mother gave up trying to lure my father home. In fact, she set me and Liz loose too, commenting in every way she could think of that our heads were as much in the clouds as our father's, trained on minutia light years away. The clearer it became that both Liz and I would be scientists, like our father, the more she threw up her hands as if we were lost causes. She devoured pop psychology and self-help books, while we took on geography and biology. The sad thing is that I think my father truly believed he had come home after we lost Timothy. He all but gave up his telescope, and therefore the universe at large, and turned his focus on Earth. In my mother's eyes, he was gone now more than ever, but in his scientist's eyes, he had traveled some 800 million miles, the distance from Saturn to Earth, toward home since that Memorial Day weekend.

I told Melody, "I quit going on backcountry trips with them when I was a sophomore. Liz and Mark went with Dad all the way through high school. Even some in college."

"Mark?"

"Oh, yeah. You know, he and Liz got together when they were fourteen. He and my father hit it off right away. You should have heard the three of them when they got back from a trip and told the stories. They were like old war buddies."

"That's nice," she says softly.

"Yeah, it was," I lie. I hated losing Liz to Mark and witnessing the intensity of their comradeship with my father. Once, in an adolescent fury, I screamed, "Mark isn't Timothy, you know!" to which I got three blank looks, from my mother, my father, and Liz. Already Timothy had become a taboo topic; no one mentioned his name, although his photograph sat, obscenely huge, on the mantel of the fireplace. I felt as if Mark were a replacement. In retrospect, I know I was wrong. Liz fell in love with Mark, who was a wonderful kid and now a fine man; that's all that happened. He fits in our family beautifully. If he replaced anyone, of course, it was me. But that didn't really happen either. Stupid childhood jealousies.

There is much less sunlight down here, off the ridge top. The trees are black and upright, the air raw and bracing. I think fondly of tonight's fire. It makes the surrounding icy blueness bearable. Even, for a moment, lovely. A plane flies overhead, the sun glinting off its steel casing, and I feel sorry for the pilot, who undoubtedly is returning to a home of insulated walls and a mattress bed. I smile at the absurdity of my thoughts. Me, exulting in the wilderness! It must be the adrenaline.

When we reach the other side of the ridge, I look up a long white ascent. It's a gradual slope, even more gradual than the one we came down. I feel strangely exuberant about being right and say, "See, not a cliff in sight." I would love a cigarette to celebrate, but I left my supply at camp. I'm sure smoking would offend Melody anyway. I wonder if meditation would help me quit.

"What time of day do you meditate?" I ask as we begin climbing.

"Morning and evening."

"Does it help?" I ask and immediately think how inane that sounds.

But she answers quietly, "Yes."

I take the lead in climbing the slope, skiing a pattern of extended zigzags. The climb takes longer than I'd expected. When I stop to rest I notice that all the pinks and yellows are gone from the western horizon. The sky is deepening into the blues of nighttime. Dusk often makes me feel as if I'm losing my grasp, but right now the failing light is tender. A softening. A letting go rather than a losing grasp. If I had the time every day to sit and watch dusk happen, it might not be so frightening.

I continue climbing and make it to the top without stopping again. But as we crest the ridge I see nothing but a scattering of trees and more snow. Somehow we have missed camp. I feel responsible for our miscalculation and say, too cheerfully, "I'm sure they're very nearby, just behind some hillock or down in a small dip."

Melody doesn't speak.

"Or this could be the wrong ridge," I say, knowing how in

the wilderness it's easy to think you're doing the most elementary thing—like skiing around the nose of a ridge—and in fact do something else entirely. In the wintertime it can be even more confusing because everything melds into white, obscuring depth perception.

Melody still doesn't answer.

"But what other ridge is there?" I ask, rhetorically, because there are ridges all around.

"We should have gone back the way we came," she says.

I look down the long slope. It's nearly dark. This has to be the right ridge. We must have overshot camp. I assure her we need only ski along the ridge a bit and we'll see camp. But in which direction? We haven't been gone more than forty-five minutes. Liz, Mark, and Lenny have to be nearby. I want to yell for them but that seems so undignified.

As I ward off panic, Melody studies the mountains surrounding us. "That biggest snow field there, the one on the haystack-shaped mountain." She points. "We were directly across from that. I think we need to ski south of here. Quite a bit."

"Okay," I agree, trying to maintain control of my voice. I feel a funny combination of fear and awe. We might die of hypothermia, but it will be a beautiful death. Fucking gorgeous, as Lenny would say. It's a relief to feel a specific fear, that of dying out here in the snow-covered mountains, rather than the overwhelming anxiety I feel so often in life. Out here at least I know my foe.

"Okay," I say again, "then let's go." I glance at Melody, whose face I can barely see in the dim light, only the white strips of her long stocking cap. I move in closer and say, "Okay?" and then see that she's more scared than me. That surprises me, her being the mountain woman and all. Her being a Buddhist and all.

"Hey." I touch her shoulder with my mittened hand. "It's going to be all right."

"Maybe, maybe not," she says.

As we ski along the ridge, the stars thicken. There is no moon, but the combination of starlight and snow is bright enough to see by. To distract us, I ask her which Jane Smiley books she has read and learn that she has read everything, even *The Greenlanders*. We exchange details about the folks in that story who endured the brutal winters by shutting themselves in drawers and virtually hibernating for months. Talking about their lives makes this little sidestep of ours seem like a piece of cake. I'm scared only in spurts.

The part I don't like is that since it's so open up here, we ought to see or hear our group, even if they're a distance away. We finish with *The Greenlanders* and ski in silence for a while, and I begin, just a little, to feel as if I'm living my worst nightmare, my Endless Task dream in which I must accomplish something plainly impossible, and yet there is no alternative. The task is always abstract, formless, and it presses on me like suffocation. Now, sliding through this endlessly white and black canvas, I feel as if my world is losing its defining edges. I anticipate a crushing numbness, the reduction of color and borders. If this progresses, it will soon be just me and the overwhelming task of staying alive. I am not there yet, but I see it ahead of me. Maybe a moment ahead, maybe an hour.

Sometimes I think it is this very moment that Liz wants most for me. She thinks that if she can get me truly lost, geographically lost, I would get over *feeling* lost, which in her way of thinking isn't lost at all. Whereas I believe she needs to admit that she—we all—are lost in our lives, however clearly we can state our goals. She and I have danced this dance for years, all thirty years of our lives since losing Timothy, this ongoing but unspoken debate about the meaning of "lost." Lostness is the gravity that keeps us revolving around each other, like two binary stars. And now I feel a surge of fury at her for letting me ski off with Melody so late in the day. Did she hope we would become confused?

Then I see an orange blink. I hear the bass note of a man's voice.

Being lost, then found, is a mighty, and strange, sensation. The hollow fear of isolation and lostness is your whole universe one second and completely gone the next.

Now another light captures my eye. Not far above the horizon, a furious ball of ice and dust with its long, sparkling tail. Worlds more magnificent than the pale smudge visible from the city.

"That was close," Melody says, oblivious to our guardian comet. "I mean, I've been in more dangerous situations before. I mean, it wasn't such a big deal. I don't know. I just got really scared."

"Me too," I say. "We would've had to build another snow cave."

"What if we hadn't found them? Poor Mark and Liz. All alone with Lenny."

"At least they'd be entertained."

Melody strikes out for the orange flicker ahead, and I follow.

She calls back, "I've noticed he likes to talk with you a lot."

"I'm a sucker for talkers."

Mark sees our shadows emerging from the darkness. "It's them!" he shouts. "Oh, man, we were getting freaked. What happened?"

We ski forward, toward the fire, not yet answering, and Mark says, "Melody?" his voice up a register. He lowers it and says my name like a command, "Tina!"

Mark stands a few feet in front of the campfire pit, in which a small fire flares yellow. He is a short black rectangle. Liz and Lenny stay seated on the logs. For a moment I'm torn between the wildness behind me, with its bright comet shooting through blackness, and the family warmth we approach.

"Well, there you go," Melody says to me. "I'm not much of a talker." She is finishing our conversation, and I think I have just been dismissed.

eight: cadaver

Mark hugs me hard, squeezes Melody's arm, searches her face for signs of damage. Her chin quivers once, twice. Then she breathes deeply, removes her skis, and takes a seat near Liz.

"Hey, we're fine," I say, taking off my skis and standing them in the snow next to my pack. "I'm sorry. It was my fault. I suggested we ski around the end of the ridge and come up the other side. But we went way too far and came up about a half-mile back there." Feeling greedy about my cigarettes, I avoid Lenny's eyes as I light one and inhale. The relief loosens me up and I toss him the pack, getting one of his beautiful smiles in return.

"You're here now," Liz says. "Hungry?"

"Definitely."

Complete darkness seems to sit down the moment we do. The firelight holds the five of us like a small golden room. Melody is quiet, having moved to one of the unoccupied logs, where she sits by herself. Lenny and Liz share a log, and I share the biggest one with Mark, who pumps and lights the gas cookstove on a pad behind our log.

"Hors d'oeuvres." Liz hands me a cracker smeared with anchovy paste. The wet fishy-flavored salt smacks my tongue.

"Soup course in about fifteen minutes," Mark says. "Seafood bisque with crème fraiche." He wags a bag of powdered milk.

I'm relieved to see Liz smile at Mark's soup joke as she hands him a cracker. When there's tension between Mark and Liz, everything tilts.

"How was the ski lesson?" I ask Lenny.

He shrugs.

"He's a natural," Liz says.

"Fearless," Mark smiles. "That guy will be skiing off cliffs soon, doing triple flips and landing upright."

Lenny tries to hide his grin by turning outward, toward the darkness, and grabbing a few sticks of firewood.

"Don't give him ideas," Liz says.

Lenny feeds the fire slowly, holding one end of a stick in the flames until it catches fire like a torch.

"We have enough wood here for four fires," Mark says.

"We may need every stick of it. I may stay by the fire all night," I say.

"You'll love the snow cave," Mark says. "We won't be able to get you out of it in the morning."

"What if I get claustrophobic?"

"I put you on the outside, by the tunnel."

"You'll be sorry for forcing me into this. Round about three A.M. my dark side emerges."

"What, you'll turn into a vampire?" Lenny asks.

"Worse." I glance at Melody. She looks once again serene with her cup of steaming soup. "Okay," I say, "if you had to use one word to describe your dark side, what would it be?"

Silence.

"Melody?" I prompt.

Mark and Liz look up.

"She-wolf," she says.

We all laugh.

"Mark?"

"Mark doesn't have a dark side," Liz says.

Mark makes monster sounds and wiggles his fingers in the firelight.

"How about you, Liz, do you have a dark side?"

"What you see is what you get. I don't have any other side."

"Is that right?" My urge to probe is an example of my own dark side at work.

"I have a dark side," Lenny offers.

"I bet you do," I egg him on. "What name would you give him?"

"Leonard."

"Leonard? That's your name."

I look at Mark and he keeps his face down near his cup but the whites of his eyes shine as he lifts his lids and looks across the fire at Lenny.

Lenny says, "My *real* self is my dark side. My light side name is Lenny."

His answer swallows the playful tone and we all tip back our cups, simultaneously draining the soup.

The firelight snags on the prominent parts of everyone's face, creating bright patches and miniature shadows. We all look a bit ghoulish. My question has made everyone shy. Mark, Liz, and I are never short of conversation, and I wonder what, or who, is putting on the damper.

Lenny keeps adding wood to the fire, and it grows. The color of the flames darkens from gold to orange with blue roots. I'm surprised neither Liz nor Mark tell him to stop; it's reaching bonfire proportions. If it weren't in a pit, the flames would be too tall for us to see each other over.

After soup we have what Mark says are enchiladas, a slop of tomato sauce, corn meal mush, and freeze-dried cheese, which tastes pretty good. I'm much hungrier than I thought and happily accept Mark's offer of seconds.

We're silent for a very long time, even as we scrub our cups with snow and hike a distance from camp to bury the toma-toey slush. As we once again take our places on the logs around the fire, Liz hands each of us a peppermint tea bag and Mark pours another round of boiling water. Liz opens a bag of Nabisco ginger snaps.

"You still take these," I say. I turn to Melody and Lenny. "They're the cookies our father always brought. The most flavor for the weight, he'd say."

I take a bite. The gingery burn on my tongue is good with the peppermint.

Still no one else talks. I wish Mark would crack a round of his dumb jokes. I can't tell if the others are enjoying the silence or don't know what to say. Liz seems content enough. I had forgotten how she expands in the wilderness, seems to become more than herself. I realize I've missed so much of Liz, the best of Liz. She seems to be, for once, at rest.

Even so, some conversation would be nice. I remember how I had longed for silence early this morning, but silence at the break of day is entirely different than silence in the black of night. And this is a seriously black night. No haze of urban electric. No moon even. This is pure night.

In a fit of courage I lift my legs over the log and turn to sit facing out into the darkness. I find the comet again, even lower on the horizon now, and think I should point it out to the group. I'm surprised Mark and Liz haven't already done so. I decide to keep the comet to myself. After all, it's at least one of the alleged reasons for my coming on this trip. I study it now so I can give Flo a detailed description: Bigger than a star, smaller than the moon, the comet appears to soar through the sky, leaving a bright trail of white-hot glitter in its wake. The next time I have to pee I'll have to tromp or ski out into the night alone. The comet will set soon and be no help to me then. Maybe I'll make Liz come with me.

Staring into the night, I do get it. I do see how this wilderness sustains Liz, but that doesn't make me feel like tackling it on my own. I want Liz in front. I want her there to bail me out. I guess Liz has been bailing me out for most of my life. Like the time I was flunking out of medical school.

I had been celibate all through college. The idea of touching another body had become repugnant to me, but I didn't admit that even to myself. I rationalized my lack of any social life with my need to make exceptional grades to get into medical school. In a weird, cloistered kind of way, my college years were very pleasant, completely without complications. I studied. Even so, those focused if dry years didn't prepare me for medical school, and especially not for anatomy class, in which I had to touch another body on the first day, a dead one.

The professor assigned four students per cadaver, and my team was made up of Herbert Babkowski, Helen Shoal, and Wally Normal, none of whom had even the hint of a sense of humor, which I recognized on that first day would be essential to finish the course sane. As the weeks went by, other teams developed codes and signals they used with one another for support, to flag a funny moment that later they would buckle over laughing about. Not Herbert, Helen, and Wally— they were deadly serious. When you figure that Herbert became an orthopedic surgeon, Helen a dermatologist, and Wally an ophthalmologist, it makes sense. At the time I thought I'd been assigned to the mentally ill team, and by the end of the semester I felt sure I belonged there.

The body comes wrapped like a mummy. Ours was a young man, only twenty-four when he died of a brain aneurysm. We later learned we were very lucky because the more common cadavers were obese old men who died of heart attacks, who required difficult carving to reach the vital organs. When I suggested to my cadaver mates that we call him Barney, Helen looked at her feet, Herbert smirked at my stupidity, and Wally watched Herbert for his reaction. Herbert handed me the scalpel and told me to make the first cut on "the cadaver," thereby nixing the name Barney and punishing me for suggesting it. I refused.

When the professor told us to unwrap an arm, Herbert motioned for Helen to do that, which she managed without touching the cadaver. When I could no longer put off taking a turn, I put my hand under the wrist and lifted. The skin was not quite spongy, not quite rubbery, something in between, and the arm was stiff and heavy. When I cut into it, there was no blood.

This was nothing at all like sequestering myself in a corner of the library, barricaded with books in a nest-like carrel. The transition from books to cadavers was so very abrupt. You'd think on the first day of medical school they might give you a rousing lecture on ethics, or boost your ego by telling you how many lives you'll save, instead of putting you in a room with dead bodies and telling you to dig in.

That night I called Liz, who was into her second year of graduate school in biology at the University of Washington. For her, lab work meant hiking mountain trails and growing plants. What the hell was I thinking? I told her I was going to flunk out.

"You've had one day. Of course it feels awful. But you'll get used to it. Everyone does. In a few weeks you won't even know it's a corpse."

"He's very young."

"Good. At least you won't have to look at, like, diseased lungs or mammoth tumors."

She took me off guard, her complete nonresponse to my description of the body. That was how it always was, though; Liz seemed to have moved on so completely.

"I wish I was doing what you're doing," I whined.

"It's hard in a different way. Look, this summer I'll be living at 6,000 feet for six weeks. No showers. Lots of hairy men with body odor. Shitty food. You'd hate it."

"Yeah, I would. But you'll love it. That's what I'm saying. At least you love what you're doing. How could I possibly *ever* love cutting up a body?"

For once, she didn't have an answer.

"I made a mistake. I should drop out now. I could probably even get my money back."

"Give it a month."

"Okay," I said. "We have a test in a week."

"That soon?"

"That soon."

"You're good at tests."

"I know."

"So study."

"I will."

"It's going to be okay. It really is."

That gave me courage. If Liz thought it would be okay, then it would. So I thought that night, but in fact it was not okay. I did very poorly on my tests that first year. The closer I slipped toward flunking out, the harder it became for me to study. Day after day we unwrapped more parts of the cadaver's body and sliced them up. In the spring, near the end of the year, the professor told us to unwrap the head.

I knew our boy was fit because of his lean muscles, but unveiling his head revealed a military haircut. Perhaps a Marine. A Marine who died of a fluke cause, and who, prior to that, had broken his nose at least once. His small, fine ears pressed closed to the sides of his head, and his prominent jaw pointed toward the ceiling.

I vomited.

Herbert shoved me away, hard enough to knock me over, but not soon enough to prevent some of the vomit from plastering our Marine's hair. I sat on the floor, surrounded by the cadaver-table legs, blinking hard to try to bring myself into full consciousness. A woman from another team knelt down and helped me put my head between my knees. Then the professor excused me for the day. I flunked a test later that week, and then another one after that.

Liz arrived. I don't remember calling her. I don't remember anything except lying in bed in my apartment, spiraling in a watery vortex. I remember the sound of the phone ringing, over and over and over again. Sometimes someone knocked on my door, but the sound came from a great distance. I remember the sunshine, softened by springtime, bathing different sections of my room as each day wore on. Most of all, I remember feeling not just worthless, but like a nonentity. Like I wasn't. The sensation of dullness caved in on itself.

First thing, Liz guided me to the couch, then washed the sheets on my bed. She opened all the windows in the apartment, shopped for fruits and vegetables, and scrubbed the toilet and shower stall. She asked for the name of my adviser and his phone number and told me to take a shower. She did all of this in half a day.

When I was clean and sitting at the kitchen table, she put a plate of pasta and spinach in front of me and told me to eat. When I finished, she brushed and braided hair.

"Your adviser says you need to get a minimum of eighty-four on your last test to pass the year."

"That's impossible. I've been averaging more like fifty-nine."

"The test is in five days. You have time."

Having Liz at my kitchen table with me was like falling back into a huge armchair after standing on my feet for forty-eight hours. It was as if the entire world were in black and white except for her.

"I'm going to get some old tests," she said.

"No."

"Everyone does it. I've talked to my friends—"

"It's cheating."

"It's not cheating. It's expected."

"I don't care."

"Don't be an idiot."

"Fuck, no, Liz! *No!*" Why, just two seconds ago, did I think Liz the safest thing in my life? Why had she felt so right sitting there at my kitchen table, rescuing me? "You don't have a choice. I'm getting the tests." She stood from her chair, as if she already knew where to go for the tests, as if she were going to walk out of the apartment right then and retrieve them.

"You're not doing this to me again."

You'd think I had struck her. Her chin jerked up and she

took a step back, as if reeling. But she didn't dare question my meaning. She didn't dare say, "Again?" What she did do, though, made me want to apologize, but how can you apologize for something you've never acknowledged happening? She drew a breath through her lungs, and I saw it fill the cells all the way down to her fingers and toes. No one knows how to summon resolve like my sister.

"Then," she said, "we'll have to do it the old-fashioned way."

For five days, Liz took care of every detail of my life. She woke me early, fed me, ran the shower water until it was the right temperature, washed my clothes. While I was in class, she read the chapters in my texts on which I'd be tested. In the early mornings and in the evenings, she drilled me. She broke down the material into sections, and we learned a piece at a time, hour by hour. At night, when I felt certain I couldn't sleep, she brushed my hair until I grew sleepy. Then she'd unplug the phone and darken all the rooms so I could sleep as soundly as possible.

On the day of my test, she drove me and dropped me off at the front door. Then she parked the car and sat on the stairs outside the building until I came out. We went straight to the Zuni Café, where we had martinis, raw oysters, and caesar salads and laughed as if we were girls again.

She amazed me by saying, "Now if you flunk out, so what!"

"What do you mean?"

"You gave it everything. If you flunk out, then fuck medical school. You can do something else."

It was so easy for her. Her philosophy of life: Go full-throttle, and if you get there, good, and if you don't, you weren't meant to be there.

"And if I pass?"

She looked blank. Ambiguity, Liz does not do.

"Do I have to stay in medical school if I pass?"

"Why wouldn't you?"

I didn't have a sentence to answer that, only the picture of the dead Marine's face, the feeling of my apartment being a vortex of dirty sheets and a total lack of resolve. After a year like this, I couldn't think of a single reason to stay in medical school.

"Let's have another martini," I said.

I passed that year by four test points.

A few weeks later I met Lucienne at Café Flore. Touching a live human being felt like salvation, especially one who asked so little of me emotionally. Big butch Lucienne held me up, has been holding me up, physically, ever since.

nine: wildflowers

I swing my legs back over the log and feel the firelight splash my face, drawing me into the picture again.

"Okay," I say, "stories. First time in love. Who wants to go first?"

I've disturbed Liz's contentment. She looks at me with an odd combination of melancholy and menace. I glimpse her dark side, the side she claims doesn't exist. It's there all right, lurking heavy and dark, fast behind her will, that fossilized will of hers.

"We already know your story," I assure her. "Mark and Liz, love story of the century, the only couple to have survived the sexual revolution intact."

"We were what, barely adolescent for the sexual revolution. As if." She turns to Melody. "Tina would have you think she remembers Kennedy being shot."

"I do! I was five years old. That's old enough to remember.

Liz, you were six. You *should* remember. You're a disgrace to our generation."

I gently kick her toe with my boot. She smiles. I've always had a better memory than Liz.

"Anyway, my remembering Kennedy being shot is nothing. Lenny remembers the Trail of Tears."

He gives me that askance look of his, probably thinking I'm making fun of him. I hold my gaze on the flames and say nothing more, and in my peripheral vision see him nod once.

Mark sighs.

"I don't even remember Armstrong on the moon," Melody says. "Hot pants are about as far back as I go."

"Who was your first love?" I ask.

"Oh!" The word puffs out as if it were an absurd question. She rocks back and forth, then says, "I don't know."

I should leave it but can't. "You don't *know*? Have you ever been in love?"

"Sure."

"Well, easier questions first: Was it a man or a woman?"

"What do you mean, woman?" Lenny asks.

"Some women like women, some men like men," I explain. "Everyone isn't heterosexual."

"I am."

"Good, Lenny. That's fine."

We all look at Melody, waiting, each of us interested.

"Maybe D.H. Lawrence," she says, and casts her eyes down.

How literary, I think. Or is she going to pull a Lenny and claim to have embodied someone's spirit in England eighty years ago?

She giggles and says, "I mean the first time I remember feeling adult passion. I was reading *Women in Love* and there's that passage where Birkin takes off all his clothes and makes love to fir trees and hyacinths and wet grass."

Melody has answered more erotically than I had expected and yet avoided saying anything personal.

"I remember that part," I say. "It was…hot."

Now I've gotten us deeper.

"Beautiful," she whispers.

"I like the scene where the two men—Birkin and the other guy—wrestle."

"Gerald."

"Yeah. Birkin and Gerald."

Liz pokes a coal with a stick. She cuts her eyes over at me and I wink. She smiles. I'm not sure if we're amused by the same thing, but it doesn't really matter.

"What about you?" Melody says quietly. "Who was your first love?"

"I guess we would first have to define love."

Liz groans. "Let's not."

"Okay," I say but continue anyway. "It's a lot easier to say what isn't love than what is." I'm thinking of Robin. "I mean, you and Mark were without any question in love since you were fourteen."

Mark nods, and Liz holds her face still.

"So tell that story," Lenny says.

Mark loves telling this story, so I'm surprised to see him shift on the log and hedge. "Tonight?" he says. "I don't know."

"I was thirteen and Liz was fourteen," I say to get him going.

He smiles.

"Not the whole thing," Liz says, almost coy, and I can see she indeed wants the whole thing.

"She was a ninth grader and I was an eighth grader and Mark had just moved to Portland from the boonies," I go on. "You want to tell it, Mark?"

"Go ahead. I want to hear your version."

Liz presses her lips together and looks apprehensive at this change. Mark always tells the story, and he's much more pre- dictable than me.

She knows her apprehension is warranted when I say, "I might know some parts you two don't even know."

Now it's Mark who looks uneasy.

"Sit back. Relax." I make eye contact with both Mark and

Liz, trying to reassure them that I'll be kind, which of course I will be, but this take-no-prisoners firelight urges me toward honesty, a rawer honesty.

"Spring of 1970, okay?"

Lenny says, "Okay."

Though Mark had moved to Portland and enrolled in our junior high school in the fall, I took no interest in him whatsoever. He was an entirely average kid. He wasn't a standout athlete, he made B's and C's in his classes, and he didn't participate in any extracurricular activities. He was very quiet, which is hard to believe now since he is the biggest ham in the family. The only thing I remember about him in those months before Liz found him was that he was a boy who walked by himself through the halls of our school, looking miserable. Kindness is not abundant in junior high school, and his obvious unhappiness served as a strong deterrent. Like everyone else, I stayed clear of the new boy.

Then one afternoon in April I went to fetch Liz at her locker, as I did every day after school, and he was there. He had shaggy yellow hair and a red complexion, which made the boyish white whiskers on his chin stand out. He looked almost exactly how he looks now except much thinner and somewhat shorter. They sat on the floor, backs against the pea-green metal lockers, a math book spread across one of his thighs and one of hers. Liz looked happy. A dry sunlight slanted in on them from a distant window, illuminating the grit on the floor and the storm of dust in the air around them. Wisps of Liz's pale hair, which had escaped from her long braid, flew around her face. They looked like two angels.

Liz said, "Hi, Tina."

Mark laughed, revealing his perfectly straight white teeth, and said, "Tina?"

"Christine to you," I said. Then to Liz, "Ready?"

"Okay," she said reluctantly.

As they closed the math book and stood, dusting off their

behinds, I remember thinking: Liz is deeper than me. I was blinded by boys and girls who were stars, who drew attention to themselves, who demanded servitude from lesser beings such as myself, but Liz always held her own council. I looked at Mark and saw a skinny kid who was several inches shorter than her, but Liz saw potential. She claims that it wasn't anything like love at first sight, that it was a simple friendship in the beginning, that she had no expectations of Mark. I don't believe her. I think she looked directly into his soul and saw his nearly fanatical dedication to wilderness, saw their farm and the goats, even saw Lenny, saw that Mark was as much a self-starter as she was. I'm sure she saw his capacity for devotion.

But back then, in that moment as they stood up, I knew only that she saw something where I saw nothing.

Mark walked down the hall with us, the air heavy with the smells of sweat and corn chips, and out the clanging school doors. He walked up the highway by our sides and right into our home. He never left.

Mark liked our whole family. He chatted with our mother about her garden. He shot the breeze with our father about adventure travel. And he included me in everything he and Liz did. I tried to construe his kindness as manipulation, as a way to wheedle his way into our family permanently, but by the summertime I had to admit that he seemed to genuinely like all of us. The following year, when Liz became mildly rebellious, it was Mark who soothed our parents, assured them she was only going through a phase. Mark was the best piece of luck to come our way in a long time.

That first spring and summer, Liz and Mark's excessive wholesomeness irked me. They—actually *we* most of the time, because even Liz seemed reluctant to leave me behind—shot baskets, took hikes, visited museums. For weeks, sex didn't even seem to be a question. They spent hours discussing the plight of Earth, the possibilities of a nuclear disaster, of ending world hunger, of reversing human population growth. Mark told us about growing up near the Rogue River, how he had spent days at a time in the wilderness alone, foraging for food and shelter. These stories were his glory, and Liz and I both admired his knowledge of edible plants and survival tactics. Later I would learn that these wilderness stays were semi-forced, a means of escape from his father's temper, a hobby of survival developed out of actual survival needs. Later Mark would tell me that he would never consider himself a victim, that there was a dialectic (yes, he used that word) relationship between strength and fear. He was nothing, he told me later, if he wasn't strong. I would know then why he and Liz held together like a nut and shell. That first spring and summer of 1970, though, I only knew that he had read books by Ralph Waldo Emerson and Henry David Thoreau, who, like Liz and Mark, believed self-reliance was the ultimate goal in life.

And while they seemed to know everything about Earth and its inhabitants, I thought they were so oblivious, then and for years to come, of the world around them. They were intent on creating a perfect life. And a perfect life excluded *most* of life, as far as I could see. Perfect seemed like such a long-shot. At thirteen I already knew self-reliance was something I would never have, that I desperately wanted people to take care of me, that need itself dragged me through life.

I held on that spring and into the early summer, trailing Mark and Liz, listening and even joining in their earnest discussions, but I knew I was being replaced no matter how hard either of them tried to prove I wasn't. More than replaced, supplanted. Liz was developing her life philosophy, actively, and its central tenet left me behind.

I fought back by buying Cokes and chips when they bought juice and granola bars, by painting my toenails red while Liz grew her leg hair, by watching television. While they dreamt of joining the green movement, I longed to become the other kind of hippie, the fuck-you Janis Joplin kind of hippie, the kind that had public sex in Berkeley. I hated that I had missed the summer of love by being a few years too young. I bought granny glasses with tinted lenses and wore a lot of Indian prints.

Mark and Liz didn't even kiss until June. I was there. We were hiking in Forest Park on an unseasonably hot day. We all wore shorts; Mark was shirtless, while Liz and I wore tank tops. Liz had her usual braid, but I had put my hair up in an elaborate bun. I thought it made me look both older and sexy. Because it was 1970, neither of us wore a bra, although I needed one. Liz was, and always would be, relatively flat-chested, but I was full-grown, already five foot eight, and should have been held in place by a C cup. Instead I bounced along happily behind Mark and Liz, who were holding hands on the trail ahead of me. In Portland, the first warm days in June are a miracle after the long, dark, wet winter. I felt euphoric, traipsing through the dappled light and watching the virginal muscles riding just below the surface of Mark's shoulders and arms, the white fuzz along his spine, the blond fur on his lengthening legs. His hair, which he was growing out, was damp with sweat. I had just read Hesse's *Siddhartha* and cast Mark in the lead role. Liz had found herself a god, his endless dumb jokes a kind of prayer to the great trickster in the sky. We were so sure of our supremacy as a generation, so on the brink of absolute rightness in life. A few years later I would crash in my huge crisis of disillusionment, but Mark and Liz would never let go of their faith in doing the right thing. In fact I don't think they ever let go of that early summer day and that holy first kiss.

The forest trail led to an open meadow. Liz and Mark knelt in the tall grasses to study the wildflowers. As they delicately touched the crimson and periwinkle petals, their bare shoulders rubbed and their white-blond heads touched like two flames. Mark said the periwinkle flower was edible and pulled off a petal for Liz to taste. She opened her mouth and he put the petal on her tongue. I knew it felt like satin and tried to imagine the taste. Chalky cream? Peppery fruit?

I could have approached and pulled a petal to taste myself, and I know that Mark would have smiled at me and asked what I thought. Instead I left them to their shoulder-rubbing—now Liz was placing a blade of grass on Mark's tongue—and wandered back to the edge of the forest. Against my back I heard them trying to remember the opening lines of Walt Whitman's grass poem and laughing. I remember thinking that they were laughing too hard. I didn't look but was sure they had fallen off their knees and were rolling on their sides in the wildflowers, maybe kicking their legs in the air like toppled insects.

I grabbed the lowest branch of a Douglas fir on the border of the meadow and walked my feet up the trunk. I hooked my legs over the branch and pulled myself up. I sat there swinging my feet, looking beyond Mark, Liz, and the flowered meadow to the dark trees and pale sky.

I heard Liz say, "Where'd Tina go?"

"She'll be back."

They could have seen me. They didn't want to. Mark picked one of the crimson wildflowers at the base of its stem and tickled Liz's ankle with it. Slowly he dragged the flower up her bare leg. When he reached her hip, they quit laughing, but he kept on with the red flower until it was at her lips. He left it there and kissed her, with the flower petals between their mouths. I could tell he expected it to be a short kiss because after touching his lips to the petal, his body pulled back. But his mouth didn't come. It was as if he couldn't pull himself away. He leaned in then and kissed Liz much more passionately. The flower must have been pressed into Liz's mouth, along with Mark's tongue. For a moment he lay on top of her, one of his legs pressed between hers, then as if he remembered I was somewhere on the periphery, he rolled off and sat up. He reached down and ran his fingers along her cheek and rested two of them on her lips. The expression on Liz's face wasn't lust; instead it was more like she wanted to fall asleep against those two fingers, as if they were the only rest she could imagine. He finally brushed them aside and leaned in to kiss her again. It was a long tongue kiss, and I was relieved to see Liz more engaged this time.

I turned around so that I sat on the tree branch with my back to Liz and Mark. Then I swung down, my knees hooked over the branch, and let go with my hands. Hanging upside down, I could now see Mark and Liz notice me. I made monkey sounds, "Hoo! Hoo! Hoo!" and scratched my armpits. Laughing, they jumped up and came toward me, looking perfect as they pushed through the tall wildflowers, their auras disheveled by desire, all gold in the gold grasses and gold sunlight. When they reached me, each took an arm and swung me out of the tree. I landed on my feet and said, "I'm going back down the hill."

"We'll come with you," Mark said.

"Actually," I said, "I'm in the mood to walk alone. I'll see you later."

I walked for most of the hot afternoon before I reached the park blocks in downtown Portland. I strolled up the park between the two long rows of benches, fervently wishing to be one of the hippies lounging there, playing guitars, or stringing beads. I finally sat down on an empty bench and a moment later was approached by a boy with long brown hair and a full beard. He said his name was Jerome, that he was nineteen and a draft dodger. I said I was sixteen, which he seemed to accept without question, although I don't know that he would have cared if I'd told him I was only thirteen. In retrospect, it's likely that Jerome was lying to me too. What draft dodger would announce that fact to a stranger?

Jerome talked and talked. I don't remember anything he said, only that he talked. He smelled strongly of something that I thought was marijuana but have since realized was patchouli oil. His arms were corded with veins and the kind of muscles wiry men have. Late that afternoon, as the heat of the day cooled and the light faded, I went with Jerome to his VW bus and had sex.

I don't tell the crew around the campfire about Jerome and sex in the VW bus. I've never told Liz about that.

Although I have entertained large groups at parties by telling my quintessentially hippie-era loss of virginity story, I know she'd be disgusted, wouldn't find it funny even now. And it would sound competitive, as if I had been racing to have sex before her. It was nothing like that. It was more like she and Mark had given me the idea of sex, maybe surrounded me in their field of desire, and I fell quite accidentally into opportunity. I do remember thinking, as I walked with Jerome to his VW, that I had the choice of waiting for love, a love like Liz and Mark's, and deciding that might be years in coming.

By the looks on everyone's face, I'm not sure how much of my story I've said out loud. Mark stares into the fire, as solemn as he ever gets, and doesn't look up when I quit talking. Melody too is gazing into the fire, in a pose almost exactly like Mark's, as if the story had been a very serious, even dangerous, one. Lenny bites a fingernail, cocking his head to get a better angle on it, but he is only bored. I finally look at Liz, knowing that her face will tell me if I have crossed any lines, and she looks back at me almost shyly. I have pleased her.

"To think that was over twenty-five years ago," she says quietly.

Mark looks up, and his eyes glisten faintly in the firelight. Tears?

"And you're still in love," I say foolishly, wanting to seal my story.

"That's a beautiful story," Melody whispers.

The sap is running too thick and sweet, then Lenny saves the day by blurting, "Me? I'm ain't gonna marry anyone. I'm having me a new woman every month."

"That could be beautiful too," I say, and we all laugh.

ten: paint job

How could I be in love with Flo when we've never even made love? And yet, sitting around this campfire, if I were to tell a story it would be about her, as if she were the raw ingredients, the uncooked recipe for "first love."

Very early one morning at the beginning of February, she showed up on my porch, rang the bell, and when I answered the door asked me, "Why don't you put your mouth where your money is and hire a Tenderloin resident?"

I was so surprised to see her that I didn't notice she had switched the objects in the sentence.

But she noticed and laughed.

"What?" I asked, thinking she was laughing at me. "*What?*"

"Did you hear what I said?"

"Yes!" I started, but then her sentence replayed in my head and I smiled. "Oh."

"Your house needs a paint job bad," she said.

I wanted to ask how she knew where I lived.

"It's beautiful. You shouldn't let it fall apart."

I looked at the rotting porch floorboards. I didn't have to look behind me at the wooden siding to see the old white paint was peeling off like birch bark. My friend Alice called my house the Addams Family mansion. It's far from a mansion, but the two-story Victorian does have three bedrooms plus all those old-fashioned extra rooms, like a full dining room, a breakfast sitting room, as well as an enclosed back porch. It had been owned by an elderly couple who lived there for forty-eight years. They had kept it in exceptionally good condition except for the last ten years, which meant, at least according to the inspector who looked it over for me when I bought it, that it was structurally sound but had lots of cosmetic problems. He wasn't kidding. The house's "as is" condition included cobwebs stretched from the ceiling to the stairway banister, kitchen walls covered with grease, bathroom cabinets with curly gold trim, and lemon-yellow paint everywhere. While I cleaned out most of the cobwebs and grease, I'd done nothing about the ornate bathroom fixtures, the tacky cabinets, and the yellow. The faux-crystal chandelier that hangs in the entryway, along with the winding stairway, are what really give the house its Addams Family feel. When I tried to clean the chandelier with a long-handled dust mop, all the teardrops tinkled and I was afraid of breaking them, so I stopped. Since then it has remained untouched, still webbed with the abandoned homes of dozens of spiders.

"I'd replace any bad wood." Flo tapped her boot toe on the porch. Then she bounced backwards down the thirteen steps and looked up at the house. "I suggest a nice taupe with navy and white trim." She narrowed her eyes. "Yeah. That would be nice. You shouldn't let this house rot from the moisture."

"If painting were all it needed…" I began, realizing that my resistance was really about my fear of Flo's ongoing presence at my house. I looked down at her standing at the bottom of the porch stairs. I could see only as far the sidewalk under her feet because an all-encompassing San Francisco fog held the two of us in a cocoon. The fog was pearly with the sheen of daybreak, and I felt the dawn right under my skin. I said, "Okay."

Flo painting my house made me feel uncomfortably domestic: the earliness and the regularity. She showed up every morning all February, usually well before eight o'clock. As I made coffee, showered, and dressed, I'd hear her scraping the old paint off the sides of my house, preparing it for its taupe coat. When I woke up in the middle of the night to rain thumping my roof, an emptiness born of knowing she wouldn't come that day prevented me from relaxing back into sleep. The third week, when she began brushing on the wet paint, I couldn't help feel the strokes as caresses to my home, a home I had neglected for so long. Not just this house, which I'd been in for only two years, but the whole concept of home. I liked it on the weekends when I knew Flo was outside, balanced on her ladder, dipping her fat brush into the gooey paint and slathering it on the boards. I knocked around the house feeling it as my big skin, something I would like to grow into.

On weekdays she was always gone when I got home at night. By then it was dark, and anyway she usually painted only half a day and spent the afternoons writing or performing. When Liz asked how much Flo was charging me to paint the house, I quickly tried to think of a reasonable sum, but I didn't even know the ballpark. I knew Flo would be fair but was embarrassed I hadn't asked. When I said I didn't know, Liz tightened her lips and looked over the tops of the buildings in my neighborhood. She always did that when she was annoyed, cast her eyes out at any horizon she could find, as if searching for the mountains, the only things that made sense to her. I could have covered my act by saying something about Flo being a Tenderloin resident, about her being a street artist; then Liz would have accepted the arrangement as charity. But of course it was nothing of the sort.

One Wednesday I realized around noon that the dizziness I'd felt in the morning was developing into a fever. Lynne found me leaning against a wall outside an exam room and said I looked peaked. She slapped a hand to my forehead, said, "Hot," then pulled me into an empty exam room. I sat obediently on the end of the table while she took my temperature. "Christine, it's 102. What the hell are you doing here?"

I was too confused to answer.

"Go home." She yanked me off the table. By the time I left the room, she had my bag and coat. "I'll reschedule the rest of the patients." I didn't dare talk back to Lynne, but I looked at her and didn't move. "Obviously if it's something that can't wait," she said, "I'll send them over to the other clinic. Go. The last thing all these moms need is for you to give them and their babies the flu. Git."

"Maybe Jon could come in...."

"He's in Guadalajara." Lynne knew the schedules of the entire San Francisco medical community.

I still hesitated.

"You don't have a choice."

I never get sick—maybe once every two or three years—so it's hard for me to accept. Or even recognize. It takes several hours before I realize I'm not just hungry, or tired, or maybe ate bad tacos the night before.

Lynne knows me. She said, "You're *sick*. S-i-c-k. Go home." She gave me a little shove toward the door.

I staggered to my car and managed to drive home. I didn't see Flo anywhere on the front or sides of my house, and the ladders were neatly laid against the fence as she always left them at the end of her day, so I figured she'd left already. Flo rode the buses everywhere. She rented a truck at the beginning of each job to deliver her ladders, paint, and other equipment, to the site. Then she bused back and forth until she finished the job. She said she got a lot of material for her poetry on the buses.

I guess the fever prevented me, as I let myself in the house and climbed the stairs to my bedroom, from hearing the shower. I didn't even notice it as I threw my bag on the bed and stripped off my clothes. I planned to take a hot bath because by now my muscles ached and I trembled with a gray foggy chill.

When I got halfway down the hall, I noticed steam billowing out of the open bathroom door and heard the shower. I didn't know what to do. I wasn't frightened. Obviously it was her; burglars didn't use the shower. But I didn't know where to go. Forward was impossible. If ever the expression, "I froze" felt literally true, it was now. My feet were like blocks of ice stuck to the floor. My entire coat of skin was tightly puckered in a feverish chill. My nipples were so hard they hurt.

Flo stepped out of the bathroom toweling her hair. She saw me and expelled a startled grunt of embarrassment. Susan B skittered out of the bathroom behind her, sat, and cocked her head at me.

There we were, two naked women facing each other: one with pale skin, fever-dry, and tight pink nipples; the other with steamy wet cocoa skin and dark blossomed nipples. In my weakness I wanted more than anything to slump to the floor. I hardly had the strength to remain standing, let alone deal with this. Of course I didn't care that she had used the shower. She had a key for using the bathroom and putting her lunch in the fridge, and she had been respectful of my privacy. She was embarrassed now, and I didn't know what to say because I was sure that I was more embarrassed.

Finally I blurted. "Fever. Flu."

"You're sick?"

Then a new bloom of mortification overwhelmed me. What must she have thought—that I had come home, heard her in the shower, stripped, and headed in to join her?

I nodded and sounded like a child when I said, "I didn't even hear you in the bathroom. I have a high fever." But not so high that I didn't notice the thighs that matched her glorious biceps. A soft covering of feminine flesh over the muscles. Rounded, easy strength. A soft belly, luxurious breasts. I thought of Alice, who once told me that she likes making love best when she has a fever.

"I'll run the tub for you," Flo said, returning to the bathroom. I followed her in and she bent over the fixtures, turning them, dropping her hand under the water, adjusting the temperature. Susan B waited in the hall.

I yanked a towel off the rack, wrapped my body, and sat on the toilet.

When she was satisfied with the water temperature, Flo stood and looked at me. "You look awful. I'll make some tea."

I didn't move as she left the bathroom, descended the staircase, and put a kettle on the stove downstairs. As I listened to Susan B's nails click on the kitchen floor, I wondered where Martin was. A few moments later Flo returned, now dressed, and looked at me again, evaluating. I could tell I looked bad. She turned off the water and took hold of me by the elbow. I stood and tilted toward the tub.

"Steady now," she said gently, and held my arms as I stepped into the hot water. I sat down, and she guided my shoulders back. Downstairs the kettle whistled. "Be right back."

After making the tea, she sat on the toilet, as easy as if we were sisters, and said, "It's steeping."

I felt as if I too were steeping. The sandpaper rawness of my skin eased in the hot water. I closed my eyes and said nothing. Flo rested her elbows on her knees and put her face in her fists. Martin came in the bathroom, walking right past Susan B, who sat at the door, and put his front paws on the tub, then jumped up. He loved sitting on the edge of the tub while I bathed, usually purring and taking occasional sips of the bathwater. Now he snarled at me.

Understanding immediately, Flo said, "I'll put Susan B outside on her leash."

Martin hated Susan B. Though he had quit putting on his ferocious act every time he saw her, he always let it be known that he could, if he so chose, scratch Susan B's fluffy white face right off. Flo had agreed to keep Susan B outside, though she wouldn't admit that the dog and cat were enemies.

My phone rang, and while Flo went downstairs to get the

tea and put out Susan B, I listened to Lynne's voice on the answering machine demanding to know if I had made it home all right and how I was feeling.

"Do you want the tea in bed or in the tub?" Flo asked.

By way of an answer, I climbed out of the tub and dried myself off. I got into bed naked.

"Don't you have any pajamas?"

I shook my head.

"A T-shirt at least? Something a little warmer than nothing?"

I was relieved to finally have covered myself and didn't want to crawl out from under the covers. I shook my head. "The comforter is warm."

"You going to be okay?" She stood in the doorway, her arms bracing either side, her hair still wet but the curls springing to life.

Don't leave.

"Can I get you anything else before I go?"

Don't go.

"Well." She took two steps toward me in bed. Stopped. Spread out her fingers like Martin does. "I'll check in on you a little later, okay?"

Stay now.

Flo turned, and as she walked out of my bedroom I felt as if I could see right through her shirt to her shoulder blades, riding her back like two glorious wings.

Lucienne had been wary of me since I broke up with Robin, and she always preferred staying at her own place anyway, but wouldn't you know she insisted on spending the night at my house that Sunday. She knows me all too well, and maybe her erotic detector picked up some activity; maybe she wanted to have a little snoop around. I think she found what she wanted to find.

Early Monday morning, around six o'clock, Lucienne nuzzled up to my back and reached around to stroke the inside of my thigh. I never said no to Lucienne. Whatever else our relationship offered, the sex was always exceptional. She made me holler every time. Every single time.

Lying on my back afterward, recovering from the journey to some place like a black hole, eternal and gorgeously spinning, I thought I heard the raccoons. A family of them lived under the house and often scampered up onto the fence then climbed to the roof to reach the figs on the neighbor's tree.

I *wanted* it to be the raccoons.

"What's that?" Lucienne asked.

"The raccoons," I said.

"No, it's not. It's your painter. What is she, some kind of voyeur?"

"As if she knew we'd be fucking at six A.M.!" I hissed. The window was cracked, because Lucienne insisted on fresh air no matter what time of year, which meant the racket I had just made would have carried outside the house. I wondered where exactly her ladder was placed. "Can you see her?" I whispered, not wanting to turn my head and look. I couldn't quite believe Flo would stare in my bedroom window.

"No, I can't see her but it sounds as if she's right outside the window," Lucienne announced.

"*Shh.*"

"Why should I *shh*?" Lucienne got up and headed for the window.

"No," I pleaded.

She shoved the window all the way open and stuck the top half of her body out so that her large breasts swung free in the air. "Good morning."

"Hiya," I heard Flo answer.

From inside the bedroom it looked pitch-black out there, but I knew from camping trips that dawn begins much earlier than insiders realize. If you're out there, the light at six-thirty and seven is actually usable. Lucienne yanked down the shade and switched on the electric light.

"Damn," I said to the unnatural glare.

A few minutes later, as I handed Lucienne her cup of coffee

in the kitchen, she said, "Everyone has sex. Why are you in such a state?"

"I'm not in a state."

"What's she doing here so early anyway?"

"How would I know?"

Lucienne sat heavily at the yellow Formica table that came with the house. I knew exactly what those little pinpricks of light in her eyes meant. They went with the epicurean smile on her mouth. She saw the part about the house being my skin and what Flo was doing to that. And it interested her. When she left a couple of minutes later I heard her walk around to the side of the house to say goodbye to Flo. I knew she was just getting a better look.

I hated myself then, me and my entire life of deception. I hated how I nested in Lucienne's love of irony and ambiguity, how she used her intelligence to obscure the rawest, simplest truths. I hated how badly I wanted to call Liz, the only person in the world who knew everything there was to know about me, and most of all I hated how lonely that made me feel.

I also felt angry at Flo, at her ability to have tantrums, at her courage to perform on the street, at the way I felt compelled to see her right now.

As soon as Lucienne was gone, I grabbed my coat and bag and went to say goodbye, or hello, to Flo.

She smiled—coolly?—down from the top of her ladder. Then, "Sorry. I should have told you I was coming early."

"No, um, *I'm* sorry."

"No big deal," she said. "I don't pay any attention to people's private lives when I'm painting their houses."

That hurt. Just another one of her clients. She resumed painting, and I leaned against the scraped but as yet unpainted wall of my house and watched. I wanted to tell her that Lucienne wasn't my girlfriend, but how could I possibly say that after she just heard me come with the woman? I felt so lost inside my life, leaning against my house.

"So how much is this paint job costing anyway?" It was a

cold question, and I regretted it instantly, but it addressed the only connection between me and Flo right then.

She looked down at me from the top of her ladder, and there it was, a pulse of anger between her eyes. Then composure, even a little bit of a smile, her acceptance of my laying out the exact definition of our relationship. "Forty-two hundred. That includes paint and supplies."

eleven: black hole

"Everything is covered with snow. It's not like the forest could burn," I argue when Mark insists on putting out the fire before we retire to our snow cave. "I don't see why we can't let it die out on its own."

Knowing that it's there, outside the snow cave, would comfort me. I imagine getting up at two or three in the morning and hovering over glowing coals.

"Can't leave a campfire unattended." Mark nods subtly toward Lenny, as if we must smother the fire for the benefit of education. But I know better. I know that we're smothering it for Mark's sense of satisfaction in doing the right thing on principle. One puts a fire out at night, and we shall. I wince as he throws shovelfuls of snow on the bright flames. All that work doused in five minutes.

"What about the morning?" I try one last time. "Won't we have a fire in the morning? The bed of coals will help."

"I doubt we'll have the time in the morning," Mark says. "We'll be packing up and skiing out. We don't want to get back to the Bay Area too late."

He suffocates the fire, and the black wilderness floods into the space it had occupied. Back to the Bay Area indeed.

I use my headlamp to find the things I might need in the night—extra socks, a book, lip balm, ibuprofen—and put them in a stuff sack. Soon we line up at the door to the snow cave, ready to enter. Lenny has made a stink about being claustrophobic, though I suspect he likes the concept more than he actually experiences its symptoms, but I give in and let him have the place next to the tunnel door. Liz will enter first and sleep against the farthest snow wall. Mark will go next, then Melody, then me, and finally Lenny.

"No worries about being cold!" Mark says, trying to cheer me and Lenny. "We'll be sardines in a can."

"Didn't Walt Disney have his body frozen to be used in future research?" I ask. "I should have left a note in my pack telling them to feel free to experiment with mine."

No one laughs.

Liz drops to her hands and knees and crawls up the tunnel, dragging her stuff sack. Mark and then Melody follow. I kneel and get that tight claustrophobic feeling in my head, like someone is about to cut off my oxygen. I like human-size spaces: rooms in houses, the cavity of a bus, even a clearing in a forest. But not entire mountain ranges and not painstakingly carved ice vaults. Lenny gives my butt a little kick, which I don't find amusing.

I pull out of the tunnel. "Don't do that."

"Then *go.*"

"I'll go when I'm ready. Don't touch me."

I crawl up the tunnel and enter the snow cave, where in the light of my headlamp I see five sleeping bags laid out on top of a space blanket and a bed of pads.

"Turn off your headlamp," Liz says.

"No way."

"I'm serious. Just do it, and you'll see what I mean."

I throw myself onto the sleeping bag designated as mine and switch off my headlamp. The cave is surprisingly spacious, and I can sit up comfortably. Two shelves have been carved into the head and foot walls of the cave, and each holds a fat burning candle. Their light leaps up the icy walls and glows. Great shadows swell and recede on the cave ceiling, making me think of prehistoric people. In the wake of my silence, Mark laughs.

Melody lies very still with her eyes open, as if she's praying or meditating, the candlelight bouncing on her face. I pull off my Gore-Tex pants and jacket and wad them up to put under my head. I keep stripping until I'm down to long underwear and zip myself into the down bag. The clerk at the mountaineering store was absolutely positive I wouldn't need a bag any warmer than one good to zero degrees, but I made him give me one rated to forty below. I realize now that it may be a very hot night. The warm cave air will only get warmer with five bodies in residence. Lying on my back, looking directly up, I see one of the four air holes Mark has poked in the ceiling with his ski pole. The ceiling, he reported, is a good four feet thick. I want to ask what would happen if those four feet of snow caved in, but he'd just have a quick answer that I wouldn't have enough information to refute, so why bother asking?

For the longest time, after Lenny settles in, we lie five in a row on our backs in deep silence. I don't break it to tell Mark he was right: This snow cave has a beauty, and even comfort, I couldn't have dreamed possible. A tent can be slashed by bear claws or ripped from its base by a strong wind. Here I feel as if I have pulled the winter so fully inside myself that it can't harm me.

"Awesome," Lenny finally says, then turns to me. "What time did you say your dark side comes out?"

"About three."

"Hopefully we'll all be asleep by then," Mark says.

"If I have to piss, can I just shoot it down the tunnel?" Lenny wants to know.

"No, you can't," Mark says. "You get up and walk a distance away from the cave. And not toward camp."

"I gotta go now."

"Aw, Lenny man. Why didn't you go before?"

"How did I know you weren't going to dig a bathroom in here too?" Lenny starts pulling his long body out of his sleeping bag and kicking me in the process. His enormous feet land momentarily in my face as he crawls out the tunnel.

"You gotta put your boots on," Mark says, seeing his stocking feet wagging in the candlelight.

When Lenny returns to the cave we're all quiet again, and I feel hypersensitive about the proximity of so many bodies. It's possible that Liz is already asleep. I hear a steady and faint whistling coming from her side of the cave. Mark rustles. Melody, by my side, lies perfectly still. I turn my head to look at her and her eyes are open. When she notices me looking, I make a mock grimace, meaning to communicate the eerie wildness of our sleeping chamber, but she only shuts her eyes momentarily like a cat and turns away. I wish I had brought Martin. I could have carried him in a Gerry pack on my chest. What's an extra sixteen pounds? He'd be perfectly happy in my sleeping bag with me, his motor purr and thick fur grounding me.

I wonder if we're going to leave the candles burning all night. I can't help but notice that there's a lot more heat coming from Lenny than from Melody, maybe because he's in almost constant motion. I don't mind. His movement keeps the shadows dancing on the blue cave ceiling. I make the shapes into Sumo wrestlers, swans on a lake, giants emerging from rock caves, four women making love.

I wish I were next to Liz. How does she stand being out here where there's no hiding, no layers, just oneself and the planet? Even with the snow cave surrounding me, I feel closer to the rest of the universe than ever before, as if I'm in outer space. Only my back curved against the Earth tells me I am *here* and not out there; the concept of *here* begins to lose meaning. In physics neither *here* nor *now* have much meaning. We could be traveling through a black hole, utterly dimensionless.

I want to ask Melody how mindfulness works in this setting. Instead I reach out a hand, seriously in need of the reassurance of a living body, and touch her sleeping bag. I find her arm. I squeeze gently, meaning nothing more than hi. But she snatches her arm away. Her eyes are still open, but now she is anything but serene. White points of candlelight waver in the tears gathering in her eyes.

I know to say nothing.

Lenny has thrown a leg against mine, perhaps for the same reason I tried to touch Melody, and I let him leave it there. Liz sighs. I lift my head to see her snuggle closer to the ice wall, away from Mark.

It's going to be a very long night.

I feel lost. Personally, geographically, cosmically.

It occurs to me that Liz's and my lifelong debate has really been a competition, and she has won. I am much more lost than she has ever been or ever will be. The kernel of her being is a crystal—sharp, clear, and radiating. She has Mark. She has the farm. She has her job heading up a world-saving organization. She knows exactly who she is, and she controls the parameters.

The center of my being, on the other hand, is a craving, an itch, an unbearable longing. Though I don't do it publicly, I can make a very good case for not saving the planet. Why should we? Science shows that life has wiped itself out, or nearly out, many times in Earth's history. Why are we so hell-bent on stopping natural cycles in the history of the universe? I hate myself for my lack of faith. The best I can do is try to relieve suffering on a case by case basis.

One summer, when Liz and I were in high school, activists climbed to the tops of some evergreens in an old-growth Oregon forest. The forest, habitat to an entire ecosystem, was slated to be clear-cut and these brave souls would topple with the trees if it came to that. Mark read the newspaper story out loud to us, and I remember how badly

I wanted to be swaying in the top of one of those trees, an owl's view of the old-growth forest canopy, the feel of that rough bark against my cheek, my body pressed against a living being that had been there for decades, even centuries. I must have said some of this out loud because Liz accused me of wanting only the romance of it, the glory. If I really cared, she said, I'd be more careful about recycling, I'd ride my bike rather than take the car, I'd be writing weekly letters to my representatives in Congress.

She was fifty percent right. I loved the men and women in the tops of those trees with a hero worship. For weeks after that, I wore red bandannas around my forehead and ripped, faded Levi's to look like them. I did glorify them, but the part Liz didn't understand, the part I couldn't help, the other fifty percent, was that I simply didn't have Liz's long-distance vision. If I didn't feel that evergreen pressed against my body, or at least hear the stories of the trees pressed against the activists' bodies, I didn't have any sympathy for the forest. Liz could look ten, fifty, one hundred years ahead of herself and see a future about which she must take action now.

Someone moves. Mark. He sits up, and I shiver with relief. Activity. Oh, please, let there be some activity. This cave is the stillest place I've ever been in.

He only leans back and then forward to blow out one candle, then the other. Now it is utterly black. I wonder if Melody is still awake. Mark is, and I'd like to speak to him but feel as if I can't. The silence is too great to break.

Once he settles, it is still again. No one is moving, not even Lenny. I snuggle closer to him, listening for a purr, any sign of life. I'm fully awake.

Mark says, "Can we have a moment of silence?" and we all crack up. The tension is broken, I'm relieved, and I decide to go pee as a way of escape.

Dressing takes forever. I strap on my headlamp but don't turn on the light. I grope for my fleece pants, my wool sweater. I pull on my Gore-Tex suit and finally my boots. Crawling over Lenny is the hardest part. I give up trying to bridge myself over him. Instead I slide right over the top of his rocklike body and slither, head first, down the snow tunnel, like a seal sliding from an iceberg into the sea. The vast wash of cold black air dotted with starlight is a relief in contrast to the silent nothingness inside the cave. I don't need to turn on my headlamp because of the starlight reflecting off the snow. It's much brighter out here than in there.

I snap my feet into my skis.

"Wait." Mark emerges from the cave. "Where are you going?"

"To pee."

"I'll come with you."

I almost object, but what does it matter out here? Do the other animals care who watches them urinate?

He's in his skis in a jiffy, and we kick and coast a hundred yards down the ridge. I stop by some scrubby trees.

"Tina." He takes my arm and turns me around to face him. "I need help."

"Shit, Mark." What. What now? And why now?

He takes a few gulps of the thin, cold air. "You're the only one she trusts, you know."

"I don't know what's wrong."

"You don't? Can't you see it?"

"See what?"

"Liz is... I can't...."

I think of the comet, the alleged reason I came along on this weekend, and I search the sky for it. Then I remember that it had been setting just as Melody and I returned from our misadventure. I think of that group of people who killed themselves because they believed that a spaceship riding in the comet's tail was going to deliver them to a higher plane of existence. How foolish to count on a comet.

Mark says, "Liz and I haven't made love in five years."

I don't want this information, though it hardly surprises me.

"That trip in the Brooks range of Alaska, that was *the last time.*" His eyes are wild with starlight. "You don't know how much I love her."

"Yes, I do."

"Do I have a choice?"

"Between what and what?" is what I should ask, but I don't want to know. So I answer philosophically, "Of course you have a choice. We all have a choice."

Anything more I can think to say will take me where I don't want to go. This is how it started between us that summer. Mark and I have always communicated better than he and Liz, though we indulge our intimacy, our verbal intimacy, only once every few years. It feels like betrayal.

I offer no comfort and turn away, skiing a good distance farther down the backbone of the ridge to find a private place to pee. I'm afraid of the stars above me, so thick the sky is more white than black, but even more scared of pursuing the conversation with Mark. I find a small tree and use it to steady myself as I pull down my pants and squat between my skis.

I wonder if Mark is waiting for me. I know he needs me as a bridge to Liz. I was there from the start, and I'm necessary. I suspect Liz has never told Mark the entire truth about Timothy and that he senses that omission, knows I'm the link to the whole of Liz. It's a strange feeling to be a conduit for something that potent, a path through which love travels to another. Of course the flow through me is ethereal, really only a concept, but it feels visceral for how closely it seems to bind us.

At one time of course it was visceral.

The summer Mark and Liz graduated from high school, Liz won a prestigious internship in Washington, D.C. They were going to the University of Washington together in the fall, so it didn't seem hard for them to separate for ten weeks. My mother, father, Mark, and I put her on the plane one Saturday morning, then we drove home to have lunch. Mark stayed all afternoon, and that evening he and I took a pizza up to the park, where we talked, mostly about Liz, until three in the morning.

That summer Mark and I spent all our free time together—whenever his days off from the day camp where he worked and my days off from the bookstore where I rang up sales coincided, which was at least one day and one evening a week. Nothing felt more natural. Without Liz, though, we tended to somewhat less wholesome activities, like overdosing on chocolate and going to outdoor rock concerts. Mark still talked about saving the planet, but he and I also talked about kids at school, our parents, LSD. It was that summer that he told me about his father, the real reason he spent hours at a time, sometimes even nights, in the Rogue River wilderness surrounding the small town of his youth. And how he had never told Liz any of this.

One very hot night in July he and I parked at the chained gate of the Pittock Mansion and hiked up the dark winding road to the big house. We sat on the lawn looking out over the city lights, still hot in our shorts and tank tops even though it was eleven at night, and talked about Liz. It was always a relief to talk about my sister, my formidable sister. The force of her will was like a wall that held me up, and it was the same for Mark. But that was frustrating too. We both needed, and resented, the fortress of her.

Finally he said, "I don't think Liz really likes sex."

"Sure she does," I said defensively.

He shook his head. "We *have* sex. But sometimes it seems like it's because she thinks we should."

"Nobody has sex because they feel they *should*," I said naively.

"I don't really mean she doesn't like it. I know she likes it. It's just…I don't know."

"Are you sad she went to D.C.?"

I asked because I was sad. And disappointed. Angry, even. This was our last summer together. It was as if she never even considered us. As if she knew she would one day direct a world-saving organization and was simply stepping onto the conveyor belt of her life. But I was part of her life too, and so was Mark. She assumed we would follow her.

"Of course not," he answered. "She had to go. It was an opportunity of a lifetime. She worked hard for it and deserves it. More than anyone."

"Yeah," I said, ashamed of my other feelings.

"And we have our whole lives. We'll be together again in the fall."

"Not me, though," I heard my small voice say. I hated my neediness in the face of their self-reliance.

"Oh, Tina," he said, more softly than I had ever heard him speak. "I hadn't thought of that. How this is *our* last summer."

I shrugged. "No biggie."

"It *is*." He scooted around so that he was sitting behind me. "Want me to braid your hair?"

I shrugged again, embarrassed by his clumsy tenderness, and then I almost cried at his idea that he could fill in for my sister. He scooped up my waist-length hair and juggled it into three clumps. As he braided, his knuckles grazed my neck, giving me shivers.

"There." He remained behind me, his knees my armrests. I leaned back and let my head fall against his chest.

"Shooting star," he said, speaking to the side of my head so that I smelled his sweet-like-fresh-grass breath. He wore a full beard then—as full as a blond eighteen-year-old's beard can be—and it tickled my temple. We stayed like that, his beard against my temple, his lips at my ear, and didn't move.

"Another," I said, and we made a game out of locating and counting shooting stars.

His arms went around me on the sixth one, and I turned to put my face against his collarbone. His chest lifted and fell, lifted and fell. Finally, Mark turned his face the fraction of an inch necessary to put his mouth on mine. He had the softest lips.

Mark believed then and has believed ever since that he was my first. I don't know why I let him think this. Part of it was his presumption, his innocent and arrogant presumption, that made him never ask. And how silly it would be to say, "By the way, you weren't my first."

Jerome in the VW bus had been my first, and the second had been a boy at school with whom I had sex throughout most of my sophomore year, usually in his bedroom after school while his parents were at work. We would fuck, then do our schoolwork. We were friends, not sweethearts, and not even very good friends at that. The sex was okay, though, and plentiful. Near the end of the year he fell in love with a girl who wrote poetry and wore only black, and he quit answering the door when I knocked after school. Mark was the third, and he and I slept together only that one time. We have never touched since then, nor have we spoken of the incident.

I see his shape, blond-bright in the starlight, waiting for me, as I ski back to camp. I dread his trying to talk more. It's funny, but all these years later I feel a greater betrayal in being his confidante than I ever did in sleeping with him. To myself—and I've never spoken of his and my summer to any-one else, not even to Lucienne—I justify our behavior by our ages. I was only seventeen. It hardly felt like betrayal at the time. I knew enough to not tell Liz, but it all seemed to fit, like it was natural, like it was my job to take care of Mark, and his to take care of me, while she was gone. Of course I'm not so naive as to think Liz would see it that way, even now, even twenty-plus years later. Still, I feel more guilty about Mark's rare confessions to me than I ever did about the sex.

"I'm sorry," he says now. "I shouldn't have spoken to you about that."

About what? is the real question, but instead I say, "I hope I can sleep finally."

"Don't you like the cave? Isn't it nearly mystical?"

"Not the word I would have used."

"Try to feel the peace. There's an overwhelming tranquillity in a snow cave. If you let yourself feel it."

"Are you feeling it?"

"Well," he hedges, "maybe not tonight."

"No. Awe maybe, but not tranquillity. Five people packed in, what, a maximum of sixty square feet? That will never be tranquil unless they're all dead."

"Tina!"

"It's the truth."

"That's macabre."

"It's going to be okay," I say foolishly. "You'll work it out with Liz." Then, to change the subject, I ask, "Is Lenny really Apache?"

Mark shakes his head.

"How do you know?"

"His mother lives in a trailer park outside of San Jose. I've met her. White, Irish-German ancestry. And his father is long gone."

"So his father could be Apache."

Mark shrugs. "It's very unlikely. His mother doesn't even knows who the father is."

"How do you know that?"

"I asked her. When Lenny started this Apache thing, I helped him do some research on the tribe. It was becoming a source of real pride for him, so I thought it would be good to check out the truth of it. I mean, if it were true, it might give him a handle on himself."

"And?"

"And so one time when I was picking him up, I sort of asked his mother, while he was in his bedroom getting ready. I mean, I tried to be respectful. It's kind of weird asking some- one who they slept with, you know?"

"So what did you say?"

"I said, 'Lenny tells me his father is a member of the Apache tribe.' I figured I'd have to say something more than that, but she blurted right out with, 'I haven't any fucking idea who Lenny's father is. How would *he* know?'"

"Oh."

"Yeah. It's a pretty rough scene at home for Lenny."

"He seems like a good kid at heart."

"He is."

"You do good work, Mark. You and Liz."

"We try."

When we reach the mouth of the cave, I want to say something more direct to Mark, want to find words that will reassure him about Liz, but I can't find any, and anyway we're well within earshot of the group. Instead I give him one of those conspiring smile-grimaces we've always shared, the meaning of which I've never examined. Maybe something like: helpless in the face of perfect Liz. Then I give him a little shove toward the entrance. He drops to his knees and goes in. I follow.

Luckily, we wake everyone up, or already had when we left the cave in the first place, and conversation ensues.

"I'm hungry," Lenny says.

"I've got just the thing. Energy nuggets." Mark rustles in his stuff sack, then throws his body across Melody's to hand them to Lenny. It's pitch-black again. The only two senses that are any use are hearing and touch. I don't dare touch anything, or anybody, so I listen.

Lenny chomps, using, it seems, an inordinate amount of saliva to digest his energy nuggets. Melody, apparently awake, takes two long ragged breaths as if she's trying to control an impulse.

Liz decides that she too has to pee and crawls over all of us to get out of the cave.

My muscles begin to relax at last and I feel sleepy, then overwhelmingly so. I force myself to stay awake until Liz returns. Once she's in place on the far side of the cave I'll be able to finally escape into unconsciousness. The anticipation is delicious.

But Liz is gone forever. I wish she would return. Without Liz, the cave seems to have lost well over half its contents. I imagine an echo if I speak.

"Where's Liz?" I ask.

No one answers for a long time. Then Mark says, "Out there."

"Hasn't she been gone a long time?"

They don't answer. I hear only their breathing. Everyone is breathing loudly.

Finally I hear her at the mouth of the tunnel. She crawls in, filling the space once again. No one speaks as she strips off her gear.

I'm asleep before she finishes getting settled.

twelve: poetry prize

What Flo doesn't know is that I was once a bit of a poet myself. In fact, I won a prize for the best poem written at Meriwether Lewis Elementary. I was twelve years old and the poem was titled "Losing Timothy." I had entered two poems in the contest and was upset that my other poem hadn't won. "Sacagawea" was a protest poem about how I thought our school should be named for her rather than for Lewis. My teacher, however, told me that politics pollute art. But "Losing Timothy," she said, was a "masterpiece of emotion." I hated the voyeuristic look in her eye as she said that. I hated even more that I had written the poem. I hated most of all that I would have to read it at the Spring Program before an audience of parents and students. If I refused, though, Mrs. Tisdale would surely contact my parents about the poem and my refusal, and that became the primary thing I wanted to avoid.

Of course, it was no secret at Meriwether Lewis Elementary

that I had lost my little brother. That is, that he had disappeared on a camping trip two years before. Everyone read it in the newspaper, saw the posters, and some teachers and even students had been questioned by investigators. Because it happened over Memorial Day weekend, just after school let out, Liz and I were spared facing the kids at school until the fall, nearly three months later, and for that I have always been grateful. I was also grateful that Liz went on to junior high that fall, leaving me alone at Meriwether Lewis Elementary for a year. I knew that what we had done locked us together for life, and back then any kind of separation felt like relief.

We were still looking that fall, full-time. My father got permission to take an early sabbatical and drove all over the West following up feeble leads that no one, especially my mother, believed in but him. He was gone most of that year, searching, while my mother coordinated the effort from home. She liquidated their savings to hire a private investigator, the only one we could afford, a discount bungler who from my point of view did little more than collect checks from my parents. Even so, in some ways I think he was the best thing going that year, because he gave my mother hope. His officiousness gave backbone and continuity to the search, even if he never turned up a thing. My mother also answered the questions of endless cops who showed up, seemingly randomly, asking the same thousand questions, apparently having no access to or knowledge of anything their colleagues were doing. They made dire predictions and suggested ugly things about her daughters' characters. Worst of all, she fielded my father's daily calls from campground pay phones and listened to long descriptions of his fruitless efforts. She was always civil, polite, speaking to him slowly and clearly like he was a crazy person. "Why are you in Nebraska?" she would ask, as if it were a just a question, but her tone said, *You idiot.* And it said, *You deserter.* She was only partly right: My father was running away—he had to run to bear his sorrow—but I think he also truly believed he might turn up something, that if he left this to the police and hired investigators he would never be able to live with the defeat.

The second year after losing Timothy was different. My mother still kept track of the police's efforts, such as they were, though she finally fired the private investigator, not because she had lost faith in him but because we had run out of money. My father came home and went back to work. He was kind, as always, and stayed home that year, but was even more distracted than usual. Studying, always studying. I'd enter a room and he'd look up, smile, say, "Hiya, Tina," then return to his concentration scowl and look back at the equation or new theory he was trying to understand. That year we all returned to our lives, but with our ears pricked up, listening, always listening, ready to snatch Timothy the moment we caught glimpse of him. As if he might walk home on his own.

My mother turned to other kinds of experts, the self-professed ones who wrote books on coping, surviving, enduring, and suffering. Though she must have been feeling sorrow, intense sorrow, what she expressed was anger. It was as if her tears had turned to bullets. If I couldn't finish my supper, she would pick up my plate saying, "You're not going to eat that?" in a tone that held me personally accountable for every single child that starved to death in Bangladesh. When Liz and I found a litter of stray kittens in a vacant lot and asked to keep one, she said, "As busy as you girls are, how do you ever think you could keep the little thing alive?" Her stacks of self-help books were testimonials not only to our failings, but to our inattention to the root causes of those failings. Looking at a book, an entire book, on *living with loss* told me I didn't know the first thing about the subject. Someone, an expert, wrote 300 pages on it, while I had no words at all. Even worse were the books on *honoring truth*. My mother's books, and the knowledge she apparently gleaned from them, left me, and no doubt Liz and my father as well, feeling ignorant and lacking in simple human qualities, such as honesty and the capacity for love. At the time, I was aware only of an acute emotional flailing and of course had no words of analysis. I was only twelve. My life was still short enough to seem like a stream. I couldn't see patterns or make objective observations any more than a drop of water traveling to sea could. But I felt my mother's icy accusations. I felt them in every book title she brought home, in her intonation every time she said "you girls," for somehow in that period after losing Timothy, Liz and I had become one in her mind, the girls. Bound in our guilt.

It was toward the end of that second year after losing Timothy that I wrote my prize-winning poem. No one in the family knew I wrote the poem, nor did they know I was going to perform it at the Spring Program. I had no intention of telling them and diverted their attention from that evening by throwing away all the announcements sent home from school. What I didn't know was that Mrs. Tisdale, my busybody teacher, thought that given the dreadful tragedy that had befallen my family in the recent past, Christine Thomas needed a boost, special recognition. Not only did she select my poem to be recited at the Spring Program, but she manufactured an award to present to me as well. She called my parents to make sure that they would be in attendance.

On the night of the Spring Program, thinking I had successfully kept them ignorant of the event, I said I was going to a friend's house to do homework. Even now the memory of this lie makes me wince because I fooled my mother so completely, and in that deception she warmed to me for the first time in so long. She smiled, actually looked at me, said, "Okay, honey. We'll see you by nine, right?" Of course she knew I was lying, but she thought I was being modest, or perhaps shy, and this touched her. She was pleased that her daughter was going to be honored. Perhaps she was particularly pleased because the honor was an artistic one; I had won a poetry prize.

I arrived at the auditorium too early. The chorus was warming up, art students were taking pictures of the murals depicting spring that they had painted and hung on the walls of the auditorium, and a crew of boys were setting up metal chairs in precise rows. Mrs. Tisdale, wearing an organdy chiffon dress that billowed out like wings as she rushed to me, made a show of stifling her smile and said that artists should never show their faces before their appearances. She ushered me backstage, repeatedly patting my back to direct me, and told me to sit. I found a hard wooden chair and she handed me a *New Yorker*. "Just relax," she said, but I wasn't nervous. If I felt anything, it was a kind of false excitement. Mrs. Tisdale thought my poem "Losing Timothy" was a "masterpiece of emotion," but I knew it was *her* emotion, not mine. I had won an award for best poem; I had tricked the entire school. I could hold up my poem like a pearl and claim to have created it, but I knew that at the core of my poem lived a worm. Mrs. Tisdale had insisted I memorize the poem, and each time I recited the words it was as if they were layers of pearly calcium I deposited around that worm. Until that moment, sitting on the hard chair with a limp *New Yorker* in my lap, there was still hope for me to come to terms with the worm. But in a few minutes I would hold up that pearl, my "masterpiece of emotion," for public admiration, and after that it would be too late.

When it was my turn to perform, I stepped out from behind the curtain and up to the microphone. Mrs. Tisdale had directed me to make eye contact with the audience as I performed "Losing Timothy," which I did, finding my family right away in the center of the third row. I felt nothing, but I observed much. My mother looked furiously cold. My father smiled absently. Only Liz really saw me. Her lips were parted and she sat forward on her metal chair, uncomfortably stiff, willing me not to hang myself. For all the times she has tried to force her will on me, it has always been as a way to save me. Even when there was absolutely nothing I could do but finish reciting "Losing Timothy," the expression on her face demanded that I find a way out of my mess. Of course I did not find a way out. There would be no point in trying to change anything; I recited the poem as it had been written.

About the lake, the stone pier, the yellow Camaro, and the man with a crew cut. For the poem I added a scar, a rotted tooth, too-tight pants. The applause sounded distant, like the roar in a shell held up to the ear. Mrs. Tisdale came onto the stage and presented me with my award.

Later, in the cafeteria, with cookie crumbs dotting the corners of her mouth and punch reddening her tongue, Mrs. Tisdale told me I had "written beautifully of loss." She said art was about speaking the truths that others dare not speak. My mother, who stood listening to this tribute, had a look on her face that said, *How could this monster be my daughter?*

"Aren't you *proud* of her?" Mrs. Tisdale hugged me tightly to her big organdy bosom.

My mother didn't even smile, which confused Mrs. Tisdale, but she wasn't a woman to let things go. "Your daughter is very talented," she said. "She's a very good writer."

"She wants to be a scientist," my mother said, "like her father."

"I do," I said, wanting to ally myself with my mother, but I realized too late that my mother's comment was another accusation, that she would prefer that I be a writer. But not this kind of writer. Anyway, she didn't hear my answer because she was walking away. I excused myself and made my way, blind with nausea, to the girls' bathroom, where I vomited into the sink. I ran the water, rinsed the sink and my mouth, and waited for Liz. I knew she would have been keeping an eye on me, and sure enough, she was there a moment later.

"That was really dumb."

"How did I know I was going to win a prize for it?"

This was the closest Liz and I had ever come to talking about it, and for a moment, the spinning I had lived with since losing Timothy stopped. I can still smell the harsh tang of disinfectant in that girls' bathroom. I can see the one-inch green speckled tiles that covered the floor and half the walls, and also the grid of white grouting separating them. I can see the salmon-pink metal stalls, the corroded chrome fixtures on the two deco porcelain sinks. And Liz's pink skin, her blond hair in a long braid, a few frizzy strands framing her face, the navy-blue sailor dress that was too short. For one moment, as Liz and I stood alone together and glanced at the truth, I felt at peace.

"Come on," Liz said. She held the door open for me, and we walked slowly down the hallway to the cafeteria without talking. I don't remember anything more about the punch-and-cookies party in the cafeteria. Perhaps we stayed another hour, perhaps we left immediately. Neither of my parents ever mentioned my poem or the fact that I'd won a prize.

Liz treated me gently that night, and all the next week, as if she were watching me descend a ladder into hell and couldn't stop me. The thing about hell, though, is that you learn to endure it. You just do. You eat, you sleep, you talk, you do your work. As the years go by you learn better and better how, when your personal hell flares in your face, to turn away.

Liz has never given up trying to save me from myself, but she has become less sympathetic in her methods. Now she just lectures. Like when I broke up with Robin. The thing is, Liz can skirt so close to the danger points, because she doesn't see that they are there.

Robin is *normal,* Liz said. She has regular interests, an easy presence. Unlike Lucienne, whose mouth is a knife, whose eyes are lasers. Liz doesn't like how Lucienne sees her, sees into her, and speaks her mind. But Robin, now there was a girlfriend who could come to barbecues on Mark and Liz's farm, who could chat—and I do mean chat—with anyone. Who, as I'm sure Liz suspected, could love deeply and with devotion. Like Mark. Perfect Robin.

But what Liz doesn't know is that Robin is a glutton for information. "Tell me," was her constant refrain. About anything.

"Tell me what you had for lunch today."

"Tell me how your parents met."

"Tell me what you see yourself doing in thirty years."

Robin's demand for information—which, if I am honest with myself, is what probably broke us up—would have sent Liz running a lot faster than it did me.

"Tell me what happened to your little brother."

"I've told you."

"No, what *really* happened."

"What do you mean, what *really* happened? I've told you the part we know. The rest we don't."

"But why haven't you *looked* for Timothy?"

"We did. Of course we looked."

"I mean now. I mean look again. He was a child then. He could be somewhere nearby. You could put ads in papers. Hire a private investigator. Research police reports. There is every bit as good a chance that he is alive than that he is dead. Don't you want to know?"

"That was thirty years ago."

"So? He's your *brother*."

"I know he's my brother, Robin. But think about it. Even if he is alive, he has his own life. What good would it do him—or us—to find him? That kind of thing just throws wrenches into people's lives."

I didn't tell her how I know this is true. I didn't tell her about the time, fifteen years ago now, when I visited that ranch in Oregon.

Robin narrowed her eyes. "It could be wonderful."

Trust me. It's not.

The odd thing was that, though Robin needled me for the truth, Lucienne's reaction to the Timothy story, many years earlier, came closer to the truth. I had told her about losing him and she had laughed. It was anything but a heartless laugh. It was an ironic laugh, the laugh of acknowledging the cruelty and stacked-deck-ness of life. It was a laugh that recognized the layers of truths and lies that we all hold inside. For Robin, there is a simple path, one straight shot for truth. It's funny because Lucienne, Robin, and Liz all have this in common: an adherence to, even a passion for, truth. But in each of them it takes a different form and incorporates a whole set of lies. Lucienne knew the truth in the *mystery* of Timothy's disappearance, a truth Robin couldn't see. Liz's truth, of course, leaps over just about everything in the present, while forfeiting everything in the past as well, to the future, but it is no less a truth.

As for myself, I don't understand how anyone can say, "This is what happened/is happening/will happen." Truth, so far as I understand it, is something we all make up. Now, as a forty-year-old woman, I'm sorry I felt so much shame over my poem about losing Timothy. Much of it was a lie, but much of it was not. After all, I hadn't yet given up; I was still trying to juggle the pieces into a recognizable form, to create some kind of knowable truth. And that had been the source of Liz's compassion toward me the night of my poetry performance. She knew I was searching for Timothy in my own way, and back then she still wanted me to. She didn't have the words to encourage me—she was only thirteen herself—but she had some weird kind of faith in me, the kind that she has always had that I might be capable of finding, or at least creating, the truth.

thirteen: spirit lake

I should have known better, but I thought Liz had invited me because it was Timothy's eighteenth birthday. I even convinced myself that she thought it would be healing for me, that she actually had understood the significance of that Marine cadaver.

It was the beginning of September, and I had returned to medical school for my second year. Liz had saved me in the spring, from flunking out and perhaps from harming myself in much worse ways, but Lucienne, whom I'd met during the summer, had given my life a whole new context. Making love with Lucienne broke much more than years of celibacy; it was as if I'd been reintroduced to the whole notion of desire. With Lucienne I learned to eat with a rapacious appetite, to listen to music so loud it made my toes vibrate, and of course to touch another body, a live one, for sheer pleasure. Lucienne taught me to appreciate desire for desire's sake, and she taught me so well that I didn't think to claim her, the physical specific person Lucienne, as my own. That summer I was so relieved to find myself alive, in the biggest sense of the word; that feeling propelled me into my second year of medical school.

When Liz called, I had to cut several days of classes to spend that one with her, but wild horses couldn't have kept me away. I drove up from San Francisco, a thirteen-hour drive, to meet her at the forest service station in Washington, the fieldwork headquarters for her dissertation on the resiliency of life and the conditions necessary for plant renewal after major environmental disruption, primarily logging. It was exactly the kind of coincidental good luck that Liz always has had: Mount St. Helens erupted all summer long, providing a textbook case for her Ph.D. thesis. Pyroclastic devastation wasn't the same as clear-cut logging, but it was far more exciting. Scientists crawled all over the mountain that summer, nervously conducting their studies in between eruptions, the most recent of which had occurred on August 7. A team of geologists, headed by a man named Donald, asked Liz, already somewhat renowned in her field, to take a look at Spirit Lake and help them assess the biological damage.

Liz called me and said, "You have to come up here. This guy Donald, a geologist, wants me to help him with a study of Spirit Lake—remember Spirit Lake?"

Of course I remembered Spirit Lake. Before Timothy disappeared from that other lake, the name of which I don't remember, that other lake somewhere in Oregon, we used to camp at Spirit Lake. In fact, I sometimes comforted myself by thinking of Spirit Lake. It was like an antidote to thoughts of that other, more barren, nameless lake. Spirit Lake was big, huge really, and surrounded by timbered lodges with smoke swirling out of chimneys, scout camps, and forests of hemlock and Pacific silver fir. Even though Spirit Lake was gigantic, it was cozy and civilized. Best of all, the glorious peak of Mount St. Helens reflected on the water's surface.

Liz said, "Donald says there's room for four in the helicopter. Can you get here by Friday?"

I assumed she knew Friday was Timothy's birthday and I didn't want to spoil it for her, the queen of inference, by saying so. I figured that was why she was offering me, rather than Mark, the fourth seat in the chopper. Thirteen years had passed since we had lost Timothy and still she wouldn't speak of him directly, at least not for long. I thought that her honoring this day, his eighteenth birthday, was a breakthrough, even if she couldn't say that was what she was doing. I said I'd pack immediately, jump on the highway, and be there sometime Thursday night.

In fact, I didn't arrive until three in the morning on Friday. The helicopter lifted off at seven, into a sky that was a deep autumn blue, whispery and layered. The pilot tilted us over the forest service building, then headed sideways toward the mountain. Sleep deprivation and levitation by chopper gave me an ethereal feeling, as if I were drugged, and I floated in the helicopter cavity thinking of Lucienne and sex, but when the mountain came into view I was startled out of my dreaminess. Mount St. Helens bellowed clouds of ash and smoke, and I thought she was erupting right then. I clutched Liz; she realized what I thought and yelled into my ear, because the engine of the chopper was too loud for normal talking, that the mountain had been doing that all summer. *"This is not an eruption,"* she yelled.

Donald the geologist, who sat up front with the pilot, turned and laughed. He was an exceptionally tall, lanky man with a long untrimmed black beard. His startling blue eyes were probably very attractive to most women, but he knew it and flashed them ostentatiously. Liz leaned forward and, putting a hand on his broad shoulder, shouted something near his ear. He laughed again.

The pilot flew us directly toward the clouds of ash and steam roiling out of the crater. Donald and Liz began a conversation I couldn't hear because they cupped their hands around each other's ears to be heard over the chopper. I didn't like the tight little smile around Liz's mouth.

Maybe she was just excited. This erupting mountain was a real heyday for her, as it was for every other scientist in the vicinity, but especially for her as it fit in so closely with her dissertation work. From our overhead view I saw the path of the pyroclastic flow, where it had devastated everything for miles around. Beyond that the blasts of hot ash had knocked down acres and acres of forest. I wondered if Timothy would marvel at this sight, if he had any of Liz's vision or my love of the extraordinary, but he was such a timid little boy, I had to admit that it was unlikely.

As the pilot made a wide circle around the crater, the billow of smoke and ash seemed to enlarge for a moment and again I grabbed Liz's hand. And again Donald laughed. He leaned back and shouted something in Liz's ear. Liz turned and shouted to me, *"She won't blow today. Donald's team can predict to the day."*

"Isn't Donald brilliant," I said out loud, knowing they couldn't hear me.

I was relieved when the pilot zipped over to the northeast and landed us near the shore of Spirit Lake. My legs were weak and shaky as I jumped down from the chopper.

The autumn sun was already bright and high in the sky, but nothing else about the day seemed to have begun. If you think the wilderness is silent, try the abolished wilderness. There were no bird calls. No tree branches to rustle in the wind. You could almost hear the sun shine. The lake was thick with mud and covered with floating dead trees that had been knocked down by the blast. The forests of hemlock, Pacific silver fir, and Douglas fir were a splintered jumble surrounding the lake.

The pilot stayed in the helicopter but Liz, Donald, and I all walked in separate directions. I bent to feel an ash-blasted log, ran a finger in the sediment-thick lake water.

Suddenly I couldn't hold back my tears. Completing my first year of medical school was the hardest thing I'd ever done, and I dreaded this second year, even with Lucienne in my life. Seeing what Mount St. Helens had done blasted open my cramped brain, at least for that morning. It was as if I could rest, vicariously, in the aftermath of its enormous expenditure of energy. Awe is very restorative.

Donald's voice carried in the still air. "Nothing. I predict nothing will come back for at least fifty years."

"I think you're wrong," Liz said in her forthright way, moving toward him. She still had that tight little smile. I wished that her contrariness was animosity, but it wasn't; it was more like flirtation. Furthermore, I could see her contradiction pleased him—in a short-term way. He would want her to capitulate eventually.

She said, "We'll see something green next year."

Donald burst out laughing. "You're joking, aren't you?"

"No," she said, and turned her back on him. "Something green next year. Probably animals even."

Oh, that faith of hers. I walked over and put an arm around my sister.

Donald said, "Five thousand black-tailed deer, destroyed. Fifteen hundred Roosevelt elk, ditto. The mountain goats on Mount Margaret, gone. Three hundred black bears, dead of suffocation. Forget all the smaller animals and birds."

"The amazing thing," Liz said, "is how the animals are curious. A couple of weeks ago we were a few miles east of here, just above Johnston Ridge, and these elk wandered into the blast zone, just looking around. Obviously they weren't looking for food, because there is none. They were just curious."

"I'm not talking about tourists from other parts of the mountain coming over for a look," Donald said."

"Have you heard about Martha's study?" she asked him.

"Who's Martha?"

"She and her team have set up seed and live-animal traps in the blast zone. They're monitoring survivors and colonizers."

"There are no survivors, and they'll have to wait fifty years for the colonizers."

Liz smiled broadly. "Next year we'll see something green. Hey, listen. Martha's traps were full of seeds and spiders! The blast zone is covered with them."

"Sure. Seeds fly around everywhere. But there is nothing—*nothing*—here for them to take root in. Seeds need soil. Every single surface is covered with thick ash. Animals need clear water. The lake and all its streams are clogged."

"There are these amazing spiders," Liz told me, "that are adapted for airborne travel. They spin webs that act as parasails. They use them to drop from tree branches and ride on the wind."

"There is no habitat." Donald again. "They won't stay."

"Bets?"

"Sure." Donald had a wolfish smile under all those black whiskers. He and Liz grasped hands and shook for too long. I was used to seeing Liz next to Mark, who is short, not to mention neat. This lunk made Liz look too dainty.

And anyway, I thought they were on official scientific business. What was all this bantering and betting? Why weren't they taking samples? Why wasn't Donald listening respectfully to Liz's opinions, if that was why he had, in fact, invited her?

Donald turned to lecture me. "The devastation is much greater than we have any idea now. They already know that the ash has dehydrated the bees in *eastern Washington*. That far away."

"Surely we can live without the full ration of bees," I said.

Liz laughed. "I told you my sister has no reverence."

This offended me. Who had no reverence? This was Timothy's birthday, his coming-of-age day, and why were we spending it with this oaf?

"What's Mark doing today?" I asked Liz.

"Working."

Donald began walking back to the helicopter. I waited for him to get twenty yards away, then said, "He's a blowhard, Liz."

She smiled, a happy smile that scared me. Behind her, steam and ash puffed out of the crater. It occurred to me that Liz was having an affair with Donald. Given my new-found lasciviousness, I was hardly in a position to be judgmental, but Mark was family. I assumed Liz had always been one hundred percent faithful to him, but what did I know? Had I been an outside observer, I would have placed even more money on Mark's faithfulness, which of course was flawed.

Finally Liz got down to the business of the day. She took samples and wrote notes while I leapt from log to log, feeling the stretch between this being Timothy's day and Liz's day. I was beginning to think that she was showing me something, but what? Was I supposed to be impressed by Donald?

When Liz finished being a scientist, we started walking to the helicopter for the ride back to the ranger station. All of a sudden I stopped her, took hold of her shoulders, and asked, "Do you even remember that it's Timothy's birthday?"

She hadn't.

She shook loose of me, turned her back on the devastated lake, and started climbing over the downed trees toward the helicopter. I caught up and grabbed her hand. "Come on," I said. "Just one moment."

"Let go," she said.

"Of what, your hand or Timothy?" I let go of neither. "Please, Liz, just say happy birthday with me. That's all."

Her mouth opened and closed. She batted her eyelids three, four times. Then that little release I have seen only rarely in my sister. I could see it between her breasts, a tiny collapse. She closed her eyes slowly this time, held them down, then opened them.

I swung her around to face the log-clogged lake. "It's his eighteenth," I told her, then called cheerfully toward the lake, "Happy birthday, Timothy!"

Liz squeezed my hand, then even hugged me.

I asked, "Did you bring me as a witness or to protect you?"

"Neither, you idiot." She jumped away from me, onto an unstable log, wavered and balanced. "Why'd you cut your hair?"

I reached back and felt where the long braid had been. We had always had matching braids, hers straw-blond, mine auburn. Now my hair hung just below my ears in a blunt cut.

"I could tell you didn't like it because you didn't say anything."

"It looks cute. It's just a surprise."

"Long hair gets in the way when you're hanging over a cadaver all day."

"That was last year."

"Okay, yeah."

"Maybe I'll cut mine too," she said, but she never did.

On the flight back, Donald sat in front again, and I sat with Liz behind him and the pilot. I draped my arm around her shoulders for the duration of the ride. If it looked proprietary, I meant it to look that way. Donald could buzz off.

He didn't buzz off, though. Liz never failed to mention him every time we talked all fall and winter.

The next summer, when she again left the university to do more fieldwork at Mount St. Helens, I asked her if Donald was around the mountain for the summer too.

"Oh, that blowhard?" she said.

I laughed, but she didn't, which made me realize how close they had come to doing something stupid. "Liz, you didn't…?"

"No," she said. "No." Then one more time, emphatically. "*No.*"

I believed her, and also knew she wasn't going to elaborate, so I just said, "Good."

"I think he's working on Mount Hood this summer."

"He didn't want to admit he'd lost the bet."

Liz laughed heartily. Because of course she had been right about the resilience of life. Already sprouts of fireweed and thistle were poking up in the blast zone. Gophers that had been underground for the eruptions had survived and now tunneled up through the ash, bringing soil with them, providing habitat for the pioneer plants.

That was exactly why Liz would save the planet if anyone could; she passionately believed in the gophers and thistles on the moonscape flanks of Mount St. Helens.

fourteen: free fall, part 1

I sleep fiercely and awake understanding the meaning of hibernation. I have no idea what time it is. I lift my head and look to my right, in the direction of the tunnel. No light enters. It must still be night. I roll gently toward Lenny and feel his solid presence. I roll even more gently in the other direction and find empty space. I keep rolling. Lots of empty space.

When I finally reach a body, it's Liz's voice that growls, "*Move.*" She elbows me. She must think I'm Mark. I roll back into my place, wondering at the depth of anger in her voice. Wondering so deeply that it takes me a moment to question where Mark and Melody are. Another pee expedition, I guess, then realize I need to relieve myself again—both of my full bladder and this silent tomb. I dress and crawl over Lenny for the second time.

The possibility of daylight shows on the eastern horizon,

a tiny blush in the night sky. I ski back to my group of scrubby trees, pee, then look for Mark and Melody. As I ski down to the nose of the ridge, I'm pleased to see the blush in the east grow slightly brighter. Perhaps dawn isn't so far away. Perhaps I can stay up rather than return to the snow cave. Perhaps I can even get another fire going in spite of Mark's pile of snow in our pit. I need only trample it down hard, pile on some green boughs, build another little tepee of twigs, and light it. If it worked once, it can work again. It would be my gift to the group.

Nearly excited, I begin skiing back to camp. I survived the night. In a matter of hours, say about eight, I will be en route to a big truck-stop meal.

The surrounding light is growing murky, still mostly dark but without the edge. The trees, down on the sides of the ridge, have taken on ghostly shapes, looking more like creatures than trees. I suppose they *are* creatures, but in this light it is as if they could bend, or throw apples, like the trees on the way to the Land of Oz.

In fact, I'm sure a tree down there *is* moving. A current of cold fear runs through me. I still my body and stare at the moving tree. I force myself to overcome the fear. It is only the wilderness. Hypothermia and avalanches are the dangers out here, not creatures. I advance toward the dark shadow and soon see that it is a human figure, two human figures.

Simultaneously, I think, *How could I have been so stupid?* and *I will kill you.*

I shove off and ski directly toward what I see now as the entangled couple. The closer I come, silently gliding down the slope toward them, the greater my dread. For I see now that she is hoisted up on him, her legs around his waist. This is something I do not want to see. It is something I do not want in my memory, as I already know it will be, forever.

They are too involved to hear me coming. I imagine spearing him with my ski pole. I consider going back for a better weapon. I could knock him unconscious with the metal shovel.

But they have noticed me. Their heads are turning. Her legs drop off his waist. I turn my face, not wanting to see what nakedness they must quickly cover. When I look back they are standing side by side, jackets unzipped but the rest of their clothing fastened. I snowplow to a stop.

Later, of course, I'll think of a hundred things I wish I had said, but now I'm silent, stunned by anger.

Mark's eyes are fixed on me. Melody turns her back and covers her face. I want to command, like a sergeant, that she get back into the moment. It is not a pretty one, but she was certainly in it a second ago. Then, as if she can hear my thoughts, she turns and looks at me too.

"I'm sorry," she says. It's weak, very weak, but I'm impressed she has spoken.

"I tried to tell you...." Mark starts.

As if telling me would make any difference.

"How long?" I finally ask. I don't know why I'm asking. I guess I'm trying to gauge the degree of betrayal, the possibilities for nipping it.

"Six months," Mark says in his honorable voice, which makes me want to vomit. Then he takes a step forward. Their skis are standing up in the snow nearby, and he must push through the snow to get closer to me. "As if you couldn't understand," he says.

"What does this have to do with me?" I ask, truly bewildered.

"You're not exactly pure." He's badger-like, his light eyebrows furry in the dawn light. Never before have I heard Mark sneer, and it makes me sad, almost.

"I don't pretend to be," I say.

"We can't talk this out here," Melody offers.

"Ah," I say, "shall we go back and include Liz?"

"No," Melody and Mark say at the same time. Mark looks humble again. He repeats, "No," and tears crack his voice.

"I want to kill you," I tell him. "If this ski pole could do it, I'd put it right through you."

His lips tremble like a little boy's.

"You're all she has," I say.

"Bullshit. I'm all she *won't* have. She has her big-shot job. She has her garden and her jar upon jar of canned fruit and vegetables. And she has *you.*"

He says "you" as if it were dirt.

"Me?"

"The two of you together. It's as if no one else exists in the world."

Melody snaps into her skis. All around us the dawn is pinking.

"What are you talking about? We're sisters. What's that got to do with you?"

I see a lifetime of unspoken feelings on Mark's face. He holds my eyes with his but doesn't speak. I say, "We're skiing back to camp. We'll pack up. We'll ski to the truck. We'll drive home. And once there, Melody, you'll find a new job."

She stops her futzing with the skis to look at me. She doesn't like me telling her what to do.

"And if you don't," I add, "I will kill you. Don't think I won't."

I believe myself completely. I think of a couple of my patients who are in and out of the women's prison at Chowchilla. They would protect me there. I could survive a few years in prison. I'm white and a doctor; they wouldn't give me life.

Now she's looking at me with the kind of hatred that non-violent people have for violent people. I am vermin.

I turn to ski back up the embankment. I hear Mark snapping on his skis. I don't hear their voices, and I guess that they aren't even looking at each other. I wish they would be forever behind me, forever something I don't have to see, but Mark catches up. "It's not so simple. Losing Timothy has bound you two in a way you can never get away from. Liz will never let go! She is so determined to never, never ever again in life lose something. She can't let go of *anything*. And especially not of you. *You* should be the one who is sick of her. She is so critical of you, yet she lives through you.

She has no use for me at all. I can't take it anymore."

"Mark," I say, and pause because I am skiing so hard uphill I can hardly breathe, let alone talk. "Liz loves you. She has loved no one but you. You get rid of this—" I almost say "bitch," but I know Melody isn't a bitch. I wave my hand over my head in her direction. "You get rid of this woman and do what you've been doing, take care of Liz."

When Mark says nothing, I know that he's considering leaving Liz. I shout, "Fuck!"

Then he switches gears and says hoarsely, "You're feeling guilty about that time with us. It's not like—"

I stop skiing and face him, gasping for air. "Wrong. What happened between you and me was twenty-three years ago. *Twenty-three years.* I do believe in statutes of limitations. I can't believe you're trying to blackmail me."

Tears swell his entire face, making it puffy, red, bursting. "I'm sorry."

"Sorry isn't good enough. You said it yourself: I'd kill for Liz."

He gurgles something. His face looks as if it has lost its structure, like it might slide away.

"I'll tell you again," I say. "You're going to pull yourself together. We're skiing back to camp. We'll pack up and ski out. Then you'll go home with Liz and do whatever you need to do to fix yourself." I almost say *Do you understand?* but he looks up now and the structure in his face has returned. He doesn't nod, but he starts skiing again. I can count on Mark's endurance; I have to count on his endurance.

Down the hill, some twenty yards back, I see Melody skiing methodically toward us. She doesn't look sorry. She moves intentionally slowly, keeping her distance, but her limbs look loose, freed. She doesn't look sorry at all. Behind her, dawn is blooming with a rosy vengeance.

fifteen: missing boys

We find Liz sitting on one of the logs around the fire pit. She doesn't ask where we've been. She doesn't even say hello. Mark skis up to her and for a moment I think he's going to kiss her good morning, but he doesn't. He removes his skis, sits on the log next to her, and asks, "Where's Lenny?"

"I don't know. Gone when I got up."

"When did you get up?"

"Just."

Mark looks around. "His skis are gone."

"He's probably gone off to take a shit," Liz says.

In this fragile light it sounds as though they are shouting.

"How'd you sleep?" I ask her.

"Like a log."

"That's good. Me too, once I fell asleep."

Mark begins putting the stove together. "Tea for everyone?"

No one answers, but he starts the stove anyway and fills

the pot with snow. I go to get a cigarette but they're missing from my pack. Damn that kid. I don't feel like building a fire anymore. I just want to get the hell out of here. I go to the snow cave and pull out my sleeping bag, pad, and sack of night supplies. I stuff my sleeping bag, return to camp, and offer to do the same for the others.

"I can do mine," Melody says, and she walks with me back to the cave. I half-expect her to try to talk, but she doesn't. I stuff Liz and Mark's bags and carry them back to camp, leaving Melody in the cave doing who knows what. I open Mark's pack to put away his sleeping bag and see a big ripstop cylinder. Curious, I pull it out.

"What's this?" I ask, holding it up.

Mark glances at Liz.

"What are you doing going through other people's packs?" she asks.

"I stuffed your bags for you. I'm putting them in your packs rather than dropping them on the snow. This looks like a tent to me."

"Yep," Mark answers.

"Why did you tell me we didn't have one?"

"Because the plan was to sleep in a snow cave," Liz says, her face stony.

This caps my doozy of a bad mood. They lied because they knew I would never have slept in the cave if I knew they had a tent. I drop the tent on the snow and take the cup of tea he offers.

After filling everyone's mug, Mark says, "I'm going to go check on Lenny."

Liz, Melody, and I drink our tea.

Finally I say, "Your hair is a mess. Want me to brush it?"

Liz looks up, surprised. "We don't have a hairbrush."

"I do." After the tent discovery, I know I'm not going to get into trouble for having brought an item that wasn't on Liz's list.

I rummage in my pack until I find the brush, then stand behind Liz and undo her long braid. I'm surprised she doesn't stop me, surprised and glad that she'll accept this.

"Are you worried about Lenny?" Melody asks.

"No," Liz says.

I loosen the braid and begin brushing.

"He's kind of young to be out there on his own," Melody persists.

"He can't exactly take a shit in full sight of everyone," Liz says.

"He's been gone half an hour."

"Maybe he's constipated."

"Still, I think—"

"Mark is looking for him."

I finish brushing all the tangles out of Liz's hair. I braid it again, careful not to pull her hair back from her face too tightly.

"Thanks," she says when I finish.

Melody looks around nervously. I busy myself organizing my pack. Liz and Melody remain on the log benches, as if they're held there against their wills. They don't speak. We can hear Mark, calling Lenny's name from a distance. Then a few moments later, we hear him shouting from a different place, in a different direction.

Finally Mark returns.

"I don't get it," he says. "How could he have gone so far as to be out of earshot?"

"Maybe he doesn't want to be found," Liz says. "Anyway, we have to go soon."

"I'm sure he'll be back in a few minutes. Have you all had breakfast?" Mark claps his hands and rubs them together like a scoutmaster.

I shake my head.

"I'll heat water for the oatmeal."

"Let's skip it," Liz says.

"We have to eat. And what else are we going to do while we wait?"

"Why wait?"

We all look at Liz. She is quietly folding up her rain pants and jacket. I wish I hadn't brushed and braided her hair because the neatness gives her a cold, calculated appearance.

"We have to wait for—or find—Lenny." I gently say the obvious. "We can't leave until he's back."

"I don't see why not. He's chosen to ski off. He's old enough to make his own choices."

"He'll die if we leave," Melody says.

"We all die," Liz answers. "The difference between dying at sixteen and dying at eighteen is greatly exaggerated. It's all the same."

"Liz?" Mark says.

"So we lose a kid," she explodes. "So what? What's it to you? Really, Mark, *what is it to you*?" She punches the last five words as if they were Mark's chest.

The scary thing about people who don't appear to have a dark side is that when it does emerge, it's very potent. I know to stay away from her, but Mark walks around and stands next to her. She looks at him for a moment with what could be hatred, but I know it's not. I know it's desperation disguised as hatred. I think, but I'm not sure, that Mark knows that too.

He reaches a hand out to her shoulder, but she steps aside before he can touch her and says, "I'm just joking. How should we organize the search?"

"I don't think you're very funny," Melody says.

Mark closes his eyes for a long moment, obviously wishing Melody would keep quiet. It is all I can do to not say, *Shut up.*

Liz ignores her and says, "Mark's right. We need to eat before we do anything. And we should eat quickly. If he's not back by the time we finish, one of us should stay in camp in case he returns here. Then we'll split up and each take a territory for the search."

The oats taste like sweet glue. I try to place each bite as close to the back of my throat as I can so that it goes down in one swift gulp. We forgo the freeze-dried peach dessert so we can get going on the search.

Wiping our mouths, we stand in a circle for a moment looking at one another.

"I'll stay in camp," Melody says submissively.

I level her one long disgusted look. Enlightenment indeed.

"Good," Liz says. "I think Tina better come with me. Why don't we take the territory north of the ridge and you"—she points at her husband—"take the south."

"Okay."

"We'll meet back here in, oh, say an hour? To check in? Hopefully with Lenny in tow."

"Liz?" Mark says. He looks scared.

"What?"

He freezes, then leans forward and kisses her on the cheek. She manages a small smile before she and I ski away. I wonder if he also kisses Melody before leaving camp.

We are down the side of the ridge in no time and start across a long meadow, shouting Lenny's name as we go. We look for his tracks, but we've made tracks all over the area so who knows which are his and which are any of ours.

I notice that the promised dawn is fizzling. The gold and pink have been bleached from the sky by a thin, high cloud cover. The air is cold.

I think about a lot of things. Of how I shouldn't have told an impressionable sixteen-year-old about losing my brother in a setting similar to this. Of how Liz and Mark have set themselves up to relive the Timothy episode year after year by taking boys out on wilderness adventures. The more I think about it, the more angry I feel. What do they expect? I'm angry at Liz for putting herself—and me—in this situation. And at Mark, of course, for not paying attention. If he hadn't been in the woods mauling Melody, Lenny wouldn't have had the chance to slip away.

I ski along behind Liz, shouting "Lenny," listening, and watching the sky.

"I'll kill this kid," Liz says, but her mood seems to have brightened. It occurs to me that this is the exact kind of predicament she relishes. She's spent her life honing her wilderness skills, thrives on knowing exactly what to do when someone is lost. I have to admit that out here, in these severe mountains, her will is entirely appropriate. To me this white tableau, this monochrome snow and sky, to which Liz subjects herself time and again, seems nearly abusive. Why would you want it? It is colorless, a wiped slate, totally empty. My memories, in contrast, are lurid in color, jumpy in their three-dimensionality. Timothy pops up over every horizon. He flashes in my face like a hallucination. Timothy would be thirty-five, I tell myself. We are not looking for Timothy.

Ahead of me, Liz's braid, the part that dangles below her fleece hat, bounces on her back as she skis too swiftly for me to keep up comfortably. I watch her bouncing braid grow more distant and think how she has never, in her entire life, changed her hairstyle.

I brushed and braided her hair maybe five times that day at the lake. We sat in the short green and white webbed camp chairs for hours while the police questioned us. Our mother paced around the campsite, waiting for our father, who, when she called him, told us not to leave until he got there. She kept bursting out at the police, "Why don't you go *look* for him? Every minute you're here questioning my girls, that man is another mile down the highway with Timothy!"

"Ma'am, we've alerted the highway patrol. The more information your girls can give us, the better our chances of recovering your son."

One of the officers was nice, the other wasn't. Whenever someone says "good cop, bad cop" I think of them, Officer Rand and Officer Norton. Both were white, both needed a size larger uniform, both had mustaches. The nice one, Officer Rand, had droopy eyelids and a habit of taking off his hat to run his fingers through his thick dark hair. The hard-boiled one, Officer Norton, was older and had millions of tiny burst blood vessels in the skin on his nose and cheeks. He came too close to our faces to ask questions, as if his coffee breath was some kind of truth vapor.

It was 1967. Our campsite was dusty and hot. While each of the surrounding campsites was shady and cool-looking, the sun poured in ours through a break in the forest, spotlighting our misery all morning long. My mother wore blue cotton pedal pushers with little slits on the hem just below her knees. She wore a white tube top and white cat-eye sunglasses with dark green lenses. Liz and I never changed out of our swimsuits, nor did we pull shorts or T-shirts over them. The next day I would have a nasty sunburn that peeled three times in the following weeks, but we endured the heat that morning. It felt like part of our ordeal, something that we could not change; it didn't occur to us to move into the shade. We drank lots of Coke. When the Cokes in our cooler were gone, Officer Rand drove his squad car up to the camp store and bought us another six-pack.

Groups of children gathered on the road in front of our campsite watching the police question us. Liz started throwing pine cones at them, and to be like her I picked up a rock and fired it at a strawberry-blond boy. The rock struck him in the chest, right between his nipples, and he howled.

"That's enough out of you, young lady." Officer Norton took my chin in his hand and put his face close to mine. "Behave."

"Don't touch her," my mother said.

Officer Rand went to check on the kid. There wasn't any blood, so he sent him back to his own campsite.

The trouble was, after telling the story once, Liz wasn't talking anymore. Since officially I hadn't been there when Timothy was abducted, it was hard for me to fill in the gaps. How I tried, though!

"Listen, girls," Officer Rand said around noon, "let's start from the beginning."

I explained how I had gone off in the woods to look for more stones. "When I got back, I saw a yellow car in the campsite."

"That's campsite number fourteen?"

I looked at Liz. She nodded.

"Yes," I said.

"Go on."

I asked my mother, "When will Daddy get here?"

"Soon."

"Go on," Officer Norton urged.

"The man in the car had Timothy."

"Did you *see* Timothy in the car?"

I looked at Liz. Her face was blank.

"Yes," I said.

"Did you see the man?"

"Yes," I said.

"What did he look like?"

"Just like what my sister told you already."

"We want your description. What did he look like to you?"

I had never been so hot in my life. It must have been ninety degrees. The sun seared right through my hair.

My father was on his way. Somehow, in my child's logic, I thought he would bring shade. We could have moved our chairs a few yards into the shade behind our tent. But we didn't. We waited for my father.

"I think he had a crew cut."

"You *think*?"

Liz had said he had a crew cut. "I *know* he had a crew cut."

"What else?"

"No shirt." I pictured a man with a hairy chest.

"Your sister said he had on Levi's. Is that right?"

"If she said so."

"Did you see the Levi's?"

"He was already in the car by the time I got there."

"Did you see Timothy in the car?"

"You already asked that."

"Just answer the questions."

I nodded.

"Did you see Timothy in the car?"

I nodded.

"Answer with words."

"Yes."

"How tall was Timothy?" This was directed at my mother.

"Three foot seven."

"And you could see his head in the car seat?"

"*Yes.*"

"You returned to the lake shore with an armload of stones, correct?"

"Yes."

"You saw the yellow car with a man with a crew cut at the wheel and your brother riding shotgun, correct?"

"For crying out loud!" my mother screamed. "That's my son you're referring too."

"Beg your pardon, ma'am," said the good cop.

Bad cop didn't even look her way. "Is that all correct?"

"Yes," I answered.

"Then what did you do?"

"I don't remember. I think I looked at my sister."

"Why didn't you help your brother? Why didn't you try to open the car door?"

"The car was already moving. I didn't know why he was in the car. I didn't know that he was a bad man yet."

"Have your parents told you to never get into cars with strangers?"

I nodded, and then, seeing the red flare in Officer Norton's face, quickly said, "Yes."

"So couldn't you assume that he was a bad man?"

"What's your point?" my mother asked. "My son got in the car. It's your job to get him out of it, not Tina's! She's ten years old, for crying out loud."

"Calm down, ma'am."

"Calm down?" My mother stalked over to Officer Norton. "My son—" she started, then broke down. She turned abruptly and went to the tent door. She stopped there and sobbed into her hands twice. Then she whirled around and said, "I'm sorry."

Officer Norton asked me, "You say that when you returned with your armload of rocks and saw your brother in the car, you looked at your sister. What was your sister doing?"

"She started screaming and—"

"She *started* screaming? She only started screaming after the guy had loaded the boy in the car?"

"It's only when *I* heard her," I said. Then, "*I don't know.* We ran to get Mommy."

This went on for hours. Liz wouldn't speak at all. The good cop tried to make her. The bad cop tried to make her. So did my mother. Later, a police psychiatrist told us the trauma made her clam up like that. Whenever the police walked away from our camp to radio something from their car or to talk where we couldn't hear them, I brushed and rebraided Liz's hair. She let me. I barely remember what our mother did all that time. I can picture her freckled skin perfectly, a film of dusty sweat on her shoulders and neck. The sun in her auburn hair, highlighting the red. I can picture the way her knees looked knobby in the blue pedal pushers. But I can't recall her doing anything other than pacing, usually behind us in our camp chairs, and smoking endless cigarettes. I was so focused on Liz.

My father arrived at two in the afternoon. Liz still didn't move off her camp chair, but I threw myself at him with so much force he staggered backwards. His face was ravaged by tears, as if he had been crying the whole drive up to the mountains and hadn't bothered to wipe his face. He stooped down and touched Liz's cheek, then hugged my mother. After he had a long private talk with Officer Norton and Officer Rand, we finally got to drive home.

I never saw Rand or Norton again, although at least a dozen other police officers interviewed me and Liz over the next few months. How many times was I asked to describe the car? How many times did the police ask if I could remember anything about the license plate? Why would a child read a license plate of a car that meant nothing to her? We learned by looking at piles of pictures that the yellow car was a Camaro. We worked with a police artist who made a composite drawing of the man with the crew cut. My parents drove back up to the town near the campground in the mountains a dozen or more times to talk to people. If they had put pictures on milk cartons back then, Timothy's would have been on one.

Liz began cooperating with the police again, just as soon as we left that campground, and she and I both went in for a few sessions of counseling. The counseling only made it worse for me, and I'm sure for Liz as well. The counselor was little different than the police. She wanted all the details. But those details were no more what happened than the composite drawing was the actual man. The two things—our descriptions and what actually happened—forked off from each other and grew more and more distant with each day. And the space that grew between all that talking and losing Timothy became a kind of Siberia, a kind of emotional work camp where nothing changed and nothing happened.

"How much time has passed?" I shout ahead to Liz.

She finally stops skiing and pulls back a sleeve and the top of her fleece mitten to look at her watch. "It's only been twenty minutes," she says.

I say, "I feel as if we're looking for Timothy," and am shocked when she answers, "I know."

We are face to face, and there is a softness around Liz's eyes. "What if we don't find him?" I ask. "Lenny, I mean."

"We'll find him. These tracks have got to be his."

I had been blindly following Liz, not for the first time, and hadn't noticed we were now trailing a single set of tracks.

She says, "None of the rest of us, as far as I know, has gone this far afield. They have got to be his tracks. I just wish I knew what he was doing."

"Would he do something crazy?"

Liz shrugs. "He has before. But listen, I'm trying to keep the pace up because he's not all that fast. We can catch up with him if we hoof it."

I'm about to say that maybe I should wait for her, that I can't "hoof it" anymore, when six feet of boy emerges from the trees ahead of us.

"Hey!" Lenny cries, his face a big grin, his legs scissoring toward us on skis. He looks vigorous and ecstatic, as if he is having the time of his life.

I feel like a shell that got stepped on. I weep, indulge my overreaction, and just weep.

Liz yells, "For Christ's sake, Lenny! That was such a fucked-up thing to do."

"What?" Lenny asks, convincingly innocent.

"Going off like that. How the hell were we supposed to know you weren't lost or dead?"

"I knew what I was doing." His grin curls, becomes a grimace.

"Let's just go back," I say, snuffling. I want my deeply cushy bed, my kitchen cupboard stuffed with cookies and pasta, heat with a flick of a finger. I want to bury my face in Martin's golden belly fur. I want to have a double espresso and heated conversation with Lucienne. I want a heaping plate of spaghetti marinara and a caesar salad. I want the clanging, roaring, stinking city.

sixteen: free fall, part 2

I set off ahead, knowing full well that Liz will ski behind
Lenny, keeping an eye on his every move. I'm not interested
in their conversation about where he has been or what he was
doing. I ski my own pace, following our tracks as well as I can
see them through the blur of my tears.

I can't stop crying. I'm cold and tired. I want to be home
so badly. When I reach the top of a short slope, I'm too
involved with my sorrow to be afraid of the speed my skis
will pick up if I go straight down rather than ski switchbacks. It's only as I start to descend the hillside that I realize I'm picking up more speed than I'm comfortable with. I
drag my poles trying to slow myself, but it doesn't help. I try
to angle the tips of my skis inward to snowplow, which
starts to work, but I've overdone it and my ski tips cross. I
resign myself to a crash landing that will hurt. This spring
snow is crunchy, not powdery, and the heavy cloud cover

has kept it firm from the night's freeze. I brace myself for pain as I go down.

I hit shoulder-first, wrenching my neck, but grateful I haven't hit my head. A sharp pain ratchets through my body, and then, while the pain remains, the source of it disappears. I am somehow midair, as if I have hit the ground and bounced up again. For what seems like a long time, there is nothing around me at all. My organs seem to press against my throat. I see my legs and skis in the air above me. It occurs to me that I am dying. Then I hit again.

I hear at least one bone snap. My head bounces down and I get a mouthful of snow. There is no pain, just frozen shock, a feeling of iciness down to my bone marrow. A silence surrounds me as if I have spun right off of Earth and into space.

Very slowly my senses return. I'm lying in a bed of snow. When I open my eyes I see the brown of a rock outcropping, its vertical face maybe ten feet high. The brown is pleasant, a welcome warmth in this white world. I try to roll over, off the shoulder on which I have landed, and cannot move.

Liz should be here by now.

Pain sets in, but it is light, to my great relief. In a moment I will sit up.

I try to recapture what happened. While descending the slope, I lost control and must have veered away from our tracks. I remember falling as I tried to snowplow. I must have slid off this rock face.

Liz might not realize that I strayed off our route. She might think I've skied down the slope and back to camp.

"Oh, Jesus," I manage to say out loud.

Then hear my words echoed. "Oh, Jesus." Liz is peering over the edge of the small cliff.

"I'm okay," I say, wincing. "I—"

When I return to consciousness the pain is excruciating. I force myself to roll onto my back so that my face isn't in the snow and so that I can look to the top of the cliff without turning my neck. Perched on the very edge, sitting in the snow with his legs crossed, is Lenny, peering down at me.

"Lenny," I wheeze.

"She went to get Mark and Melody."

"Ugh," I answer, thinking, *And she left you to watch over me?*

"Did you hurt yourself?" he asks. I try to concentrate on the warm details of his face, a lighter shade of brown than the cliff face.

"Don't leave me," I manage to say.

"I ain't going nowhere. You think I'm crazy?"

I'm grateful that he answered me, and with feeling. I need distraction in the worst kind of way, so I ask, "Where did you go?"

My words are apparently too garbled for him to understand, so I have to repeat myself two times. Drawing breath into my lungs hurts.

"You mean this morning?"

"Uh."

"I told you before. A vision quest. I left right before dawn, right after you left the cave."

I think, *An hour makes a pretty short vision quest*, but I say, "And did you have your vision?"

Lenny looks beyond me and then stands up. He thinks I'm mocking him.

"Don't leave."

"I told you, I ain't going nowhere. It's cold sitting in the snow."

"Please talk to me."

Lenny shakes out each leg. He looks huge from below. I see his monster boots, his long legs, his wide shoulders. He says, "I saw my great grandmother."

"The one whose body you inhabited on the Trail of Tears?"

He nods.

Nausea sweeps from my feet to the crown of my head. My vision grays over. I'm about to black out again.

Lenny shouts, "Hey!" and claps his hands hard. Shock rips through me.

My eyes fly open, and I see the brown cliff with snow on top and Lenny's long figure.

Lenny crouches, looks worried. "Better to stay conscious." He glances over his shoulder, then turns back to me. "They're coming."

For a moment I see a stream of Indians, four and five abreast, trudging toward the cliff edge. Bleeding feet bound in cloth. Then I realize Lenny means my sister, Mark, and Melody.

I close my eyes. The pain is increasing in my shoulder, and I'm pretty sure my ankle is broken. There's no way I can ski out. I can't imagine a single solution other than dying. Liz, of course, will have lots of ideas. Thank God, I think, she isn't the one who has broken bones. I'm sure she's much better at first aid than I am, particularly in this context, and further-more, if our situations were reversed I would have to fight the urge to break a few bones myself to see what she was feeling. I would much rather be the problem than have to solve it.

First Liz, then Mark and Melody, look over the edge of the precipice. "Not so close, Lenny," Liz says before addressing the problem of me.

"She's conscious," she says. "Tina, can you hear me?"

"Yeah."

"How are you?"

"Not so good."

"Have you broken anything?"

"Pretty sure my ankle. And my shoulder is either dislocat-ed or separated."

"Hang in there, Teen-Teen," Mark says, and I manage to arch an eyebrow at him. He catches my look and crouches, smiling wanly. He doesn't speak, just sits there on his haunch-es with his forearms resting on his thighs and his hands dan-gling between his legs.

Then he stands suddenly, as if something big has been resolved, and says, "Melody, you and Lenny stay with Tina. Liz and I will ski out for help."

We are all surprised. He is teaming himself with Liz. He is making a decision.

"Yes," I second his proposal as forcefully as I am able. "Yes," I say again.

"No," Liz says.

"Honey." Mark takes her hand.

"I'm staying with Tina."

From here, ten feet below, and perhaps because of my pain, everyone's face looks distorted. I see their chins first, their nostrils, barely see eyes at all unless they bend to address me. Melody does not bend to address me. She nods hard when Liz says she's staying with me. Melody wants Mark. She wants him enough to do just about anything to get him. I see it in her body. She is moving already, moving away from me and Liz and Lenny, moving away with Mark. She even reaches over and touches his hand, which now dangles at his side. Liz, on the other side of him, cannot see this, but I can see it and Melody knows I can see it. She doesn't care. She knows that contact, physical contact, will sway Mark. She caresses his palm with her fingers. He heaves a big sigh. I see him try, weakly, to disengage his hand from Melody's. She hangs on. He pulls away more firmly and takes Liz's shoulders in his hands and says, "Please."

"Just go," she says without looking at him. She keeps her eyes on me, so that finally he looks at me too.

"What are we going to do with Tina?" he asks. "Do you think we can get her to the snow cave? She would be protected there. You could keep her warmer until we return."

They peer over the sheer and crumbly rock face.

Liz says, "I don't see any way to get down there."

"Hey, it's easy," I tell her. "Just do like I did."

They ignore my joke.

Liz says, "Even if we could get down there, I don't think we can move her."

The way they talk about me in third person makes me feel as if I'm dead already. I look to Lenny, who is standing off to the side, staring down at me, waiting, as I am, for the verdict. In a small fit of clarity, I resolve to give Lenny all my attention. Having faith in his vision, even if my faith is secondary and the experience is his, seems important, maybe crucial.

"Lenny," I say, and he nods. "I'm glad. I'm glad you saw her."

He crouches and trails a gloved finger in the snow. "She was plain as day. I mean, I saw every wrinkle in her face. And she spoke to me."

Leave it to a teenage boy to stay centered in his own experience in the face of someone else's crisis.

"What did she say?" I ask him, glad he can understand my pain-garbled speech.

"Well, she didn't *say* anything exactly, but she communicated a lot."

I maintain eye contact with him so that he'll continue.

"It was like she wants me to keep her inside me. Then I'll be able to figure things out."

I close my eyes to concentrate, then open my mouth to ask Lenny what his grandmother thinks we should do now.

I hear Mark shout, "Lenny!"

I open my eyes and see Lenny's legs dangling over the brown outcropping, his arms stretched across the top, gripping the snow. Like in the movies, I zero in on his spread fingers clutching the snow, slipping, slowly slipping. Until they give way and he crashes down, his chest and the front of his thighs scraping along the rock wall. He lands next to me. He has purposely thrown himself over the edge to come to my aid, and I'm more grateful than he could possibly know. Still ignoring the others, he crouches down and looks at my face.

"You're not going to pick me up, are you?" I ask. "I don't think it's a good idea to move me."

Lenny stands and looks at the short cliff. "There's no way I could carry you back up there, anyway," he says.

"We could make a sling out of a space blanket and some rope," Mark offers. "Lenny could roll her onto it and we could lift her up."

"That was really dumb of you, Lenny," Melody says. "How are you going to get back up?" She's standing too close to

Mark. This new development has interfered with her plans. She wants to be on her way.

"With ropes," Mark says, nodding at Lenny, acknowledging that he's done something brave.

I want to tell them it won't work. Even if I could bear being hauled up in a sling—and bounced against the rock face as I went—they would still have to drag me back to camp. I open my mouth. I can't even get out the word *no*.

Liz says it for me. "It's too dangerous. Look at that drop-off on the other side of her. Mark, you and Melody ski out for help. Lenny and I will stay here. I'll go back to camp and get the tent, sleeping bags, food. We'll keep Tina safe and dry here. It's morning. There should be no problem getting a rescue by nightfall. It'll be okay."

Despite my pain, I can't help looking at Melody to see how this registers. Oh, it goes down well. She even smiles. She alone will ski out with Mark. He gives up, resigns himself to anger. I see it pass through his body. He glances at Liz and then at me as if to say, yes, you two have each other as always. I can leave now. I can leave you two together.

"Well, *go*," Liz says. "You don't need anything. It's only a few miles. Do you have the truck keys?"

Mark says, "I'll get them at camp. Come on, Melody." He looks down at me and opens his mouth to speak, thinks better of it, and leaves. Melody follows in silence.

I expect Liz to ignore their departure, but she turns and watches them ski away, watches for a long time. When she turns back to me, her face is scrunched up.

"Liz," I say.

She sits down in the snow, ten feet above me, and cries into her hands. A moment later she pulls out her green kerchief, wipes her face, and blows her nose hard, once.

Then she stands and says, "You're pretty much stuck there for now too, Lenny. Don't try to climb back up. I'll start getting our gear over here."

Liz puts on her skis and leaves. Just like that.

Lenny says, "Another couple of feet and you'd be dead."

He points beyond me, in the opposite direction of the rock face I skied off. I turn my neck slowly, see a great expanse of air. Rotating my eyes, I try to inspect the rest of my surroundings. I seem to be on the edge of another, apparently much higher, promontory. In fact, I've landed on a rather small shelf. It's not much bigger than the floor of our snow cave, and I'm much closer to the edge than to the rock face.

"I'm going to take your ski off," Lenny says, carefully stepping toward my legs and feet. One ski, the one attached to the surely broken ankle, is vertical. In fact, it may have saved my life, spearing into the snow like a lampoon, stopping the momentum of my fall and breaking my ankle in the process. As I stare into the gray void beyond my small shelf, I think a broken ankle is a small price to pay. I also think I'd like to be moved closer in toward the rock wall.

I scream as Lenny grasps my foot and unlocks the ski. He sets the foot gently on the snow. "I'm sorry," he says. "But you couldn't keep it twisted in the air like that."

I turn my head to the side and vomit instant oatmeal.

"Okay," Lenny says softly. "Okay." He jams the ski into the snow next to the cliff, then uses his boot to scoot the vomit snow away from my face and off the precipice.

"Do you think," I wheeze, "do you think you could move me away from the edge?" I know it'll hurt like hell, but one small earthquake and I'll be a goner.

"Yeah," Lenny says. "I was going to do that next." He squats next to me and places one hand on the outside of my hip and the other under my armpit. "This okay?" Without waiting for an answer, he slides me across the snow until I'm close to the rock outcropping. I gag rather than scream, because it hurts too much to scream.

He sits right in the snow then, beside me, to wait for Liz's return. "Here," he says, unzipping his jacket and reaching into the front pocket of his flannel shirt. He pulls out a cigarette and puts it between my lips. As he lights it, we meet eyes, and I watch him realize he's been caught. He shrugs and says, "Stole them. Last night from your jacket. Sorry. But I only took half."

"It's okay," I mumble around the cigarette he holds to my lips. I'm glad he stole the cigarettes so he can give me one now.

Liz returns and slings off the backpack in which she has stuffed a ball of rope and the makings for my bed. "We can't afford to lose a thing," she tells Lenny. "So I'll lower everything with the rope." She waits while Lenny helps me finish the cigarette, then one by one she ties and lowers two pads, a space blanket, and two sleeping bags.

As Liz skis off for more of the gear, Lenny has to move me again so he can put the space blanket and a double layer of pads beneath me. He covers me with the two sleeping bags, and I begin to shake violently.

The next time Liz returns she has brought the tent and painkillers from the first aid kit. At first she thinks Lenny can set up the tent right on the ledge, but the ledge isn't big enough, so she sets it up on top of the cliff to use for gear storage. After several more trips she has moved all of our stuff to the tent, and she sits on a pad in front of it and looks down at me and Lenny.

"Are you both warm?"

The sleeping bags help, but I can't stop shaking.

Lenny says, "I'm okay."

"Hungry?" Liz asks.

"No," I say.

Lenny says, "I can wait."

Liz tosses him an energy nugget. "I'll make some soup. We should all stay fed." She unfolds and lights the stove, stuffs snow in a pot, and digs cheese and crackers from her pack.

Now we will wait for hours. How long will it take them to ski out? For a rescue crew to mobilize? There will be a rescue crew, won't there? This is a national forest; maybe rescue crews have been cut out of the budget.

I look up at Lenny, who sits at my head like a greyhound.

Liz says, "I'm making a basket of sorts out of this rope. I'm going to lower soup down to you."

I can't possibly eat anything. Besides, how can Liz lower the soup to us? The idea of boiled soup splashing across my face triggers the impulse to vomit again. I gag to the side, sending knives of pain across my collarbone and shoulder, but produce nothing more from my stomach. Of course Liz does manage to fashion a little basket out of rope and lowers a lidded cup of soup without spilling a drop.

Lenny peels off the lid and sniffs. "Tomato."

Liz tosses down a spoon, which Lenny catches. He scoops a bit of red soup with the spoon, blows on it gently, and tells me to open up. I don't want the soup but think what a lovely boy he is, hovering over me with the spoonful of soup, his brow knit with concern.

"It might burn my mouth."

"Mmm," he says and tastes it. "No. It's not too hot."

He scoops another spoonful, blows on it again, and lowers it to my mouth. I'm obliged to open up. As the soup spills over my tongue I'm surprised at how pleasant it feels. Lenny feeds me a few more spoonfuls until I convince him I've had enough. He finishes the soup and polishes off a couple dozen cheese and cracker sandwiches, plus another energy nugget. I can't see if Liz eats anything or not.

Eventually she says, "He's not coming back."

I'm alarmed only for a second. Alarmed, that is, for my own safety. He will come back to *us*. He will complete the rescue mission. She means come back to her. The only thing I can think to say is, "You don't know that."

"I know that."

"Why did you agree to this trip?" I ask, not sure exactly how much she knows about Mark and Melody.

"Sometimes moving toward something is the best way to get rid of it," she says. Liz and her take-the-bull-by-the-horns philosophy of life.

"But everyone has their limit," she continues. "And he's hit his."

"He loves you."

I have a good view of Liz's clenched jaw from here. She says, "I thought you might like her."

I'm confused for a minute, then realize her meaning. "You were trying to foist her off on me?"

Liz shrugs. "You might have liked her. She might have liked you."

"So you thought that if you threw me into the mix, maybe I could take her off your hands?"

I don't like the look on her face. Dark side is an understatement. "You're good at seducing women. Why not?"

"You're scaring me! I'm broken, lying on a snowy ledge in the mountains. I didn't do anything to you. Melody did."

She says, "I know. I'm sorry," but isn't convincing.

"Melody ain't worth shit," Lenny says, catching on.

His loyalty is touching, and I look inside for my own. "Liz," I say, "if I had known, and thought it would help, I would have bedded her down on the lake ice yesterday morning. I would have used all my powers of seduction. I'm sorry. I'm really, really sorry about what's happening. I thought you were setting me up with Melody because you don't like the women I choose."

"I guess I just wanted to see how far they'd go," Liz says, staring into the vast space beyond my ledge. "You should have seen Mark's face when I invited her. It was priceless. I mean, he can fuck his secretary in the barn, but he acts appalled when I invite her on a ski trip. And Melody, cool as can be, just says, 'I'd love to. That sounds like fun.'"

"I hate her," I say. "She makes me sick."

Liz's face scrunches up again. She stands, then paces out of my view.

"Shit," Lenny says. "Where'd she go?"

"I don't know," I whisper, and unsuccessfully try to close my mind to cold thoughts. I think of television specials about people dying in the wilderness—that woman huddling with her baby in a rock cave while her husband walked through a blizzard for help, or those people on Mount Everest, all experienced like Liz, who died scattered along the climb route. I think how this kind of crisis, a physical survival crisis, is the pinnacle of human experience for Liz. That somehow her emotional survival is dependent on the severity of the threat to our bodies.

She stays away for what feels like a very long time, but every time Lenny lifts my wrist to check my watch only a minute or two has passed. He asks me lots of questions, his panic rising, but the sadness is swallowing me whole and I can't answer.

I should have figured everything out a long time ago. Six months, Mark said. That explains that day last fall. Lucienne agreed to spend a Sunday afternoon at Liz and Mark's place, which took quite a feat on my part because Lucienne doesn't believe in family. She has almost no contact with her own, all of whom are in Paris. She believes the concept of family is dead. She believes in her absolute individuality. Which is why she treats Liz like some appendage of mine that needs to be removed. Of course, I see a strong resemblance between Lucienne and Liz's autonomous personalities, but that's the thing about autonomous personalities—they deny connections to other people.

To get her to go with me, I appealed to Lucienne's sensuality. I told her how beautiful the live oaks would be, how delicious whatever Liz or Mark cooked would be. It was stupid of me to lure her. I knew she would hate the afternoon. Mark would walk us around the land—Lucienne hates vigorous walking—and show us their various improvements. Eventually he would show us the most recent volumes that his firm has published, which would interest Lucienne more. Liz would be much quieter, particularly with Lucienne present, but she would be the one to tell us about their latest trips or rescue efforts.

It was a gorgeous autumn day. I felt particularly happy, happy that Lucienne was with me, happy that the weather was fine. We had wanted to make love in the morning, but Lucienne had to fax a letter somewhere before nine, I had to run home to feed Martin, and before we knew it we were already late. Still, we were happy. And I expected to find Mark and Liz happy. They always were.

The day didn't go at all as I thought it would. Mark was uncharacteristically dreamy. He sat in the den reading

Elizabeth Bishop, which made Lucienne snort, though I'm not sure why. Liz regarded Lucienne suspiciously and tried too hard to be comfortable. We drank coffee at the kitchen table and didn't look at any of their new projects. Lunch was a thin vegetable soup and salad with only a squeeze of lemon for dressing. We should have just left after lunch. There was so much tension on the farm the air was crackling. Liz, Lucienne, and I took a walk to the top of the hill, where there is small grove of live oaks. Liz carried a canvas sack to gather acorns.

I knew Lucienne was hungry—lunch had been minimal—and being hungry made her angry.

She said, "You look thinner, Liz."

"Do I?"

I put together her thinness and the meager lunch and asked, "Are you dieting?"

"A little. We're hoping to do some climbing in South America next year. The lighter I am, the better."

That shocked me. Dieting seemed so, well, against her principles. Besides, she's a thin woman to begin with, not skinny, but compared to her I'm hefty.

I should have pieced it together, figured out that something was seriously wrong, but I bought the "getting thin to be a better climber" story. My almost desperate desire for a full meal, next to her calculated desire to climb some major peak in South America, made me feel trivial.

We reached the live oak grove, and Liz knelt to gather acorns. Lucienne lowered herself onto the ground with a grunt. She wore her usual jeans, white T-shirt, and tweed jacket. "How hunter and gatherer like," she said.

I laughed and wanted to kiss her, but instead came to my sister's defense: "Liz makes a great acorn pâté."

I was serious, but Lucienne laughed like I had told a joke. I could just hear her in a few days time, telling her friends, "Acorn pâté!" and howling with laugher. "Is that with or without goose fat?"

Liz threw down her half-full canvas bag. The acorns made

a pleasant knocking sound as they hit each other and the ground. "Just what exactly do you like, anything?" she asked Lucienne.

Liz fired me a furious look, then picked up her sack of acorns and strode down the hill alone.

"Whoa," Lucienne said.

"Wow," I said. Rarely had I seen Liz overtly angry.

"I'm sorry," Lucienne said to me, making an exaggerated grimace. She had promised to be "good."

Now Robin, with whom I had just broken up—*she* would have been on her hands and knees helping Liz with the acorns. *She* would have asked for the pâté recipe. *She* would have wandered into Mark's study and lured him out with warm conversation.

But Robin wouldn't have done what Lucienne did next.

"I'm sorry, baby," she said again. "I really am."

Lucienne, full of faults, was quick to admit them even if she made no effort to change them. Later that afternoon, she went to Liz and apologized and meant it. Not that it mattered to Liz. Liz preferred people to act properly from the start. At least to apologize immediately.

Lucienne didn't. She lay back and looked up at the blue sky through the gnarly black live oak branches. I sat beside her, watching my sister march all the way back to the farm house, far down the hill.

Two ravens called me back to the bed of autumn leaves. On the ground, pecking toward us, they stopped, nearly side by side, and cawed.

"What?" I said. "What did we do to you?"

Lucienne sat up, pulled off her tweed jacket, and laid it out like a blanket. She took my arm and pulled me toward it. I lay back on the satin lining of the jacket and heard the dry leaves crunch as I extended my body. There's nothing like the weight of a big woman. Total encompassment.

There have been times, when we are making love, that I have felt as if I could be with Lucienne forever. My physical response to her is whole; every bone in my skeleton wants to wrap her, every drop of blood rushes to meet her. I have held back from saying, "Oh, God, I love you," so many times. For so long. And why? Because I don't know if it's true? Or because it would send her running? Sometimes I wonder if she's just waiting for me to say it. That if I said, "Lucienne, you are the one I love," she would smile and say, "Okay," and that the next time we made love, she would say, "I love you, Christine. I love you."

Other times, like after we made glorious love there in the live oak grove, and as we walked back down the hill so that Lucienne could apologize to Liz and we could leave her and Mark to their mysterious distress, I think that the tension holding Lucienne and I together is this refusal, this refusal of commitment.

Though Liz was gracious enough in accepting Lucienne's apology, she called me later that night. "I don't know what your problem is," she said.

"What?" I asked, unused to Liz's anger.

"That woman."

"You must be referring to Lucienne."

"I'm sorry, it's your life, but Robin was a gem."

"You're right, Robin is a gem. She also can't admit she's wrong, ever. And at home she is far from that bubbly cheerful woman you know. She's prone to nightly depressions, during which she reiterates the details of her life, which are not perfect. And she doesn't make my synapses sing."

"When are you going to get over your synapses and use your brain?"

As if there's a difference. That's the point, that's the whole point of sex. Of touch. But I let that slide and pulled out my ace. "Let me tell you how perfect Robin is. She's been badgering me ever since I've known her to launch a full-scale search for Timothy. She wants cops, the Bureau of Missing Persons, milk cartons, notices in newspapers nationwide, the whole nine yards. What do you think of that?"

I stunned my sister to silence, but only for moment. Then, "What does that have to do with anything? I have to go." And she hung up.

I wish now that I had seen that afternoon and evening phone call in a larger context. Liz's nastiness surprised me, but I let it go, figuring she had a right to stressful periods like anyone else. I should have known that the stress would have to be of big proportions to alter the behavior of my sister the bionic woman. Mark was leaving, she knew it even then. And she also knew that while my loyalty would be with her, my compassion might well be with Mark.

Is it? I know this: Loneliness is an animal. Touch deprivation can make you fierce. I do understand Mark.

seventeen: storm

Liz appears once again on the lip of the cliff. She has been crying and her red face is a brick—hard, rough, and impenetrable. I feel as if that brick has been hurled at me when she says, "I also know about you and Mark."

My body feels as if it is breaking. The pain pills have done nothing for my snapped ankle bones and torn ligaments. The drug only contributes to the nightmare quality of what is happening. I'm lying broken on a tiny ledge in the late-winter Sierras, wrapped in a dull white world of cloud and snow. My sister stands above me, far above me, and calls me on my betrayal. Stupidly I ask, "What do you mean?"

"The summer of 1974."

"How do you know?"

I look up into her nostrils as she laughs. "It was obvious. It was obvious from the start. In his letters Dad would mention how much time you two were spending together, but both of

you concealed it, acted as if you were only together occasionally. There would be only one reason for your lies."

Shame slushes through me. Saying "I'm sorry" would be
like throwing a single pea to a starving woman. No response
could be adequate. So I allow myself to slide into self-pity and
ask, "And you didn't hate me?"

Again, the harsh, dark-side laugh, as if I have asked a stupid question. Stupid how? Of course she *did* hate me or of
course she *did not* hate me?

She says, "If that had been the first time, maybe I would
have."

"What do you mean, the first time? The first time of
what?"

"You were always the one who told the truth. Or at least
that's how you presented it. You and your relationship to your
skin, everything right at the surface. Or so you make it seem."

"All right," I say. "All right, then. There *is* one more lie,
isn't there? You want me to tell it?"

And that is when she leaves. She leaves for what feels like
hours. I imagine she has traveled into that space between
what happened and what we say happened. The pain is like a
fist around my body. It squeezes and the truth comes out.
There is not space on this tiny ledge for anything but truth.
No space in this wracked body of mine for the excess of lies.
Listen to me, Liz. Please listen to me. I love you. You are my
geography. You are the mountain next to me. I could not separate myself from you any more than one mountain in this
landscape could move away from another. Mark may or may
not be back. But I am here, and I will never go anywhere.
Ever. You could commit a grisly crime and I would still be your
sister. That is why we are here in this web of lies now. We have
stood by each other. Even when you were eleven and I was
ten, my deepest instinct was to protect you above all else. But
I may have destroyed you. I may have accomplished the exact
opposite of what I wanted to do.

I pity Lenny, who is trapped on this ledge with me, trapped
in this thirty-year drama between me and Liz. He has been

stomping his feet, trying to keep warm, muttering "Shit," then, "Fucking shit," and finally, "Women!" as if this were a cat fight, a sisterly hissy fit.

Now that Liz has disappeared, he hopes to be back in the picture. He says, "What the fuck does she mean, he's not coming back?"

"Their marriage," I say. "He'll come back for us. Or send someone. We were talking about their marriage."

Lenny crouches next to me so that I can see his face. His lips are chapped, his nose dripping. He says, "I don't get it."

"Me neither."

"Melody is pretty," he says, considering, "but she seems kind of dingy." He falls back so that he is sitting in the snow, still thoughtful. "I think Mark's making a big mistake."

"Me too."

The confusion on Lenny's young face is exquisite. I mean the way his smooth brown skin, the stubble of virgin whiskers, and his chapped lips look like they hurt with this news of betrayal. He frowns, concentrating, as if he can understand if he thinks hard enough.

Lenny gives me hope. I keep my eyes on him. He sits by my head, alternately looking at my face and out into the white void off the edge of our ledge. I am sure that he's scared, but he's enjoying his bravery just the same. Perhaps this isn't nearly as bad as standing before a judge in juvenile court or enduring whatever torments a boy must endure in a high school. With his size, Lenny may well be a tormenter more often than the tormented, but I don't know. I don't know anything.

A light snow begins to fall. At this altitude, in this amount of pain, everything is otherworldly, and I begin to hallucinate about my future. Would Mark and Melody rush to call for help, or would passion stall them, demand that they stop, now that they are truly alone, for a quickie in the truck before taking steps toward our rescue?

They wouldn't. I know they wouldn't. I know Mark wouldn't. Yet reality is tilting badly up here on my ledge. Skewing, diving.

The flakes of snow hit my face and land on my down sleeping bag, making little wet spots. A wet down sleeping bag is useless. In a matter of minutes, my source of warmth will be destroyed. Lenny says, "Fucking shit." He stands and looks up at the top of the cliff, searching for my sister.

"Liz," he shouts in a deep man's voice. "Liz!"

And amazingly she comes. She has the tent fly in her arms. She knows exactly what the problem is, the immediate problem anyway, and drops the fly down, holding onto one corner of it until Lenny has a firm grasp.

"Use that as a cover. But if it really snows," Liz says, "we're going to need to set that up somehow."

"If it really snows," Lenny says, "ain't no helicopter gonna come into the mountains."

Lenny and Liz didn't need to say "if," because it has already begun, quite suddenly, to really snow. We are wrapped in a white cloud and bombarded by tiny flying lace doilies. I study one that rests on the taffeta of the sleeping bag, a valentine from the angels, until it is sucked into the bag, just another wet spot.

Liz says, "I can use the tent as a bivy sack. Do you think you could use the tent poles, and maybe the ski poles too, to somehow prop up the fly for her?"

I am only a "her" now. I wish she would say my name.

Lenny flaps the tent fly over me. Liz dismantles the tent and hands down the poles, and he goes to work putting up a makeshift shelter. I can see his boots shuffling around the edges of the tent fly. If a wind comes up, I don't see how this shaky piece of thin cloth draped over thin bendy sticks is going to stay up. He manages, though, to create a tension in the materials so that for now the shelter stands.

I try to speak up, but my voice is little more than a whisper. "Lenny, you can't stay out in the snow. You have to come in here with me."

I don't think he hears me, and certainly Liz doesn't, but I hear her shout down, "Lenny! Get in there with her. You can't get wet. You're going to have to lie down under the fly."

"Nah. I'm okay."

I can picture him, all six feet of his youth, his dark hair flopped over his forehead, his big nose jutting out, shifting from one foot to the other, waiting. Waiting for the helicopter.

"I wasn't offering you a choice," Liz says, "I was *telling* you. Go on. Now. Before you get wet."

I imagine Liz standing ten feet above us, in the snowfall, waiting for Lenny to crawl under the tent fly with me. Then I guess she will retreat to the collapsed tent and wrap it around her like a bivy sack. Our situation is getting serious.

Lenny crouches, lifts a corner of the fly. He looks in.

"Come on, Lenny," I say. "You have to get in here, under the sleeping bags with me. I won't bite."

It's funny how tenacious embarrassment can be, even in life and death situations.

"I don't want to knock down the setup," he says, and he's right: To get his big body in here will be a delicate operation.

He has two more pads that Liz has lowered to him. He slides them under the tent fly. Then he lies down in the snow and rolls under the fly edge and onto the pads. He brushes the fresh snow off his clothing, pushing it out under the fly as best he can.

The two sleeping bags are tucked around me, but not zipped up. "You have to get under the sleeping bags too," I tell him. Shaking, he does. He's scared now, maybe more scared than me.

eighteen: *first loves*

We lie side by side silently. Being so close to, yet barely touching, another human makes the tears snarl in my chest. Then they rise up and I am crying, which scares Lenny even more.

"Sorry," I blubber. "It all hurts so much."

Lenny lies stiffly, and yet shaking, beside me. We are both shaking, from cold, shock, and fear. I cry harder, the sobs wrenching my shoulder, intensifying the pain, making me cry more, until it is one big wet aching circle.

I'm concerned about his fear, aware that I'm an adult and he is not, and worried that his feet are sticking out of the bottom of the shelter. But I can't stop crying. I try, heaving in a big gulp of icy air, swallowing, but then I choke on my own mucus and cry more to expel it.

Lenny shifts to his side, scoots closer, and puts an arm around my waist.

"You can blow your nose on my shirt," he says. "I do it all the time."

"Thank you," I say. I can't move my left arm, and my right arm is pressed between us. Snot is running all over my mouth, down one cheek. He props himself up on an elbow, unzips his jacket, pulls out the tail of his flannel shirt and wipes my face with it. Then he gathers the other tail of his shirt and bunches it under my nose. I blow, then blow again. He tucks his shirt back in.

"Does it hurt a lot?" he asks.

"Yes." I breathe for a while to get more energy, then say, "Are your feet under the tent fly?"

"I can't tell."

"You'd better check."

"How?"

"Can you feel them?"

"No."

"Sit up and look."

Very carefully, Lenny bends at the waist and folds his upper body over his legs to reach his feet without knocking over the tent poles. I hear him working with the tent fly. Slowly he lies down again.

"Now wiggle your toes," I say. "Can you do that?"

"Yeah."

"Good. Keep wiggling them as much as you can."

"What about your feet?" he asks.

"At this point, with the pain in my left ankle, I'd really love it if I got frostbite and lost all feeling."

Lenny thinks this is funny, and I'm glad I've cheered him up.

Then we're quiet again. I worry about what Liz is doing. Is she wrapped in the tent as she's supposed to be? Or is she wandering around in the snowstorm? What if her mind has snapped? What if she takes this opportunity to show all of us how much we love her? I imagine her turning herself over to the mountains, the only lover she would let take her completely.

No, I console myself, that kind of drama would be mine. Liz would never do something like that.

Lenny is surprisingly warm. He has put his arm around me again; I am grateful and press my face against his chest.

"I need you to talk to me," I say. "Tell me something."

He remains silent.

I pull my face away and look at him. "Hey, can I ask you something?"

He remains impassive.

"How come a boy with a heart as big as yours gets in so much trouble?"

"Bored, I guess."

"I don't believe that."

"It's all just for fun. I don't hurt anybody."

"The 7-Eleven holdup must have hurt someone."

"Nah."

He withdraws his arm and lays it along his own side. I hadn't meant to push him away. I am aching for contact. *Talk to me, Lenny,* I want to scream. *Tell me the absolute truth. About anything.*

"You're scared, aren't you?" he says, not gently.

Somehow I know that he is not talking about the developing blizzard and our ledge, but I answer as if he is, "Of course I'm scared."

"I mean about what I did."

"What are you talking about?"

"I know you're scared." He belts out a "*Ha!*" like some redneck. I have a feeling that Leonard has just arrived.

I say nothing.

"Nobody asked for *my* love story last night."

Oh, boy, I think, and try to weigh which would be worse: silence or Lenny's love story. I hope that Lenny's great grandmother is on board now. We may need her.

"So tell me," I whisper hoarsely.

"You don't want to hear it."

Dealing with adolescents when I'm in the prime of health is challenge enough, but now, in this state...I don't know. Of course, now, in this state, choice isn't a player. So I say, "Yeah, I do. I want to hear."

That's all the coaxing he needs. "I'm dating my math teacher."

"Oh."

"She's fucking gorgeous."

"Isn't that against the law?" I rasp.

Lenny is quiet for a few moments, then in his tough guy voice, maybe the voice of Leonard, he says, "We keep it under wraps, know what I mean?"

"Mmm." Noncommittal.

"She's fucking brilliant. Her brain is like a computer. You can call out a list of ten numbers—like I say, 'eighty-five, four, nineteen, fifty-one, sixty-four, eight, twelve, ninety-nine, twenty, seventy-one,' and then say, 'Add,' and she'll tell you the sum in a second. Then I can say, 'Multiply,' and without me even repeating the numbers, she can tell you how much it is."

"That's very impressive."

"Yeah. But only with two-digit numbers. All the numbers have to be under a hundred."

"It's still pretty impressive."

"Yeah, it is. But that's not what I like about her. She's fucking gorgeous."

"How often do you see her?"

"Every day. She's my math teacher."

"Oh," I say, relieved, "so you don't see her outside of school."

His mind seems to drift, maybe because I've called him on his little fantasy-lie. He rolls onto his back, away from me, and I feel the cold air surge into the warm place. Finally he says, "Sure I do." Then he laughs, rolls back, and drapes the arm over me again. "Scared?"

"I already told you: yes."

"I mean of me."

I lift my head as well as I can, forcing myself to look directly at his big calf eyes. "No, Lenny, I'm not scared of you. I've just had a terrible thing happen with my sister. I'm scared of that. I'm scared of this ledge and this snowstorm.

I am not scared of you. In fact, I'm counting on you. Sorry to disappoint you." My speech exhausts me.

"I'm not disappointed," he says, dropping his eyelids. His long lashes curl up toward me. "And anyway, my great grandmother says it wasn't like Ms. Brewer said it was."

"Ms. Brewer?"

"My math teacher."

I wonder if Liz is on the top of the ledge. I wonder if she could hear me if I yelled. I don't think I have the strength to yell.

"I'm good in math. She said I could go into computers or maybe work for NASA. She said it would be no problem."

He's quiet for a long time, and I'm torn between being grateful for the time to think about Liz and desperate for him to continue so I don't have to. Finally I say, "What happened with Ms. Brewer?"

Again, he needs no coaxing. "Right before Christmas she started baking things for me. And inviting me to her house to eat them. We'd watch a little TV. She's, like, fucking gorgeous, but I would never—" His voice cracks, and in a quick instant, Leonard becomes Lenny once again. He gulps once, attempts to wrench his mouth into a snarl, but is unsuccessful. His lips fall open and a bit of drool runs down the side of his chin. He wipes it away.

"Then in January, like out of the blue, she called me in after school. She said she was going to have to tell the principal. But I hadn't done anything. I just sat on her couch and watched TV. I mean, once she started, I, like, did it. But she started everything."

"Does Mark know about this?"

"Everyone knows."

"What do you mean 'everyone knows'?"

"She said she was telling the authorities."

"Have you talked to Mark about it?"

"No way. I mean, I, like, mentioned that I was in a little woman trouble. You know. So that he knew that I knew he knows."

"Has the principal talked to you?"

"Not yet."

"Lenny," I say. "I don't think your math teacher said anything to the principal. Or to anyone else."

"What do you mean?"

"I mean what she did would get her fired in a second. She blackmailed you. She never told a soul."

Lenny lies on his side with his eyes wide open, staring at the blue taffeta a few inches above our heads.

"You're a doctor, right?" he finally asks.

"Yeah. What exactly did your math teacher say she would tell the authorities?"

Lenny cringed. "I'm no pervert."

"I know, Lenny. I'm asking you what exactly she accused you of." I cannot, absolutely cannot, believe I am having this discussion on a ledge in the mountains, in a blizzard, with a broken body.

"The word starts with an *r*."

I struggle to bring forward my professional self. "She's wrong. You're sixteen; she's at least twenty-something. She's your teacher. She initiated all the touching, right?"

"Hell, yeah."

"If you wanted to, you could talk to the authorities yourself."

"Oh, right." Spit flies out of his mouth. "What, you think they'd believe me over her? Me who has a record? Whether she's told or not, she's got me by the balls."

How many times in the clinic have I talked to kids about this stuff? But right now Lenny's need is more than I can handle. My own bones are broken. My own life is threatened. My own sister is somewhere up above us in the snow with much more broken than bones.

"She said she loved me. Before."

"Oh, Lenny."

His tears have come loose. "She said all kinds of stuff. That I'm a math whiz. That I could be a computer genius."

It's very difficult to pull my arm out from between us but

I do. I wipe away his tears as he had wiped away mine. "I'm sorry, Lenny." I brush hair off his forehead, tuck it under the edge of his wool cap.

He cries for a minute or two, and then, as if he has to make amends for his moment of tenderness, he asks, "They let dykes be doctors?"

"Yeah, they do."

"I don't really care," he says, "you being a dyke."

"That's good, because you're stuck with me for the time being."

Then he says, "But you didn't answer either."

"Didn't answer what?"

"Your first love. You never said."

nineteen: crystal chandelier

Even when I was fourteen I was embarrassed by how deeply Janis Joplin's phrase, "Freedom's just another word for nothing left to lose," moved me. I suspected it was flawed, and yet it seemed so perfectly true. It fit beautifully with Mark and Liz's philosophy of self-reliance and simple living. If you gave up everything on your own, you couldn't lose anything, right? That was freedom.

I have this feeling, lying here on this icy ledge, of having stopped for the first time in thirty years, since losing Timothy. It is as if since that day I have been moving so fast that I haven't had time to accumulate anything I might lose. Including a first love. Which must mean that I have been very free.

Oh, I could lose Lucienne, all right. I will lose Lucienne. I think I have already lost her. Lucienne, who will have sex in the car at Marine World. Who will take me to the mat on the construction of a sentence. Who reads books on epistemology for fun. Lucienne, who refuses to dance, ever. Who can party harder than anyone I know, but still isn't an alcoholic. Lucienne, who sends me off to other lovers, knowing I will always come back, not just grateful but relieved, not just relieved but awed by her in compari-son to what I have had. It's not arrogance, but a choice: If I don't come back willingly, if I don't come back awed, she doesn't want me back. Not spite, just her adherence to the highest level of passion.

Lucienne, who will treat a meal, perfectly prepared, in the same way.

Lucienne, who couldn't make a commitment if her life depended on it. Which leaves desire pure. And there's noth-ing wrong with that. Desire can never be taken away, only the objects of desire.

But desire is movement, and now I am no longer moving. I have been stopped, stopped by the gravity of the planet, the cir-cumstances of my life frozen in this moment. I have nothing but reflection until that helicopter comes.

Two weeks ago, as I left for work on a Friday morning, Flo told me that she would be finishing that day. Surprises are almost always bad ideas, but I planned one anyway. I came home from work early, toting two big bags of groceries.

She had a surprise of her own. I found Flo in the front hallway, on the top of a paint-splattered stepladder, polishing the chandelier, teardrop by teardrop.

She said, "I always do something a little extra at the end of a job."

Of course that hurt my feelings, her making it clear that this wasn't anything special for me, just something she did for clients, all clients.

"I have a surprise too," I told her. "I'd like to make you dinner."

She hesitated, and I opened my mouth to tell her that I understood if she had other plans, but before I could speak she let go of the tiny scowl and said, "Great. But I'll be at least another hour with the chandelier."

"You don't have to do that. You could come talk to me while I cook."

"This thing has been driving me crazy for six weeks. You have this beautiful house, with this glamorous centerpiece, and it's covered with spiders and dust."

"Well, it's not like it's real."

"What do you mean, not real?"

"Not real crystal."

"Like hell it's not. What, you thought these were plastic? This thing is worth a small fortune."

I laughed uneasily, preferring to believe the chandelier was a fake. "I guess I'll have to throw a ball."

I carried my groceries to the kitchen and began unloading them onto the counter. I could hear the squirt of Flo's dusting spray followed by a tinkle sound as she wiped and let go of each piece of the chandelier. It reminded me of lying in bed during the last earthquake, listening to the eerie music of crystal drips shaking against one another. I kept expecting the whole thing to crash to the floor.

First I made a pear tart and set it aside so I could bake it at the last minute and serve it warm. The rest was easy. I stuffed porcini mushrooms with shrimp, roasted Japanese eggplants, and drizzled arugula with an extraordinarily virgin olive oil. Just as I finished making dinner, she called me in to look at the chandelier.

I have seen it in many kinds of light, but always webbed with spider silk and clotted with dust balls. Now the last light of the afternoon snuck in through the dining room door, a thick rectangular shaft, striking only half of the chandelier. That half dazzled. It was too much. I wanted to throw my arm across my eyes, emit harsh sounds, walk backwards, scream no. It was a shining, a Hitchcock detail in my otherwise ordinary house, and for a moment Flo's smile also looked demonic, like she had brought this thing to life on purpose. She climbed up on her ladder and, taking hold of a branch of the chandelier, shook it gently. Tiny rainbows danced all over the walls to the earthquake music.

I said, "Thank you," not too warmly, then, "Ready for dinner?"

"I need to shower. Is there time?"

"Sure."

"I won't be long."

But she was long. She bathed rather than showered, soaking in the tub for at least thirty minutes. I kept walking to the bottom of the stairway, wanting to go up and see if she was okay, then thinking better of it. I tried not to look at my refurbished chandelier, now glittering faintly in the hazy light of dusk, some husk of a royal ghost.

Finally I went into the front room and sat with the animals, waiting. Susan B lounged on the couch while Martin lay on the mantel, one eye open. When he saw me he let out a long guttural growl to let me know how much he hated Susan B's presence, but he didn't even lift his head. He had gotten used to her. Susan B gave me an Eddie Haskell smile, like I didn't know she was pulling one over on me. By the time Flo finished her bath and came down the stairs, I was as grouchy as Martin.

She wore fresh chinos, rolled at the cuffs, and a dark purple corduroy shirt. Her hair was towel-dried and she looked dewy, fresh, and damp. I swallowed and gestured her toward the dining room, where I had set the table, but I suddenly wished I had set the kitchen table, where it would be warmer, friendlier. I almost gathered up the plates and utensils to move us, but Flo sat down and said, "Ah, dining in style."

Because the dining room was cold, literally, I turned up the heat, but it was also lacking decor, the walls empty. The table was too big for two people. I had planned to serve in courses but instead, hoping to at least visually warm the room, I brought in the mushrooms, eggplants, and arugula all at once. On a whim, I piled whatever fruit I had in a bowl and put that on the table too. Flo served herself big helpings and dug in.

"I didn't know you could cook. This is good." She dropped

chunks of shrimp-stuffed mushrooms down to Susan B, who had moved from the front room to sit at her feet. "She doesn't like eggplant."

"Or arugula probably."

"No. But anything with shrimp she loves."

We talked about ordinary things, people we knew in common, mostly the priests and nuns from the church, and her students, who were also my patients. I loved the way she talked—not just the words she used, though certainly that as well, but the way she formed the words with her tongue and lips, the way they left her mouth like juicy little parcels. She laughed at my stories too, convincing me that I was at least amusing.

I tried to ignore the chandelier glimmering in the dark of my peripheral vision. Instead I allowed my entire being to surge to my kneecap, which occasionally brushed hers under the table, and then like a tide washing in another direction, to my nostrils as they caught the essence of her smell even through the scent of my own soap. Finally, I brought out the warm pear tart and coffee, which we ate in complete silence.

Then, abruptly, she thanked me for dinner and said, "Do you mind if I leave my ladders by the side of your house until I get my next job? That way I'll only have to rent a truck once."

"Of course not." We stood under the chandelier, which even now in the dark, like fresh snow, captured enough light to glow. "Flo. I hate the idea of not seeing you anymore now that you're done painting my house."

"Hey, we run into each other all the time. You know, on the street."

I nodded and followed her outside. Standing on the freshly-painted porch, I looked out over the buildings. The sky was hard and black, no stars. I took her hand and pulled her toward me, but she didn't allow more than a quick kiss. She stepped back and looked at me. "Sometimes I can't see you in your eyes. It's like you disappear."

"Flo," I said and stepped closer.

She shook her head.

"Why not?" The humiliation of desire. Was I begging?

"I'm celibate."

"I don't understand."

"No," she said, "I know you don't."

"That sounds patronizing."

"I'm sorry." She turned as if to leave, then sat on the top step. I waited, standing. She asked, "What about your girlfriend?"

"You must mean Lucienne."

"Big woman, short hair. Looks sort of like Gertrude Stein."

I laughed. "That's Lucienne. We don't have any kind of commitment."

"How long have you been seeing each other?"

"The answer to that question is misleading."

Flo waited.

"Ten years."

She lifted an eyebrow.

"We've been seeing less and less of each other. It's a mutual pact of dancing so lightly our feet don't have to touch the ground."

"That's just how I think about you sometimes."

"How?"

"No place to set down your feet, just like you said. No place on the planet to call your own."

"Give me a break. We're all lost. If you're waiting to know exactly where you are before you have sex again, it's going to be a long wait." But I knew she was telling the truth and almost realized it was that truth-telling of hers I wanted most.

She was silent, so I backpedaled and asked, "What do you mean, a place on the planet?"

"I'm sorry. I didn't mean to be patronizing. Celibacy for me is like a period of visceral silence, that's all. I don't know for how long."

"How long so far?"

"Almost two years."

"That's impressive."

"It's not like...." She shaped her hands as if she were trying to give form to something that would never have form. "I still have desire." Then that dimpled smile. "Lots of desire."

I didn't ask for what, though I wanted to know.

"But a lot of times, not always but a lot of times, my rage slash-burns my desire. Do you know what I mean?"

I shook my head.

She asked, "Have you ever felt rage?"

"I've been angry."

"Not anger, rage."

I had a feeling I hadn't, not the kind she meant, and shook my head again.

"It's like a very high fever on speed."

I snorted, then realized I was jealous. I didn't say so, but I thought rage sounded pretty good. It had an energy, even a direction, so that, potentially, it could run its course. If you *found* its course. But not having a place on the planet, well, that was pretty vague, wasn't it? I could search for fifty lifetimes and come up empty-handed. There was no energy to being lost, nothing to expend. While Flo learned to hold on to her own energy, or use it, I would be constantly in search of a source, a current of energy from the outside. Susan B climbed in her lap and whimpered. Flo hugged her.

I said, "I guess I'll go in."

Flo moved Susan B off her lap and stood up. She jammed both hands in her front pockets, then took one out and touched my cheek. "It's not you," she said softly. "It's me. I have a feeling we'd be too much like a plug in a socket."

"Isn't that sort of ideal?" I couldn't keep from asking. "Isn't that like a fit?"

She shook her head. "A voltage provider and a voltage receiver isn't a fit, but it's very attractive."

"That's too simplistic," I said. "'No' is fine, but I don't buy your voltage theory."

She bounced down the stairs backward, like she did that first day she came to my house to ask if she could paint it. "Good night, Doc."

When she was almost out of sight of my porch, she turned and said, "Susan B! Say good night to the doctor."

Yip.

I reentered my house, shut the door, and pressed my back against the inside of it, forcing myself to look at my newly polished chandelier. The sun had set long ago and there was no moon, no apparent source of light at all, and yet the Gothic fixture gleamed in the blackness like the comet. I slid my behind down the inside of my front door and sat on the floor, staring at it. I realized what disturbed me was the chandelier's clarity. Nothing inhibited the light from traveling at top speed through each dewdrop. Nothing masked the true essence of the crystal. Without the dust and cobwebs dulling the chandelier, my house felt bigger and colder and lonelier than it ever had.

I was very free in the light of my crystal chandelier, free in the Janis Joplin sense of the word, and utterly alone. I pushed myself to my feet and found my phone. I called my sister and left a message that I would go on the snow-camping trip after all.

twenty: poodle pimp

A couple of weeks later, I left the clinic, stepping into a late-winter urban dusk, ashy and cold. I knew it would be many degrees colder in the mountains. We were leaving the next day directly after work, which meant I had to get completely packed tonight. I found where I had parked my car, after looking for half an hour, and stuffed the parking ticket in my overcoat pocket. I drove home slowly and found Flo sitting on my front porch. She wore a worn brown leather bomber jacket, a couple of sizes too big, which I'd never seen on her before, and she sat with her elbows resting on her spread knees.

"Hi!" I cried, jumping out of my car too enthusiastically. I had not seen her since our dinner together, although her ladders had disappeared from the side of my house a couple of days ago.

"Hey."

"You okay?"

She shook her head. "Susan B is gone."

"What do you mean *gone*?"

"One minute she was at the bottom of my ladder, the next she wasn't."

"Where are you working now?"

"Three blocks from here. For a couple I met while working on your house."

"When did she disappear?"

"About ten this morning. I've been all over the neighborhood fifteen times, all over fucking Bernal Heights. Then I walked back to my apartment, thinking maybe she had some reason to go home. I don't know what to do now."

I sat beside her on the porch and tried to think. "I can't remember: Does she wear a tag?"

"No. I don't have a telephone and I've changed addresses so often, what's the point? And anyway, she's never out of my sight."

"Have you talked to the people whose house you're painting?"

"They haven't seen her. They're having a dinner party tonight. I've been by three times, and the last time they were very annoyed."

"Shit."

"I've looked all around your house. I thought maybe she came back here. Maybe she likes Martin's company. Or the comfort of your house. Maybe she's sick of the Tenderloin, of living with me." She squeezed her eyes shut and said, "Sick of *working* for me."

"Susan B adores you," I said. "You know she would never leave you on purpose. Let's look now. We can take the car."

"I've been looking since ten this morning. She's not anywhere within a five-mile radius. I've got about six blisters on my feet." She stood and clunked down the stairs.

"Let me at least drive you home."

She hesitated. I had often offered her rides home and she had always refused, but now she shrugged and said, "Okay."

Once we got to the Tenderloin she directed me to a small

dark-brick building, and I pulled to the curb. She closed her eyes, as if she could shut out the pain. "I don't know what to do."

I reached over and took her hand. "You're going to find her. I'm sure."

She sucked in a wet breath and, opening the car door, said, "First daylight and I'll start looking again."

"Are you going to be all right tonight?"

"I don't know," she said. "I don't know."

After she went in, I sat in front of her building for a few minutes, paralyzed. I thought I should stay with her but I doubted she wanted me to, and besides, I had to pack. I had promised Liz I would go on the snow-camping trip. No matter what I chose to do right then, I felt as if I would be turning my back, unforgivably, on someone.

It was eight o'clock when I got home. I felt as empty and saggy as the rented backpack and sleeping bag sitting on the floor in my hallway under the chandelier. I forced myself to hold Liz's packing list in front of my face and to gather the items on it. I piled the stuff—toothbrush, flashlight, ibuprofen—on top of the other gear. Each time I returned from my attic or basement or bathroom with another item, I stepped outside on the porch, smoked a cigarette, and called Susan B. I wished I had made Flo show me the house where she now worked. Three blocks away, she had said. Susan B had to be nearby. I yelled her name as loudly as I could, tried to cast my voice as far afield as possible, ready to tell any complaining neighbors to fuck off.

By eleven o'clock I had finished packing and went to bed, but I couldn't sleep. I hadn't called Lucienne. Not that I should have. Not that I said I would. But it would have been a nice gesture. I lay in my bed feeling disoriented; this was not a good time for a wilderness trip. But when would be? And there was no way in the world I could back out now. Ever since I had called Liz to tell her I would come, she had latched onto my participation like it was the point of the trip. She called me daily, asking ridiculous questions, like would I prefer sweet and sour tofu or cheese enchiladas for dinner. Tonight there was a message on my machine informing me that she had booked us motel rooms for Friday night, and was it okay that I had a single, or did I want to share with Melody to save forty dollars? I knew that my being on this trip was important to Liz, but I didn't know why. I lay in bed, dreading the trip and thankful for Martin's huge body, with its thick polar coat, wedged against my hip. I petted him as I waited for sleep.

Around two o'clock I finally started to get that melting feeling in my knees that meant sleep was imminent. I steered my thoughts away from Flo—Flo of the visceral silence, Flo who was heartbroken over her missing poodle—and eased myself into unconsciousness.

According to the clock, it was only fifteen minutes later when Martin sat up and growled. I would have ignored him but he jumped to the window and stood on his hind legs, his front paws on the sill, and growled more. I lay in bed and listened for a moment, and, sure enough, heard a faint, raspy *yip*. I got up and pushed open the window. There she was on the ground, looking up two stories, her voice tiny and hoarse, as if she had been barking all day and night.

I pulled on jeans and sneakers and ran down to get her. Susan B limped down the side of my house to meet me, then flopped on her side at my feet, crying. She had a bad cut over her left eye, and her white curls were clotted with blood. I checked her legs, back, and abdomen before deciding I could pick her up, carefully, and carry her into the house. Martin was waiting on the stairway and looked almost concerned. He didn't growl, anyway. I cleaned up Susan B's cut, which didn't look like it needed stitches, with hydrogen peroxide, and then examined the rest of her body more carefully. She had some bruised ribs and a sore paw but seemed to be otherwise all right. I suspected she had gone off to explore the new work site, wandered into the street, and gotten hit by a car. She must have crawled into some bushes to recover and perhaps gone into shock. I had to admit that she was a smart dog to know to come to my house. I also couldn't help but wonder how she knew the way: From the one trip with the ladders, or had Flo taken a few walks by my house, indulging feelings she wouldn't otherwise admit?

I wrapped Susan B in a fleece blanket, told Martin to hold down the fort, and drove fast across the deserted city to Flo's building. The front door was locked and the entryway so dark that I couldn't read the names next to the buzzers. I backed up and looked at the building. Because I didn't have any other choice, I rapped on a ground-floor window. Nothing. I rapped harder.

The window opened a crack and a mouth appeared in the space, looking like a sea anemone in the ghoulish light of a pink neon sign across the street. "What the fuck?" said the red opening in a voice I couldn't identify as male or female.

"I have an emergency message for Flo. Florence Hughes." Then, hoping he/she could see me better than I could see him/her, and also hoping that he/she knew Flo and Susan B, I opened the fleece blanket and exhibited the poodle. "Her dog was hit by a car."

"She's in C." The window shut. A moment later I heard a buzzer and lunged for the front door, but the neon light didn't make its way into the dark entryway, and, fumbling to find the door handle without dropping Susan B, I wasn't fast enough. The buzzer went off and the door was still locked shut. I went around and knocked on the window again, then took a chance on his/her understanding the problem and returned to the door immediately so that I'd be ready. I figured right. This time he/she leaned on the buzzer for a full ten seconds and I got in the front door.

Climbing the stairs to Flo's apartment in total darkness, I held the bundle of dog and fleece against my chest. I knew I was bringing Flo the best possible gift anyone could ever bring her, and that humbled me. On the second floor I fingered the surfaces of the two doors, one on the left and one on the right, and luckily the apartment letters were made of brass, not paint. I made out a D on the door on the left and a C on the door on the right. I knocked and took a breath to call out that it was me, but Flo, wearing a white T-shirt and underpants, opened up before I had a chance to say anything. I put the fleece-wrapped bundle in her arms.

"Oh," she said. "Oh, God." She unwrapped the blanket gingerly, and I realized that she wasn't sure if Susan B was alive or dead.

The poodle blinked at her, then gurgled love and threw her paws up on Flo's chest, even as she whimpered in pain. Flo sunk her face in Susan B's bloody, muddy fur and sobbed.

"Careful," I said. "Her ribs are bruised. And she has a sore paw."

Flo carried her dog inside the room, which was lit by dozens of burning candles, and sat on a mattress on the floor. I watched from the door for a second, then quietly retreated down the stairs.

"Doc," she called. "Don't leave yet. Wait, please."

I climbed back up to her doorway.

"Come in. Just for a minute, okay?" Her face was wet and swollen. "Please."

I entered her small, candlelit room and gently shut the door behind me. Flo rocked and cuddled Susan B on the mattress, her sobs ebbing and flowing but her grief at full tide. I found a red corduroy beanbag chair and lowered myself into it. Two walls of Flo's room were nearly covered by big pieces of red velvet. Photographs, poems, and drawings were pinned all over the plush fabric. Besides the beanbag chair, there were cinder block and board bookshelves, stacks and stacks of books, a small desk and chair, and the mattress on the floor, which was covered by what looked like a homemade quilt. I saw a toilet through the door to the closet-size bathroom, and along the wall behind me were the makings of a minimal kitchen, a small fridge, and a hot plate. In the opposite corner was Susan B's bed and her food and water bowls, and, hanging on the wall at a good dog height, a portrait of Susan B. Anthony. Every horizontal surface in the room held a burning candle; there were dozens of them, as if this were a chapel in the heart of Portugal. The only other light was that coming in the one window that looked out onto the street, just at the level of the pink neon sign. It was a martini glass, with a swizzle stick and an olive, flickering faintly. On the floor beside the beanbag chair were a cluster of seven candles in glass cylindrical containers covered with paintings of saints and prophets. The one closest to me was called "*Oración al ángel de la guardia.*" The small print read, first in Spanish and then in English, "Angel of God, my guardian dear, to whom God's love commits me here, ever this day be at my side to light and guard, to rule and guide. Amen." The room smelled like cinnamon.

Flo babbled in dog talk to Susan B and still wept. I felt I really shouldn't be there, so I rose and again tried to leave.

"Stay, stay," Flo pleaded in her soggy voice.

I stayed, though I didn't know why. I felt awkward, out of place, not just a third wheel but the wrong species even. I said, "I cleaned her open wounds. I'm almost sure the paw isn't broken, but she should probably be checked out. I know an all-night emergency vet."

"There's a guy in the building next door who used to be a vet. He'll check her out for free in the morning. Do you think she'll be all right for a couple of hours?"

"Sure."

"Wait, okay?" She rose and carried Susan B to her bed. Crouching, she petted then kissed the dog's head and told her to stay. Flo returned to her mattress, pulled a tissue from a box on the floor, blew her nose two, three times, then looked at me. "Wow," she said, making me laugh. "I don't know what I would do without her."

"I'm glad you don't have to find out."

"It must be the middle of the night."

I looked at my watch. "Three-thirty."

"Why don't you stay? It's too late for you to go back home."

"No, I don't think so." I was too exhausted to feel insulted but didn't like the idea of being offered a reward for rescuing Susan B.

Flo realized what I thought and said, "As friends. I don't want to be alone."

I glanced at Susan B.

"I need a human friend tonight."

I was surprised to hear her acknowledge the difference. Stalling, a little confused, I said, "I'm leaving tomorrow evening for the Sierras."

"The trip with your sister! You decided to go?"

"Yeah."

"The comet will be awesome. Here, you can wear my pajamas. The building has no heat." She pulled a pair of flannel pajamas, blue with white dots, from under a pile of neatly folded clothes next to the mattress, and held them out to me. I never wear anything in bed, but I took them and looked around for a place to change.

"Sorry, no dressing room."

I pulled off my jeans and sweatshirt and put on the pajamas while she crossed the small room to kiss Susan B one last time. I could barely button the top over my breasts and wanted to just leave my T-shirt on but was too embarrassed. I sat carefully on the mattress on the floor and folded my arms over the gap in the pajama top. "I figured she slept with you."

"No. She likes her own bed." Then softly, "Inside or outside?"

I looked at her blankly.

"Next to the wall or not?"

"Oh. Whichever."

"I'll take the outside then, if you don't mind."

"I don't mind."

Then, lying in bed on our backs, she made me tell her every single detail of what I knew, or hypothesized, about Susan B's ordeal: about how I called and called her, how I fell asleep, how Martin growled, what exactly Susan B looked like from my window, and how she responded to being rescued. I explained my theory, based on her injuries, of her being hit by a car and going into shock.

"What's Martin's favorite thing in the world? I'm going to get it for him. He saved Susan B's life."

"Martin hates Susan B, and you know it. He was *growling* at her. Even if he knew it was her outside the window, his reaction was extreme annoyance, not love or even animal solidarity."

"You don't know that."

I admitted that once I brought Susan B into the house, Martin had looked concerned.

She said, "However Martin and Susan B feel about each other, for some reason you're one of Susan B's favorite people."

"For some reason?"

"I mean, well, yeah, for some reason. *I* like you, but she doesn't always like the people I like. Susan B is usually right about people though. She has impeccable taste."

I watched the candlelight shimmy up the walls of her room and said nothing.

She said, "All night I've been praying to the gods, goddesses, and spirits of every religion I know anything about. I felt like losing Susan B was the penance I paid for pimping her. I promised if they returned her, I'd never ever pimp her again."

"Susan B likes working with you."

"No. No, she doesn't. She wants to be a regular dog. She wants to run in the park, be my pal. It was wrong to pimp her. I'll never do it again. Besides, the only reason I do the street performance is to find an audience for my poetry. Some audience! Hardly anyone stays for the poetry anyway. It's time to try something different."

"Like what?"

"I don't know. Maybe I'll get an arts grant this year. Or paint more houses."

I rolled my head to the side so that I could see her face.

Her eyes closed as she repeated, "I don't know." And now quiet, her mouth, her beautifully expressive mouth, relaxed. She folded her body into a curl, touching me lightly in the most innocent of places, her knuckles against my shoulder, her knees kissing my hipbone. I watched her fall asleep, her chest rising and falling more and more slowly.

When she was irredeemably unconscious, her breathing steady and deep, I heard the quiet clicking of claws on the linoleum floor and a moment later felt a presence step into the space between Flo's and my bodies. Susan B settled in with a long sigh. I put my fingers in her curls and found the top of her head to scratch. The love of Flo's life. Once Susan B was snoring, I lay on my back, feeling both afraid of and cradled by this red velvet nest of hers. So this was her place on the planet, I thought, knowing that she never meant an actual place, a real geography. Still I felt her presence here, her absolute presence, absolutely here.

When I closed my own eyes, I saw Timothy, exactly as he had been the last time I laid eyes on him. His thin, white-fleshed chest. Scrawny arms dangling. Sunken belly. His hair wet and cowlicked to the side, his ears like small round wings. Rose mouth. Baby pug nose. Needy eyes, lashes clumped with lake water.

Did the man wrap him in a towel? A warm shirt?

I began to fall asleep, with Timothy locked onto my mind's eye. I tried to shake him loose before I lost consciousness, didn't want him shivering the whole night through in my dreams, but he stayed. He stayed like a reflection in a lake that won't disappear no matter how many stones you throw at it. He stayed, standing knee-deep in the icy water, watching me for a signal.

It came to me then, in that transitional state that is neither sleep nor awake, that I would never shake off loneliness, that cold winter animal, until I found Timothy. I fell asleep with all the candles burning.

twenty-one: the raft

I returned from peeing in the woods. In my arms were three big stones. They were extra smooth round stones. Better than the others I had brought. Liz had asked for smaller stones now, but I had found these good ones. They were better, much better. They were perfectly smooth, nearly perfectly round.

I was barefoot, and I stepped on something sharp. A flash of nausea lit my belly. Then the dull pain in my heel. I put down the three rocks and lifted my foot. A ragged pebble was stuck into my flesh. I flicked it off. I picked up my stones. That was when I saw the Camaro in the parking spot of campsite number fourteen. It was a yellow car. I have no idea what the driver looked like. I barely remembered the yellow. I knew I had to move, move quickly to get out of the way, because I didn't know if the driver saw me. The car was backing out of the campsite. Perhaps the driver, or the driver and passenger, had stopped only to look at the lake for a moment. The car didn't stay in the campground, that part is for sure. Otherwise the police would have found it. Maybe the person in the Camaro pulled off the highway for a look at the lake, that's all. A quick cup of coffee from the thermos. I don't know. I didn't give the Camaro a thought, other than to get out of its way. Mostly I was excited about my extra-good stones, and I continued on down to our pier-in-progress.

The raft was floating. It was fifty yards, maybe even farther, from the shore. A brown raft on a brown lake. Blue sky, a rim of green trees. Tiny lapping sounds.

Liz's face. I saw a scream but never heard it. She moved toward me in her red and white plaid bathing suit. She was looking past me, so I looked behind me. The yellow Camaro was slipping around the corner, out of sight.

I was so proud of my stones that I ignored her screaming face for a moment, maybe I pretended that she was playing at fear, and started to show them to her. But she was running past me.

"What?" I yelled. I had no problem getting out a real vocal cords scream. "What?"

I looked back at the empty raft.

Then I took off after her.

"Mommy!" Liz said in a strangled voice. "A man took Timothy."

Moments later, our mother was on the campground pay phone to the police, the forest service, and our father.

I wonder how many children have played on that raft since. Surely it has rotted by now. But in the interim, these thirty years, how many children have floated on its slivered surface?

twenty-two: *bivouac*

The blue taffeta lightens. I think Lenny is asleep. His eyes are closed, his chest heaves gently. I lie still. The me of me, the essence of my being, feels tiny and dry, like a shriveled pea knocking around in an oversize pod, my wracked body. But the tent fly, inches from my face, has begun to pale, is even turning yellowish.

"Lenny." I whisper, as if there is someone else I don't want to wake. "Lenny."

He groans and opens his eyes.

The human urge for survival is enormous. The lightening tent fly triggers the release of adrenaline into my bloodstream and, compared to a few moments ago, I am nearly vigorous. "Is it clearing?" I demand to know. "Can you look outside?"

Lenny shuts his eyes again. I'm impatient and say his name two more times until he heaves over onto his other side, his back to me, and lifts the edge of our makeshift shelter. A puff of light, reflecting off the snow covering our ledge, breathes into our tiny space. He grunts, then tries to get onto his hands and knees, but his back strikes a tent pole and the whole thing collapses, just like that.

"Shit," he says. "Fucking A."

The poles fall toward our feet, and the taffeta, heavy with fresh snow, flops into my head, dumping its load. I try to move my right arm to wipe my face. Slowly I can get my hand up and push away the wet snow. What I see almost makes up for the catastrophe of the fallen tent—the sky is clearing in that instantaneous way that happens only in the mountains. The clouds are hustling now, moving south very quickly, like armies, leaving big patches of blue. Sun, a late in the day buttery sun, strikes my face. The adrenaline has flushed out the pain, even the dull slush of the drugs, and my senses perk up, respond to everything at once. The honey fragrance of the sun is like a crooked finger beckoning me toward a crazy place, and I long to go.

Lenny's bustling distracts me from my reverie. He curses the collapsed, snow-laden tent lying across my body. That enchanting sun is already hovering above a ridge in the west, will be gone in a moment.

I don't want to spend the night on this ledge.

Where is Liz? Where is Mark? Where is the helicopter?

Lenny pulls the corners of the tent fly up and off me, then carefully drags the whole thing, including the load of snow, to the side. One of the poles breaks loose and slides. It makes a silky s-s-s sound as it glides across the snow toward the edge, then is silent as it goes airborne. I listen for the clatter of it hitting the side of the mountain, but hear nothing. Perhaps the drop-off is hundreds of feet, even hundreds of yards.

"Fucking A," Lenny says. There are tears in his voice. After all, that was half of the skeleton of our shelter for the night.

I cannot move. That transparent, nearly hallucinatory quality of my pain has been replaced by a weight, like stones sinking to a place of extreme forbearance. Maybe, I think, *this* is my place on the planet. Maybe I have finally landed from the fall that began the day Timothy disappeared. But how can I possibly land without Liz? Without Timothy, for that matter.

"Where the fuck are they?" Lenny says. I can see his big boots and long shins pacing the short length of our ledge. I tilt my head until I see his chest and then his clenched jaw. He bends to look at me and seems to be about to make a decision. I hope that he is. Any decision would be good now. I try not to watch the sun, sinking at an alarming rate, and keep focused on the sky, try to find sustenance in its color, wait for Lenny to come up with something.

A long shadow falls over me. A figure stands on the ledge above, and I find the strength to cry out, *Oh, thank God Liz where have you been I'm thinking about Timothy and you and the lake and the man.* But then I realize I actually hadn't found the strength after all. The words were screaming in my head but otherwise silent. And anyway the figure isn't Liz. It's Mark. I must be truly hallucinating now, for no helicopter landed, yet my brother-in-law has appeared.

"Your eyes are open," he says. He looks a bit like a madman, his sunlit hair spiked and golden, his mustache caked with snot, his eyes metallic with fear and exhaustion.

I search my auditory memory. Did I sleep through a helicopter landing? No. No helicopter landed. Is he here to tell us that no helicopter will be coming? The federal budget, he will explain. Rescues are no longer possible. I force myself to consider that this may be my permanent place on the planet, the end for me. Rather than frightening me, though, the thought shatters the last of my fear. What really is there to fear? I think how silly my life so far has been, this long hunkering bivouac.

"How'd you get here?" Lenny asks.

"Where is Liz?" Mark demands.

"Dunno," Lenny says but adds, "She said she was going to wrap herself in the tent."

Mark disappears, and now I'm sure I hallucinated him. But then why would Lenny be shouting to the top of the cliff? "Wait a second! Hey! Wait!" He claws the wet dirt, desperate for a handhold. I see him lift a big boot and place it on a small boulder that immediately loosens and falls away when he puts his weight on it. Lenny continues anyway, gripping the rocky face with his gloves, but it's too wet and crumbly. When he gives up, he drops to his haunches beside me and stares out where the sun has now sunk. Tears wash down his cheeks and he doesn't care that I see them. I join him and cry my own tears, a flash flood ripping through me, sluicing out everything in its path. The tears are a fun-house lens on my eyes, and I look through them in the direction of the drop-off, which must be the south, and stare at the miles of peaks, arranged like sharks' teeth, row after row, covered with the fresh snowfall. The sky is a fragile periwinkle as it prepares for twilight.

"It's you and me, Lenny," I rasp.

"Yeah," he says. "Looks like it."

"Do you think we're going to die here?" I ask, more out of curiosity than fear.

"Hell, no!" He wipes his wet cheeks with the back of his glove and falls off his haunches and onto his behind. "I'll get us out of here." I can almost see the bravado rising in him, like mercury in a thermometer. "Die? You're fucking crazy," he tells me. Then he pulls his flannel shirt tail out from under his parka and pants and dabs the tears running down my temples. He holds the fabric at my nose for me to blow, which I do. "Just give me a minute to think this through, okay?"

"Okay," I say.

He stands, puts his hands on his hips, and turns slowly, 360 degrees, as if he will see something useful at hand, as if there is anything out here but air and distant, darkening mountains.

"Where the fuck did you go?" he says, and I see that now there are, or appear to be, two figures on the ledge above us.

"Liz?"

"How're you doing, Tina?" Softly.

"I'm fine," I say.

Both Liz and Mark smile at that.

Mark says, "Now that's what I call living on the edge."

I'm grateful for his cornball humor, and yet it's like a knife in the stomach because it used to mean safety and now what does it mean?

"Lenny's taking good care of me," I say.

"Lotta pain?" Liz asks.

"It comes and goes."

"The helicopter should be here any time now," Mark says. "They had to wait out the storm."

"It's gonna get dark," Lenny says. "Soon."

No one answers him.

"What happened to the shelter?" Liz wants to know.

Lenny explains about the collapse and jettisoned pole. I see Mark and Liz exchange a look and know they are silently debating whether they should scare us by discussing plans for the night or sit tight in the hopes that the helicopter will indeed show up soon. Mark says, "Why don't we have a seat and enjoy this beautiful evening for a moment?" He tries for the same jocular tone but doesn't achieve it. He sounds stupid and knows it. For a moment he stands stunned, by everything, and Liz takes the wadded tent out of his arms. She unfurls it and spreads it out on the snow. Mark piles two pads and two sleeping bags on top of the flat tent, and they both sit down, cross-legged. Mark tries to take Liz's hand, but she withdraws it and turns her body at a forty-five-degree angle to his.

There is much I don't understand, but I can't quite formulate the questions. Luckily, Lenny asks, "So what the fuck is up? What are you doing just sitting there?"

Good questions, partner.

"I showed the search-and-rescue crew our exact location on the map, but they have to wait for the storm to pass before they can get in here. So I drove back to trailhead and skied in so I could be with you all. They won't have any trouble finding us. They should be here any minute."

Lenny cranes back his head and searches the sky. "When?" he says. "When exactly? Where will it land? How can it get me and Tina?"

"These guys are experts," Mark says quietly. "They'll get us, all of us, out of here."

"Where's Melody?" I have to ask.

"I dropped her off at the bus station in town."

For the first time in hours, I laugh.

"She was weird," Lenny says, as if she is gone for good, riding Greyhound into the sunset. "She was too quiet." He kicks at the short cliff and a miniature cascade of wet soil and rock covers the toe of his boot.

"I agree," I say.

Liz is looking east, at the darkest part of the sky, away from Mark, beyond me and Lenny. "And what about you?" I ask her. "Where'd you go?"

She turns and looks down at me. "Into the trees to stay drier."

"I was worried about you."

"*You* were worried about *me*?" She gives me her big sister grin. "You're the one on an exposed ledge with broken bones. I had a comfy little bivouac."

"Comfy?"

"Well." She shrugs. "I dug a trench. Had the tent to wrap up in."

"You could have gone back to the snow cave."

"That was too far away," she says, then adds, "from you."

Lenny fires up a cigarette, takes a drag, then holds it to my mouth. The rush of nicotine lights my brain, and I say to Liz, "While you were gone, I was thinking about Timothy."

Mark says, "Not now, Tina."

But Liz says, "Me too."

"I was thinking about finding him."

"Tina! For fuck's sake," says Mark, as if he is protecting Liz and not himself.

"Your language, Mark," Lenny says.

"This is a crisis," Mark argues, "and in a crisis you can curse."

"Then when the fuck is the helicopter coming?" Lenny asks.

"I know where he is," Liz says.

"The helicopter pilot?" Lenny asks.

"*Timothy*?" Mark asks. "You know where *Timothy* is?"

"Sure. And so does Tina."

"For fuck's sake," Mark says again. "Now? Do you have to now?"

A bivouac, I think, is only a temporary shelter, a place to cocoon until the environment is safe or until the shelter itself is destroyed, forcing you out.

"Honey," Mark tries now, gently, to summon Liz, but she isn't listening to him. Neither am I. We are listening only to each other.

twenty-three: coyote hides

Liz never knew, at least I didn't think she ever knew, about my trip to Oregon fifteen years ago, when I was twenty-five years old, to visit the Eggerts. It happened so quickly that my own memory of that day and night is encapsulated, more like a short story I read than something that actually happened in my own life.

One morning, shortly after I graduated from medical school and had begun my residency, I read an article in *The New York Times* about a group of survivalists living in Clackamas County, Oregon, not far from the small town of Canby. The article was the third part of a series, and I had relished the first two parts on Idaho and Alaska, where there had been whole communities of survivalists who grew weird crops and stockpiled ammunition. This third segment, however, was weak. The group in Oregon was composed of just two or three families who weren't a community, not even quite neighbors, but who shared a philosophy of isolationism and self-determination. On the front page, below the fold, was a picture of one three-generational family standing on their farm, staring hostilely into the camera. They wore nineteenth-century clothing and claimed to eat squirrel.

As I read the article, I mused on how these families were different from Liz and Mark. Of course they *were* different. Liz and Mark participated in society, held jobs, and most of all didn't sound like crazy people or evangelists when they spoke. But it was true that Liz and Mark *did* distrust society at large, believed in providing for as many of their own needs as possible, *were* experts in survival. I had to admit that it was probably just a matter of degree, and that was a scary thought. Twenty, thirty years hence, would I see Mark and Liz's faces on the front page of *The New York Times*, examples of survivalists? It didn't take a big stretch of the imagination to picture. I wondered if Liz would think this was funny. If she did, that would be a good sign. If she didn't, it meant she already identified too closely for humor.

The story continued on pages ten and eleven, where I read about the third and last Oregon family profiled. Mr. Warren Eggert called himself a rancher, though apparently he had only a half-dozen Holsteins, which are milk cows, one field that at the time of the reporter's visit was not planted, and a large vegetable garden tended by his wife and daughter. Eggert and his son collected old cars, which they were in the process of restoring. The reporter suggested that this restoration process did not appear to be moving quickly.

The Times was far from kind to the Eggert family, and I suspected that Eggert made it into this article not so much because he was a survivalist—although the two other Clackamas County families vouched for him on that account—but because he was a good story. Eggert had become a bit of a local celebrity by shooting coyotes and stretching their hides on the highway fence. When he had eleven on display, a young, newly employed Canby elementary school teacher, Mr. Henry Trowbridge, had his third-grade students write letters to Mr. Eggert asking him why he killed the coyotes. Mr. Eggert wrote back that the third-graders should mind their own business. Coyotes were vermin, no more than dog-size rats, and if God meant for children to drink the milk of his cows, then God also meant for men to shoot the coyotes who preyed on those cows. Mr. Trowbridge was outraged by Eggert's cruel response to the children, and he paid a visit to the Eggert ranch to complain.

The schoolteacher arrived on a cold winter morning. A hard freeze made the usually muddy and potholed dirt road leading up to the Eggerts' house slick, and Trowbridge's Volkswagen bug fishtailed twice on his way in. Later, reflecting on Trowbridge's account, I had to laugh at the thought of Eggert, who stood in the entrance of his barn, watching this schoolteacher skid and lurch up the road. Unfortunately for Trowbridge, he arrived at a bad time. He reported that when he got out of his car he heard shouting coming from the house. Mrs. Eggert and her daughter, Cynthia, were arguing in the kitchen. He had the bad judgment to knock anyway, and Eggert, who had been watching him from the barn, approached and asked Trowbridge what the fuck he was doing on his land. When Trowbridge informed Eggert that he was the teacher of the children who had written the letter, Eggert said, "Follow me," and walked around to the back of the house.

Trowbridge, delighted to have won an audience with the rancher so easily, followed him, expecting a cup of coffee and a sit at the kitchen table. But at the back door to the house, Eggert said, "Wait here." A moment later, Trowbridge heard him tell the arguing woman and girl to shut up, then Eggert reemerged with a rifle, which he braced against his shoulder and aimed at the schoolteacher. Trowbridge says he was "astonished," and he walked backward, around the side of the house and toward his car, with his arms in the air. When Trowbridge arrived at his car, Eggert closed one eye to take aim, and Trowbridge cried "I'm leaving!" but that didn't stop Eggert from firing one, two, three shots over the school-teacher's head. Trowbridge told the *Times* reporter that it was not at all clear to him whether these were purposefully missed shots. Trowbridge dove into his car, started the engine, and began sliding back down the melting but still slick mud road.

Eggert shot out one of his back tires, disabling the vehicle. Trowbridge says he sat in the driver's seat and waited for Eggert to come kill him. In his rearview mirror he saw the man laughing and approaching jauntily, swinging the rifle at his side.

Trowbridge wouldn't roll down his window, but he heard Eggert say, "You got a flat, son. You best get out, fix it, and get off my property." Which Trowbridge did, the whole while with a gun aimed at him. Trowbridge finally made it back to the highway unharmed, physically anyway, but he pressed charges. The charges went nowhere in that small Oregon town, because after all, he had been trespassing. Trowbridge tried to get revenge by writing letters to the press, but until *The New York Times* played the story, he was made the fool every time he appeared in print.

"We just want to be left alone," Eggert is quoted, saying in the local press, and requoted in the *Times*. "My family and I bought this land so we could live a God-fearing life with Jesus Christ as our Savior."

When the *Times* asked him about the coyote hides, Eggert said, "I'm just sorry I can't stretch a schoolteacher hide alongside them." Furthermore, "So long as God sends coyotes—and schoolteachers—to my land, I'll shoot."

I had seen the picture on page ten of the coyote hides stretched out on the barbed-wire fence, along with a sign that said NO TRESPASSING MEANS NO TRESPASSING, but I'd been too engrossed in the story to look at the picture on page eleven until I finished reading. Two men sit on the hood of a wrecked '57 Plymouth, their knees spread. They both wear mud-caked boots, dungarees, plaid rancher's shirts, and wide leather belts with wallet-size buckles. The older man, Warren Eggert, is leaning back on his hands, which are placed behind him on the car hood. Eggert Junior holds his hands in a ball between his legs, his back curved forward, but his head tilted up, as if a moment before the shutter was released someone rebuked him for cowering. Next to Warren Eggert, who is barrel-chested and greasy-haired, the younger man's slight frame and sensuous mouth make him look winsome. The caption read simply, "Warren Eggert and his son Timothy Eggert."

I left at five A.M. the next day, driving fast and with a perfect calm, as if for the first time in my life I was doing the right thing. Oddly, I didn't think much about Timothy at all, except for the occasional tickle that I should be figuring out a story for my arrival, some kind of introduction for myself. But the pristine air of an April dawn, the deeply leafing spring trees, the purple water of Shasta Lake against its red banks, my sense of purpose, so on target I could have been a human laser, seemed enough. My meeting with Timothy would unfurl from this spring morning, these flying miles, the inevitability of it.

I stopped only two times, to pee and to make phone calls. I called the hospital at eight and told another resident that I wouldn't be in, and when he asked what he should tell the attending physician, I said, "Nothing." Then I revised that and said, "I have to take care of some family business, but I'll be in tomorrow for sure." I also called Liz, at both stops, but hung up before she answered. I don't know what stopped me from telling her: fear of her being too shocked, of her not believing me, of her being angry I didn't bring her with me. I guess I didn't bring her because I didn't know how to tell her I had found Timothy. But in truth there was more. I wanted him to myself. I wanted this moment in its biggest, fullest possibility, and I wanted it all.

At the second rest stop, I even dialed my parents' number, out of a sense of duty. Surely I should tell them. I would eventually, of course, and how would I explain that I hadn't immediately? My concern for Timothy answered this. What was he going to do with *me* let alone an entire family descending on the ranch to claim him? So I hung up the phone before either of my parents answered. Then, to stretch my legs, I walked the perimeter of the rest area, where there were great lilac

bushes, nearly twice my height. I collected the perfumed purple blooms and carried an armful of them to my car. After
placing them in the front seat, I went back for more. Then
back again until I had a lilac-bloom passenger in the front
seat with me. I had picked a whole section of the shrubs
clean, and a big woman wearing a paisley house dress and
using a walker told me I might leave some for others to enjoy.
But I didn't feel guilty. I felt a strange and overwhelming
greed that day, as if my lifelong hunger would finally be satisfied. I drove the last 300 miles in a cloud of lilac molecules,
so fragrant they seemed to stick to my skin.

I made it to Canby in ten hours, arriving at three P.M.,
and realized I was starving. I had brought a bag of peanuts
with me, but other than those I hadn't eaten since the
night before. I considered getting a meal in town, collecting my thoughts, devising a way to approach the family. But
I didn't. I drove the highway out of town until I came to the
coyote hides and NO TRESPASSING MEANS NO TRESSPASSING
sign and turned down the dirt road. So enmeshed was I in
the truth of my mission and the wash of feeling welling
inside me that it simply didn't occur to me that Warren
Eggert would aim his rifle at me. It was something different, more like not wanting anything between me and my
reunion with Timothy, that caused me to park the car along
the dirt road and walk the rest of the way. I walked slowly
until I saw the yellow house and, behind it, a gray, weath-
er-beaten barn. I knew from *The New York Times* article
that the barn wasn't full of cows and milking equipment,
but I wanted it to be. I wanted to discover Timothy living a
wholesome life, and already I was revising what I had
learned from that reporter. Journalists exploited human
lives for a story, right? They took one aspect of a person and
presented it out of context, didn't they? Timothy, after all,
had five years of love and decent values from our family.
The psychologists say that the first six months are the most
crucial. Well, Timothy had five years.

There was no answer to my long knocking at the front door

of the yellow house, so I walked back to the barn. A whole side of the barn was open, a big dark cavity, leading into a car-wreck graveyard. At least a dozen rusted car hulls sat in the dirt like great inert beasts. Car parts, in no kind of organization, littered all the surfaces. A few shafts of yellow late-afternoon sunlight shot through holes in the roof, striking a shattered windshield here, a pile of bald tires there. The place smelled rank, like wet minerals and mildewed rags. The Plymouth featured in the *Times* photo was nowhere to be seen. As my eyes adjusted to the dark, I searched for the Camaro too, but all of the cars were in such a state of decline that I couldn't determine their make.

I had made my way to the back of the barn and was holding a detached steering wheel when a girl's voice asked what I was doing. I rushed back toward the entrance and sunlight, where I found a young woman, maybe eighteen years old, with pale features and blond hair parted in the middle, hanging like a curtain down the sides of her face. The hair was too thin to cover her ears, which stood nearly perpendicular to her head. She wore jeans and a black T-shirt.

"Hi." I held out my hand. "My name's Christine. You must be Cynthia."

She said nothing but seemed interested.

"I was looking for your...for Timothy."

"He's gone."

"Will he be back soon?"

"If you're a reporter, you better git." She sat on the fender of what may once have been a Porsche and watched me. I don't think she did want me to git.

"Oh, no. I'm not a reporter."

"Nah. You don't look like one."

Suddenly I was very self-conscious about how I did look. I hadn't given it any thought this morning at five, and I realized then that I certainly should have. I had on sneakers, beltless baggy khaki shorts, a midnight-blue T-shirt which suddenly felt too tight. Sometimes, particularly when I'm nervous, particularly when I'm around lithe, wispy women, my breasts feel as if they have a life of their own, as if I'm three people instead of one. I raked my fingers through my hair a couple of times. If I couldn't reign in my breasts, I could neaten up my hair.

"You have pretty hair," she said. "Red highlights."

"Thanks."

"Anyway, Timothy isn't here."

"Do you mind if I wait a bit? See, I'm from California. I mean, I'm visiting my family in Portland now. But I went to elementary school with Timothy. When I saw him and your family in the newspaper I thought I'd, um, visit."

That feeling I'd had all the way up in the car, the purity of my mission, corroded with my lies. It was finally dawning on me that the path from introducing myself as a stranger to introducing myself as Timothy's sister was going to be a rocky, steep one. I couldn't simply say, "I'm Timothy's sister," then to Warren Eggert, "Are you the man who kidnapped him?"

"Where you from in California?"

"San Francisco."

"Daddy don't like people from San Francisco."

"I'm originally from Oregon."

"Are there lots of hippies there? In Frisco, I mean."

"Some. Not as many as there used to be."

"Homosexuals?"

"Yeah, there're some of those."

"Oh," she said, as if we were discussing the fauna of Africa. "I'll get Mom."

When she left, I sat on the fender she'd vacated and seriously evaluated my situation. If I didn't want to lose my residency, I had better be back at work in the morning, which meant I had to be on the road by nine tonight. That gave me about six hours to reach Timothy. How the hell was I going to do that?

Cynthia returned a moment later and said her mother had a headache. Then she said, "I'd like to see that prison they have in San Francisco."

"San Quentin?"

"The one on the island. The one they escape from by swimming."

"Alcatraz. Only they drown when they try to escape."

"Some make it. I've seen a TV movie." She tucked her hair behind her prominent ears and watched me. Her eyes were unnerving. Though they were dull, she pinned them on her subject like suction cups.

"Hey, I have this crazy idea," I said. "As I told you, Timothy and I went to elementary school together. It's sort of fun to sort through childhood memories, know what I mean?"

She looked at me blankly.

"Well," I stuttered stupidly, "anyway. What I was thinking was, while I wait for Timothy, I'd love to see pictures of him as a kid. You know, like when he and I were little. Do you have albums?"

The girl took a step back and shook her head. Her hair once again fell forward into her face, and I felt as if I'd lost the tiny opening I'd gained. I was counseling myself to back off, go slowly with this family, when the sound of a truck coming up the dirt driveway diverted both of our attentions.

A spanking new black Chevrolet Blazer ground to a stop in front of the house. Warren Eggert grunted down from the driver's seat, and on the far side of the car another man leapt out of the passenger seat. "Is that Timothy?" I asked Cynthia.

"The one and only."

I smiled, hoping to keep this girl as my ally if I could.

Mrs. Eggert emerged from the house. "Oh," she said mildly. "It's lovely, Daddy."

"*Lovely?* You'd call a truck *lovely?*" Mr. Eggert said. Then, "Where's Cynthia?"

As he asked the question, he saw us in the entrance to the barn. Cynthia began walking slowly toward her father, so I followed.

"Who's this?" Eggert asked his wife.

"I don't know. I haven't seen her until now."

"That your car down the drive?"

"Yes, it is, Mr. Eggert. My name is Christine Thomas." I

approached him with an extended hand and my best smile.

"She's not a reporter, Daddy," Cynthia said. "Nice truck."

I was grateful to have arrived on the day he bought a new truck, because he seemed well-pleased with himself, and maybe that would extend to others. I knew I had to ingratiate myself with him before getting any kind of chance with Timothy, so I patiently trained my attention on him, not Timothy, who anyway remained standing on the far side of the truck, as if he needed a barricade.

"I'm an old classmate of Timothy's," I said.

"Classmate, huh? That's a good thing, honey, because has anyone told you I shoot schoolteachers and reporters on the spot?"

"No, sir," I said. "I mean, I did read that. I did see the article about you. That's how I found out Timothy was here. But I swear to God I'm not a reporter."

"What do you want?"

"Just wanted to say hello to Timothy. We were friends in school."

"Yeah, you said that." Warren Eggert looked at me good now, in that way men look at women that has more to do with them wanting you to know they're looking than with them actually looking. He started at my ankles, did my legs, then rested his eyes on my breasts for a long time. That's when he smiled. I'm not sure he even made it to my face.

"You remember this girl?" he asked Timothy.

Timothy stepped around from the other side of the Blazer. Could he possibly recognize me? We had been ten and five. He glanced at my face, then back at the dirt in front of his boots. "Yeah, I think so. How're ya doing?"

"Daddy?" said Mrs. Eggert. She nodded toward the house while her hands fluttered uselessly in front of her.

"Sure," he said, "put on some coffee. You want to stay for supper, sweetheart?"

"That would be nice," I stammered. "Thank you."

"Just bought this here Blazer." He tossed his head in the direction of the truck. "You like new-car smell?

"Oh, yes!" I said, too enthusiastically.

He mimicked me under his breath, "Oh, yes," then said, "Well, hop in. Tim, take the lady for a ride, why don't you." He winked at his son.

Timothy lifted his head enough to look at the dirt at my feet but didn't answer his father. I worried about leaving as Mrs. Eggert was making coffee but was glad for the chance to get alone with Timothy right away. I didn't like this family. The heat of the afternoon doubled in their presence. Mr. Eggert's voice felt like a rag stuffed in my throat.

"Cindy, help your old man in the house." The girl, who now had the presence of a five-year-old, came to her father's side. He slipped an arm around her waist and dug his other hand in his pocket. He slung the keys at Timothy, who just barely caught them. Then we both watched Warren and Cynthia Eggert enter the house.

"A ride sounds great," I said to Timothy.

I wanted more than anything to take his face in my hands, to make him look me in the eye, to have him tell me right now every detail of his life since he left us. I wanted to know what he remembered, what he didn't remember. I wanted to spend the few hours we had piecing together our lives. But I could see that he was still as timid now, at the age of twenty, as he had been as a boy. I girded myself for patience.

Timothy climbed in the driver's seat, and I got in the other side and rolled down my window.

"There's air conditioning," he said, so I rolled it up again.

Once we were down the drive and on the open highway, I said, "Nice truck."

"Yeah."

"Have you always been into cars?"

"I guess so."

We drove in silence for a few minutes, and finally I couldn't keep myself from reaching over and touching his shoulder, the tip of his clavicle. He flinched. I asked, "Timothy, you don't really remember me, do you?"

"I can't say that I do." He glanced at me and grimaced. "Sorry."

"That's okay. We were really young."

We arrived at an intersection and Timothy parked the truck in front of the one building, a small general store. "Want anything?" he asked. I shook my head, and as he went in the store I felt like I were on a high school date, waiting in the passenger seat for him to come back. He carried a Styrofoam cooler, a bag of ice, and two six-packs of Bud. I turned and watched him through the cab window as he placed the cooler in the truck bed and broke each beer from its plastic holder and put it in the cooler. Then he slammed the bag of ice on the parking lot pavement to loosen it, tore open the plastic, and dumped the ice on top of the cans of beer.

"Tualatin River is just north of here."

I realized it was a question, so I said, "Okay. That sounds great."

I didn't touch his painfully bony shoulder again, but I couldn't stop staring. He wasn't handsome. He wasn't even winsome, as the *Times* picture had made him look. I tried to match up the five-year-old Timothy with this twenty-year-old one. His mouth was no longer so red, and his lips had thinned, but he still had pretty eyes, green like mine. The slouch in the newspaper photo seemed to be a permanent one. Timothy hung over the steering wheel as if he were driving in a snowstorm.

We didn't talk until we got to the river. He parked the truck, hefted the loaded cooler, and we walked on a thin path through dry, scratchy, shoulder-high shrubbery until we came to the river. He placed the cooler on the pebble beach and sat next to it. "Want a beer?"

He popped it open for me. I took a sip and looked around. It would be difficult in this state known for its beautiful rivers to find an ugly one, but Timothy had. The Tualatin River at this spot was not so much languid as sluggish, its color greenish-brown, and not a tree in sight, only these shrubs that were browning even now in April. The sound of the nearby highway was much louder than that of the river. I imagined that this wide ditch was where the Canby High School boys drank their beer on weekends.

By the time I finished assessing our surroundings, Timothy had downed his first beer and opened a second. After drinking what looked like about half of that in a couple of gulps, he said, "You knew me in grade school?"

The beer must have given him confidence, because for the first time he looked at me directly.

"Yeah."

"How come I don't remember you?"

"I only went to school with you until I was ten. We moved to Portland. I live in San Francisco now."

He nodded and looked away.

We stared at the stones, the river, the shrubbery on the far side. I had to think of a way to talk to Timothy, but I hadn't eaten all day and the beer went straight to my head. When he offered me another, I took it, drinking it like it was food.

"Why did you want to look me up?" he tried again. Now he held my eyes, and I saw a hardness behind his tentative facade. I took this as a good sign. A hardness was something to work through.

Even so, my answer was lame. "It's sort of a hobby of mine, looking up old classmates."

"Funny hobby."

"Timothy, how old are you?"

"Same age as you, I guess, if we were classmates."

"I'm twenty," I lied.

"Yep." He tossed a couple of rocks into the river and took a long pull on the beer while I watched his Adam's apple hitch up and down with his swallowing, amazed at this manly feature on my little brother. Then he said, "Actually, I do remember you. I always thought you were pretty."

Delighted, I beamed at him, and he smiled back at me.

"You still are," he said.

Then I realized Timothy was flirting with me. I looked away quickly and he opened another beer.

"So you work on, uh, your father's, uh, ranch?"

"Yeah. I want to open a garage, but I don't have any money."

"Couldn't you start it at the ranch? I mean, you have all those cars out there."

Timothy laughed and looked at me like he was sizing up my intelligence. With a few beers in him, he looked more intelligent himself, oddly enough. "*Nothing* happens on that ranch," he said. "Nothing."

"What do you mean?"

"I mean my father makes sure nothing happens."

"That *Times* article said you two restore old cars."

Timothy laughed again. "You believe everything you read?"

"No," I said. "Definitely not."

"My father wouldn't know the difference between a gas line and a garden hose."

"But you do."

"Sure." He nodded and picked through the nearby stones in search of flat ones for skipping. These he piled up between his feet. "I want to restore vintage cars. See, you can find wrecks and buy them for a song. I've found some real gems. There's a '65 Porsche in the barn. I spent two years finding all the parts. You find them in junkyards, used-parts shops, catalogs, trade magazines. It's a shitload of work, but I got every fucking 1965 part for that Porsche and had that sucker complete except for body and paint work. She was gonna be a beaut, a complete beaut."

"What happened?"

"What happened?" he mimicked, suddenly sounding like his father. "What do you think happened? The old man got stinking drunk and took a sledge to it."

"Shit."

"You got that right. That thing would have been worth eighty, maybe a hundred grand."

"Still, you're only twenty, Timothy. You have time. You could leave the ranch." A whole scheme bloomed in my head. I could finance Timothy's garage! "How much money do you need?" I leapt up onto my knees in front of him, right there on the river stones.

Timothy looked at me oddly. "Just call me Tim," he said.

I laughed and settled back on my heels. "I can't do that. I know you as Timothy."

He looked at me funny again but didn't say anything.

I knew I couldn't offer him the money right then, but I said, "You could just leave, you know. Get any kind of job somewhere. Then all you'd need is a driveway to do auto restoration, right?"

He shrugged. "Ready to go?"

I said okay, but he opened the cooler and drank one more beer before getting up. His disinterest in my idea about leaving the ranch depressed me. Suddenly the whole place depressed me. I wished we could have gone somewhere less desolate than this barren river basin.

We walked back to the truck and he loaded the Styrofoam cooler into the bed. He took out two last beers and held one out to me.

"I'm still working on this one," I told him.

He shrugged again, looking as if he had gotten depressed as well, and carried the two beers up to the cab. When he got in, he put one between his legs and pulled open the other, took a long pull, then put it in the new drink holder. This seemed to give him satisfaction, and he smiled. He looked so out of place to me, sitting in that big black Blazer, his almost delicate hands resting on the steering wheel, his smile of appreciation for the design of the drink holder. I thought of that barn full of vintage auto bodies he had collected, his knowledge of acquiring old parts, the yearning in his voice when he talked about restoring cars, and realized that Timothy was an auto restoration artist. Him driving this big old Blazer was like a fine illustrator being forced to paint road signs. I wished I knew a way to kidnap a twenty-year-old man.

"Maybe I'll have that beer after all," I told him, and he handed it to me. We sat in the truck and finished the beers and he went around to the back to get a couple more before pulling out of the parking lot and turning onto the highway, squealing the tires and laying down rubber just like some small-town kid. I felt as if he had taken a sledge to my admittedly drunken fantasy of him as an auto restoration artist.

"Damn, Timothy," I said.

"Tim."

"Why do you have to do that with your new truck?"

"It's fun."

He did have a nice smile when he let it go full tilt. I decided now was not the time to be the judgmental big sister. I decided that when in Rome I should do as the Romans do, so I sat back and pretended I was his redneck sister. I prepared myself to enjoy the next time he laid rubber or spewed gravel.

Once we were on the open road, I asked, "Timothy, were you adopted by your parents?"

"*Tim*. You ask strange questions."

"Well, were you?"

"Not that I know of, but if someone told me I was I'd be happy to know it."

"I think you were."

"You're a crazy chick."

"I'm serious. Tell me this, do you remember being with your parents before you were five years old?"

He threw back his head and poured a long guzzle of beer down his throat, tossed the can out the window, and opened the one between his legs. "What is this, twenty questions? Are you hungry?"

"I'm starving."

Five minutes later he pulled into a diner, and I was greatly relieved that we weren't going back to the ranch. He raised his eyebrows when I ordered meatloaf, mashed potatoes, peas, coffee, and apple pie. "I have money," I told him. "Order what you want."

This seemed to make him angry. He only ordered pie and didn't want to talk while we ate, but when I had finished he laughed and said he had never seen a chick eat so much. When I pulled a wad of bills out of my pocket to pay, he said, "What are you doing? Damn. Where do you come from, Mars?"

Through the dull blur of all the beer and the huge meal,

I thought I should tell him that this wasn't a date, but it was so obvious to me that I felt stupid saying it. So I didn't. Instead I drank another beer with him, sitting in the truck outside the diner. Then we both opened one for the road and drove the darkening highway, now with the windows down, in what felt to me like a companionable silence. It was enough to be with Timothy. I didn't have to make him understand that I was his sister tonight. I could come back in a few weeks. It would take time. Tonight I'd just be with him. So I drank more beer.

I don't remember when we returned to the ranch. I don't remember parking the truck or if we went inside the house at all. I do remember walking into the barn and Timothy shining a bright flashlight on each and every wreck in that black cavern, explaining the car's year and features, describing vintage parts he had acquired or knew where to acquire. I remember being possessed by my wanting him to start his restoration business. I even remember telling him that I was so confident he could make it work that I would invest in it, that I could give him most of the start-up money. He laughed and told me again that I was one crazy chick.

I remember at some point asking him what time it was.

"Late," he said and laughed.

I laughed too. "But I have to be at work tomorrow."

"Call in sick."

"I can't. *They're* sick. I'm the doctor."

He thought this was very funny.

"I'm serious. I'm a doctor and my job is in San Francisco. I'm AWOL from the hospital. I have to be back in the morning."

We could barely stay on our feet for laughing so hard. He grabbed my elbows and I held his as we doubled over, gasping for breath, recovering for a moment, then laughing all over again. We laughed until our stomachs hurt. Then he pulled me to him and kissed me.

"No, Timothy," I said, trying to back up.

I woke up alone in the barn. A greasy quilted blanket covered me. My head rested on a partially inflated inner tube.

The air around me smelled of rust, grease, and vomit. When I tried to sit up, my head felt as if it splintered into pieces. Bright sunlight poured in from the open side of the barn. I managed to stand up and stumble outside. I had on a big green sweatshirt that didn't belong to me and I was barefoot. It took a long time for my brain to formulate any thought at all, but when it did the thought was something like this: I'm twenty-five years old; I'm a doctor; I'm not supposed to be in this situation.

My car keys were no longer in the pocket of my shorts, so I walked to the front door of the yellow house and knocked. This time Mrs. Eggert answered right away. "What do you want?" she asked icily.

"I wonder if you've seen my car keys."

"I think you had better leave."

"I can't go anywhere without my car keys."

Cynthia appeared behind her mother and looked at me with wide-eyed interest.

"Can I have a cup of coffee?" I asked.

"Just leave." Mrs. Eggert shut the door, and as I slowly made my way back to the barn to look for my keys, I heard a shrill scream. Then womanly shouting. Cynthia and her mother fighting again, I guessed.

A few moments later, as I rummaged through car parts for my keys, Cynthia entered the barn carrying a large mug of black coffee, which she handed to me.

"Oh, God, thank you."

"Did you want cream or sugar? I hope not because it was hard enough getting this."

"This is good. Just like this."

"Tim isn't here," she said, as if we were back in our initial conversation here in the barn yesterday afternoon. I wanted it that way. I wanted to let time collapse in on itself and cancel out this last episode of my life. I drank the coffee and found my keys by sheer luck. They were ground into the dust, back near the tire pile, but a beam of sunlight caught the metal ring and the glint caught my eye.

"I'm off," I told Cynthia.

"Are you coming back?" she asked.

"Definitely," I said, still holding to my story that this was just the first visit in many to come with my brother.

"I don't believe you," she said.

"What? What don't you believe?"

"You ain't no old classmate of Tim's."

"Then who am I?"

"I dunno. None of us has any idea. Daddy said maybe it was some kind of joke."

It made me uncomfortable that they had already had a family discussion about me. Cynthia seemed to believe that it was possible that my visit had a legitimate purpose, but I wasn't about to confess anything to her. There would be time later.

Of course, there wasn't a later. I never went back. I never went back even in my memory. Hunting people down like that is a terrible mistake.

twenty-four: wild silence

Flo, though a poet, doesn't believe in word trickery. For her, words are bald. Unlike Lucienne, she would not question that a word and the thing it names are one and the same. And though she tells stories with her poems, her poems *are* life, not a description of life, not something separate like I have kept the story of her in my own life.

I start by telling Liz, who sits on the lip of the cliff staring down at me, that Flo is the reason I am on this trip. It is not only that she encouraged me to come view the comet, though that too, but it is how she showed me that words can be used as muscles, that stories are useless unless they are true.

"Flo?" Liz says. "Who's Flo?"

When I awoke in her candlelit nest in the heart of the city, just two mornings ago, I had no idea what time it was, though it was clearly past dawn. Susan B laid under the covers in Flo's arms. Moving as quietly as I could, I slipped off the flannel pajamas and dressed. At least half of the candles were still burning, and I couldn't bring myself to leave Flo and Susan B alone with the fire hazard so I tiptoed about the room and blew them all out. Since putting out the candles was probably already a transgression, I allowed myself a quick peek at the things she had pinned to the red velvet wall coverings. Most of the pictures seemed to be of Susan B, though there was one of a young white woman in a black beret, cramped John Lennon wire-rim sunglasses, bell-bottoms, and a handful of droopy wildflowers, a 1960s hippie girl, and I knew that it was Flo's mother. An Emily Dickinson quote pinned below the old photograph read, "Life is a spell so exquisite everything conspires against it." I looked over my shoulder at the candles I'd just blown out, tiny wisps of pearl-gray smoke swirling above each one, and my stomach clenched. Had I broken some covenant she'd made with her gods and goddesses? Was I a part of the conspiracy? At the time, I read the word "exquisite" to mean delicate, as if life, like a candle, could be extinguished with one puff of breath, but now I think she meant the opposite. I think she meant perfectly made, exquisite like a crystal with its extraordinarily strong structure.

Liz listens to my fragmented stories about Flo and accepts them as a necessary prelude to what we both know we will talk about next. Finally I turn the corner and say, "I don't remember the name of the lake. Do you?"

"No."

"Can you picture it though?"

"Perfectly."

"What lake?" Lenny asks.

"The lake where we lost Timothy," I tell him.

Lenny scratches his head, says, "I'm starving."

Mark, relieved for the diversion, gets up and disappears. When he returns, he tosses three energy nuggets and a bag of dried fruit down to Lenny, who opens the latter and noisily consumes the withered pears and peaches.

Liz says, "It was big for that elevation. At least a couple

hundred meters long. Muddy at the edges, brown water. Except in the center, there the water was flint-gray, hard and cold. Half the lake was bordered with trees—no, more like two thirds of it, mostly Pacific fir. The other shore, across from where we were, was stone, a big slab stone wall and some boulders."

At the lake that morning, I went into the woods to get more stones. I got distracted. I played, got a little lost in that magic forest. Then I came back to you and our stone pier. As I approached, you were absorbed, completely absorbed, in building the pier. You didn't even answer my first question, which was, *How many more rocks do we need?* I remember feeling jealous of how your intensity could be funneled into one project. You have always been that way. My intensity blasts out of me in every direction. Which was why I probably forgot all about you and the pier while I played in the woods, and why I forgot about you for a moment just then, even after asking you a question, and looked out at the lake. I saw the raft floating at a distance and my first thought was, *She lost the raft!* I wondered if we could swim that far to get it. Then, only then, did I wonder where Timothy was. I looked back at you. You were still fitting small rocks into the spaces between the big rocks. I looked behind me. That yellow Camaro was just disappearing down the campground road. I asked you, *"Where's Timothy?"*

"How about the car?" I ask her now. "Can you picture that?"

Liz stands up, so from my position I am looking at a distortion of her: shins, knees, underside of breasts, chin.

Mark reaches for her hand and says, "The helicopter should be here any second now."

"No," Liz says to me. "No, I can't picture the car—only my picture of the car, not the car itself."

I close my eyes and try to see the car, the real car.

"I can't picture the man either," she says, her voice closing like a fist. "Not at all."

"What about the raft?" I ask.

"The raft…?"

After the yellow Camaro, which probably did exist but who knows, disappeared, you followed my gaze out onto the lake. I know you too saw the floating raft.

"The raft," I say. Even as I see, perfectly, the fear in my sister's eleven-year-old face, as plainly as if it were before me now, I press on the bruise of her lie, press hard to cause pain. "Can you picture that?"

Liz rallies. "Yes, of course I can picture the raft."

Quick, you said. *We have to get Mother.* I remember you said, "Mother," not "Mom." And I followed you, of course; I would always follow you. We ran back to camp and found her reading her novel in the hot sun.

A man in a yellow car, you told her. Later by looking at pictures we would identify it as a Camaro. *A yellow car took Timothy.*

Mother grabbed you by the shoulders, and I remember how raw her hands looked. She shook you and said, *Say it again. What? Say it again.*

Finally she turned to me and asked what happened. As you know, I corroborated every detail of your story.

Soon you were asked to describe the man and exactly what he did, and you were able to do that. I also claimed to have caught sight of him, but just barely. I thought that was safer, to back you but not mess up your details. You said he had a crew cut and wore Levi's but no shirt. You said he was a medium height and had the bristle of the beginning of a beard. You said you called for help and that you pulled on Timothy's foot. You said that he parked his car, got out, and walked toward you where you were working on the pier and Timothy was sitting on the shore. You said he picked up Timothy from behind, inserting his hands under Timothy's armpits and lifting him. But that is what *you* did when you put Timothy on the raft. That's when you said you screamed. And ran to pull on Timothy's foot. But the man, you said, was fast, and put Timothy in the front seat of his car. He drove off as I appeared. Yes, I said, I had seen the man at the wheel of the yellow car and I think he had a crew cut. Yes, I'm sure he did. Together we ran to the campsite to get Mother.

You never once mentioned the raft. We never did. Never once did we mention the raft to anyone.

I can see it now, the brown raft floating on brown water, but it is detached from my consciousness, adrift like the spots behind tightly closed eyes.

"Tina. Are you listening to me?"

I nod. I know she is feeling the urge to devil me as much as I am feeling the urge to devil her. I realize we both feel as if we are the only one who possesses the truth, that the other is the fatal liar, and we are both angry about that.

She says, "When we left the campground late that afternoon, the raft had drifted across the whole lake and rested against that boulder wall."

"You looked for the raft when we left that afternoon?"

"Of course."

"Of course? I don't understand. What do you mean 'of course'?"

"Yes, you do know what I mean. But here's what I don't understand. I don't understand why the fuck you backed up my story."

Her question disarms me. "Wait," I say.

Lenny forms a snowball and fires it into the void beyond our ledge. Then he makes another and throws it at Mark. "Stop it, Lenny," he tells him.

Lenny throws another one at him. Mark doesn't even brush away the snow from the front of his parka. He looks miserable sitting next to Liz's two fleece-encased legs. At least before he was her protector. Now that the beast is on the loose, and he can't cage it, he doesn't have a purpose that he can immediately discern.

Liz suddenly squats and balances herself by putting a hand on Mark's shoulder. She says to me, "I really want an answer. Why did you back up my story?"

"I didn't want to get you in trouble."

"You didn't want to get me in trouble! You can't be serious."

"Listen," Mark says. "I know what you're talking about is

important. But I think we had better start figuring out—"

"Mark," Liz says with unnerving tenderness. "The helicopter either comes or it doesn't. If it doesn't, Tina and Lenny use the tent and fly as best they can. We go to the snow cave. We have at least an hour of light left."

"You got everything all figured out, don't you?" Mark says. He leaps to his feet, toppling Liz, and paces out of sight.

She watches him go, then turns back to me. "Well?"

"I was scared. You were older."

"But you were the one who always told the truth. Always. Shit, we'd steal a quarter from Mom's wallet and you'd feel compelled to tell her. You were always the smarter one, always correcting me, getting everything *exact*. The little scientist at age ten. Then suddenly, bam, when it matters, really, really matters, you do a switcheroo on me and skillfully back up every detail of my story. My *fabricated* story."

Lenny says, "So what happened to Timothy?"

I look up at his big brown eyes and think that it's a crime not to answer him.

Liz says, "I was going to tell the truth. I was going to in a minute. I just needed a cushion of time, a little moment. I don't know why I didn't swim out there. It was like the lie came up in me so fast, instantly. Maybe I could have…"

"Probably not."

"It's possible that I could have. Admit that it's possible we could have saved him."

I remain quiet.

"I never meant the lie to stick. I expected Mom to save him. I don't know. I just thought it would come out. But you were there repeating everything I said like some kind of parrot."

"What lie?" Lenny says, and I'm touched at his insistence at being a part of this conversation, at his willingness, unlike Mark, to hang in here with me and Liz.

I say, "Our thirty-year bivouac. *That* lie. I only wanted to protect you, Liz. I'm sorry."

Then we sit, the three of us staring out at the darkening

sharks' teeth mountains, and wait. All around there is this silence, this wild, wild silence.

Lenny eventually lights another cigarette and places it at my mouth. I shake my head, so he takes long, hard drags until he has smoked it down to the filter and then he snuffs it out in the snow. For the first time, he pockets the butt. Then he reaches over me and pulls the sleeping bag up, tucking it under my shoulders. He says, "Timothy drowned, didn't he?"

For thirty years I've been afraid, most afraid of all, of those words, and yet their effect isn't what I expected. Instead of more pain, I feel less. It is as if Lenny's words were the last stretch of trail through a wilderness and I am delivered to a clearing, an open vista of possibility.

My first thought is of Flo.

As I stood at the door to her room two mornings ago, about to leave, I turned one last time to watch her sleep. She opened her eyes and for a moment looked panicked. "Are you leaving?"

I nodded.

"Hey, you know what?" she said sleepily. "You're right. My voltage theory is bogus."

When I didn't answer, she said, "I'm scared."

"Me too."

"Will you come back?"

I almost asked *Do you want me to?* but said, "Yes."

"When?"

"Soon."

Her body looked Florentine, twisted in the bedclothes, lovely and full, toasty skin against creamy sheets.

"Have a good time in the mountains."

"Soon," I said again, blew her a kiss, and let myself out.

I understood then that the path to Flo meant passing through the terrain of Liz and finding Timothy, but I had no idea what I would see on the way. As I lie on this raw ledge in the last moments of daylight, as I lie here and look up at Lenny's blinking cow's eyes, and then out on the mountains, as I consider the possibility of forgiveness between my sister and me, a possibility the color of steel, the flint-gray center of that lake, I wonder if just being alive is enough.

After a while Mark returns, and rather than letting him break the exquisite silence, I do. "How could the parents have believed us?"

"They didn't."

"What do you mean? They hired an investigator for a year! Dad searched five states."

"The investigator was an idiot. If they really believed Timothy could have been found, they would have sold the house, anything they needed to do to hire a good one. And Dad was only doing what he always does, wandering. Sure he thought he was looking for Timothy, but he was just traveling, on the go."

"Oh."

"Our story gave them hope. What choice did they have but to believe it?" Liz says. "For a while, anyway."

"You always knew? *Always*?"

"I was *there*, Tina. So were you."

I *was* there, and yet for all these years I have believed the story, Liz's and my story, more persistently than I have believed what I knew to be true. We were so convincing that we not only engaged our parents' hope, I permanently separated myself from ever knowing a real border between fact and fiction. I've never known the solid ground of truth, the assurance of an absolute. The truest experiences in my life have been free falls in which, while plummeting, some kernel of truth gets pressed into my throat by the force of gravity.

"But if he—"

"Timothy."

"If Timothy—"

"Drowned."

"Why didn't he…I mean, wouldn't he have…?"

"When water is cold enough, they don't resurface."

That she has scientific information on drowning appalls me. That she has been that meticulous in researching not only the truth, but the *details* of the truth, without cluing me in, infuriates me. "Shit, Liz. I believed you. All these fucking years I believed you. You fucking lied and I believed you."

"I'm sorry," she says.

But I knew he drowned. I did know that. I have even imagined it, like a nightmare that lives just outside the perimeter of my consciousness, an eternal drowning. Wispy brown hair, nearly the same shade as the lake water, trailing over his head like reeds. Face flesh pushing upward, toward the surface. Thin limbs flailing, spiraling down into the lake water too cold for release. Then the one fatal gulp. The icy water too, too cold, claiming the small body and forcing it to the lake bottom. In a warmer lake, the corpse would have floated to the surface. That one fact might have changed our lives, the temperature of a lake, but this water was so cold, it was too early in the season, and the lake ate Timothy whole. If he had screamed, we would not have been able to hear it. For Timothy, underwater, the silence was complete, his loneliness absolute. Perhaps out there, well beyond the shore, the basin was not so gushy, squirmy with invertebrates, perhaps it was a lovely pebbled basin onto which he landed.

"So, like, all these years you've been pretending some guy kidnapped Timothy, but really he drowned. Whoa." Lenny pops an energy nugget into his mouth and thoughtfully chomps it down.

I laugh. I actually laugh. Whoa, Lenny says, and then eats. When I look back up at Liz, she too is smiling. Poor Mark is standing slightly behind her and to the side, his arms dangling, his face blank like a scarecrow. I can only imagine what he is feeling. His heart must be aswirl with the lust of the new relationship, the heartbreak of hurting Liz, and most of all our eclipsing his crisis with a different one that has nothing at all to do with him.

"Yeah," I tell Lenny. "That's about the sum of it."

Above my head lies a ski pole that had been helping to hold up the tent fly. I reach up with my good arm, and it hurts but no more than it did when I laughed, and close my fingers around the pole. I bring it over my head and adjust my grasp so that I have it by the handle. I reach the basket end up toward Liz. She looks quizzical for a moment until I tap the highest place on the cliff I can reach with the pole. Then she smiles, leans back toward the pile of gear behind her, and grabs her own ski pole. When she reaches it down, the tips of the ski poles click and the baskets engage.

Connected to Liz by our ski poles, I stare at the azure-going-black sky until my gaze pierces its surface. Ripples of sky fold back like waves. If I were Lenny, I might have a vision now. I might enter the sky or the sky might enter me. This late-stage twilight has concentrated all color, as though I am seeing the wilderness through stained glass. The blue mountains, red cliff, purple sky are color shards. Viewing them hurts, yet it is a pain so deeply imbedded in beauty that what emerges is grace. It occurs to me that beauty itself satisfies desire. If this is a culminating moment, a moment that required all the moments before to be as they were, then I would not change a single event that led me to now. I suddenly realize that my desire for Timothy, my eternal hope that he will ski over that ridge toward us, as a child or as a man, that longing has defined me, *is* me, and I can no longer call it loss.

"Liz," I say. "Hey, Liz. Listen to this." I tell her and Lenny, and Mark if he wants to listen, about Timothy Eggert, that self-imposed decoy, a story I tossed off to one side to confuse the part of me that hunted for the truth. I tell them about the *New York Times* story and picture, the coyote hides, my drive up north and the lilac blooms, the Eggert family as I found them. I tell about the Tualatin River and the endless beers. I consider leaving my story there, but continue with the parts of the night and morning that I remember: the kiss and waking up in the barn, the mug of black coffee, finding my keys.

Throughout my story, Liz keeps saying, "Damn, Tina!" and when I finish we start laughing. Then we can't stop. We laugh so hard I am sure my ribs will split apart. I would never have dreamed that a person could endure so much physical pain for the sake of laughing, and yet I do.

I'm not even sure when my laughing evolves into crying. It is as gradual as the way the day is shifting into night. The crying hurts as much as the laughing, but I do it just as relentlessly.

about the author

PHYLLIS CHRISTOPHER

Lucy Jane Bledsoe is the author of *Working Parts*, winner of the American Library Association GLBT Award for Literature, and *Sweat: Stories and a Novella*, a Lambda Literary Award finalist. Her fiction has been awarded a 2002 California Arts Council Individual Artists Fellowship in Literature as well as a National Science Foundation Artists & Writers in Antarctica Fellowship. Her work has been widely published in anthologies and periodicals such as *Ms.* magazine, *Newsday*, *Fiction International*, *WIG magazine*, *Girlfriends* magazine, *Blithe House Quarterly*, *California Wild*, and *Northwest Literary Forum*.